APHRODITE'S WAR

BY DONNA MILWARD

Cover Design: Terra Koster, KMS Design

Edited: Sara Johnson
Heather Savage

Staccato Publishing
Zimmerman, MN

First Edition: September 2013

ISBN: 978-0-9892027-6-3

I would like to dedicate this novel to the following people: Sensei Stephanie Bozzer, Joseph Kim and Dan Gyoba.

I will forever cherish the lessons I learned from each of you. Thanks for working so hard with me. You taught me discipline and pride among other things. It was an honor to train with you, and I will remember my time with you for as long as I live.

CHAPTER ONE

"You shall wear a trench in the marble," Ares said. Aphrodite glared over her shoulder at him in contempt and continued to pace.

"I am sick of hearing you say that."

"Then perhaps you should stop doing it. I grow weary of your posturing."

Aphrodite rolled her eyes. It had been decades since they had anything interesting to say to each other. The turn of the century saw them resort to petty bickering, not unlike a mortal married couple too afraid of change to leave a union of misery.

If only it were that easy, Aphrodite thought. If only I could simply walk away.

But it was not an option. This was the only place she called her own.

She stared past the vine-wrapped stone pillars of the pantheon to the Earth below. Aphrodite shivered in this fabricated hell she had willingly traded for the eternal beauty of Eden so that she could harness the emotions of humans and become a goddess. What a tragic folly.

Aphrodite cast another glance at the lean and tanned Ares lounging on his throne of bloodstone. He stroked his beard like a conceited cat. She loved him once, left Hephaestus for him.

She came to regret following him, and wandered Olympus like a ghost, forever bored and lonely.

"You are jealous because I have more power than you." Ares stretched forward, sneering. "I always have. Nothing has changed."

"That is false," she said. "Everyone believes in love. No one wishes for conflict."

Ares threw both arms in the air, exasperated. "Yes, I know. All mankind wants world peace." He held out his hand and one of many nymphs crept to his side with a full goblet. "But this realm has never known true rest," Ares spoke and considered his wine. He drained most of the cup and waved it around, sloshing leftover wine dregs like splatters of gore. "If you added all the years without war on this planet, it would not amount to a single decade."

Aphrodite shrugged. "Humans have delicate tempers." She peered out to the green and blue vista below Mount Olympus, breathed deep the ripe scent of olive trees. "It requires little talent or skill to set them against each other."

The comment had the desired effect. Out of her peripheral vision she saw Ares stiffen. His rage washed over her with such force she braced herself on a pillar.

Not that she feared him. Causing Ares aggravation pleasured her, one of few satisfying amusements. She suppressed her laughter, but it mattered not at all. He was well aware of her disdain. It was hard to keep feelings to oneself when everyone around her could exchange thoughts.

"Harpy slut," His lips curled in rage. "You think yourself superior to me?"

Aphrodite faced him, almost shocked by the ugliness in his expression. Veins appeared like cracks in his skull and his brown eyes became black pits. Saliva dripped from his cruel mouth.

"Humans do not need you to teach them to fuck."

A crowd gathered. She heard the babble, both spoken and unvoiced.

Not this again.

Third time this year alone.

They never tire of it.

Wish they would both be silent.

A new presence arrived. Aphrodite glanced to the skies to see storm clouds building before Zeus appeared between her and her old lover.

"Enough, both of you," His roar filled the room. "You need to cease this constant nattering at each other." Zeus ran his hand down his rich chestnut beard, stroking the curls.

Aphrodite gauged his temperament. Zeus' anger simmered. True, she and Ares had been at each other's throats for a few decades, but the confidence she once admired had become smarmy arrogance. She considered it her duty to remind him of his inadequacies, lest Ares become insufferable.

Zeus pinched the bridge of his nose. "A noble idea, Aphrodite, but it is unpleasant to listen to. Everyone here..." He motioned behind him with a heavily muscled arm. "...is sick to the teeth of the noise."

Several murmurs of agreement filled the room, rustling the trellised ivy.

"She started it," Ares blushed, seeming to realize how childish he sounded. His gaze dropped to the floor. "She goads me to occupy her time."

Aphrodite opened her mouth to protest, closed it again. She must admit, the endless tedium of her existence caused her moodiness. And Ares provided a convenient target for her frustration. She had come to this dimension because of him, and for that he should suffer.

Zeus' stormy blue eyes flashed. Lightning blinked over the throng and thunder shook the ground. The smell of ozone wafted to Aphrodite's nose. "It must stop."

His shoulders rose then fell with the weight of decision. "One of you will leave Olympus."

"What?" Ares said, dropping his goblet.

"Are you mad?" Aphrodite asked. Her hands became imploring claws. "This is my home."

Ares sneered at her. “Mine as well.”

“Nevertheless, one of you has to go. Our sanctuary must have quiet,” Zeus stepped away from the quarrel to face the assembly. “Ideas, anyone?”

Voices rose in pitch as the other gods, nymphs, and pet mortals weighed in. One opinion rang out over the din of the mob.

“A contest!” The voice belonged to Artemis. Aphrodite’s heart sank. Leave it to the huntress to suggest such a concept. “Winner stays on Olympus, loser departs.”

A wicked grin spread over Ares face. He liked to compete. Aphrodite used to find that desirable. Now it was to her disadvantage.

“But what kind of contest?” Zeus asked.

“I believe that one is obvious.” The slurred statement came from Dionysus as he made his crooked way forward. Judging from the alcohol and vomit stench of his last belch, Dionysus and his worshippers started devotionals early.

“She is the goddess of love.” The god of wine and ecstasy spilled dribbles on his violet robes, the floor, and his entourage as he gestured. “Let her do what she does best. She always goes on about how love is the strongest force on Earth.”

“And he always tells her love leads to hate,” Artemis said, her silver eyes dull with apathy. “That it is easier for humans to fight than to choose friendship, affection, or goodwill.”

Several gods and goddesses nodded and applauded. They all remembered the fights between Ares and Aphrodite over the years. The topic remained the same.

Zeus pursed his lips. Aphrodite noted by the way he fingered the twists in his facial hair that he liked the idea. As did she. Aphrodite never doubted herself, not with love. Ares could do whatever he wanted. She never failed. She could almost taste the sweet victory like honey on her tongue.

"I accept the challenge," she said. Ares eyebrows lifted high, lending him a comical vulnerability. "I anticipate having something new to do for a change."

And she would defeat him. She pictured herself roaming the lush gardens of Olympus, dancing between the vine-covered marble monoliths...without the lewd and brash presence of the war god tainting its loveliness.

She studied the sharp angles of his handsome visage before staring Ares in his raven-dark eyes. She wanted to remember this precise moment. Soon he would be gone. She may never have to see him again. "You can do your worst."

Ares' grin spread like a scourge across his face. "I will. I also accept."

"Then it is settled." Zeus rubbed his hands together. A static charge of blue light shimmered between his fingers. "We need to establish ground rules. Everyone, be seated."

Ares went back to his throne and Aphrodite reluctantly sat in hers. She appreciated the splendor of the mother-of-pearl and sea shell inlays on her chair, but it was placed next to him. That meant enduring a whiff of his rank musk whenever the breeze blew north.

Sure enough, once settled, Ares exuded the odor of sweat and alcohol. Aphrodite stopped stroking the scallop shells of her armrests and brought her hand to her mouth and nose.

First thing I shall do when he leaves is scour all traces of him from that spot.

Ares put both hands behind his head and smirked. Aphrodite refused to react to the overwhelming smell. Why encourage him?

“We need a location.” Zeus waved a hand and a map of Earth appeared in the center of the room, hanging like a translucent tapestry. “The duel will take place in the New World.”

The visual focused on the landscape of North America with lush fields of wheat, corn, and canola. Flat plains gave way to craggy mountains. Occasionally, a city or village interrupted the open spaces.

The New World? That sparse wasteland of technology and materialism? Aphrodite uttered an unfeminine oath. The Mediterranean, or even Europe, would have been preferable. There the humans revered her in art and books. Many still lived by the old ways.

But it was not the Middle East or Asia where constant war and revolution made Ares strong. For that she was grateful.

The New World had no use for either her or Ares. They were too busy chasing wealth and power to fall in love or fight.

Understanding dawned.

“A wise choice, mighty Zeus,” she said with a demure smile.

“No advantages,” Ares said. “I concur.” A small wonder they finally agreed on something, Aphrodite thought.

“I give you all of North America to choose,” Zeus said, presenting the image between his massive hands like an offering. “Aphrodite, you select first.”

She felt her lips widening. She knew just the girl. Aphrodite recalled her lineage and her love of cultures new and old.

“Her,” Aphrodite said. She waved away the map and placed in its stead a visual of her chosen champion. “I choose this human.”

Before them hovered the image of a young woman in her twenties. She wore her glossy black hair long but bluntly sheared. Streaks of pink and blue burst through her bangs. Her twinkling brown eyes were lined with kohl. Her skin shone a light shade of olive, healthy from within and etched with ink. Mythological creatures merged with tiger lilies, hibiscus, and roses. Silver jewelry decorated her ears and throat. A single diamond perched on her cheek like a teardrop.

"She is a strange beauty." Zeus stared at the depiction, doubt crinkling his brow. "Hardly the epitome of femininity. Are you certain?"

"Your vanity is greater than your will to win." Ares chuckled, a sickly imitation of merriment. "This mortal wears Aphrodite's likeness across her back. Not to mention 'Aphrodite' is her second name."

Aphrodite narrowed her gaze at him. "Those are not the sole reasons." She faced Zeus. "This one has a Greek father. Her parents teach classic literature. They have a deep love of all the legends of our time, as well as each other. Good breeding and intelligence are more attractive than appearances."

Ares guffawed but Aphrodite ignored him. "More importantly, she is newly single."

She folded her arms and tilted her chin at Ares. "Your turn." Sarcasm oozed from her lips. "Lover."

CHAPTER TWO

Poetry heaved her sack of tools across the threshold of her apartment and relaxed. She stretched her aching back as she sauntered into the kitchen, nearly tripping over sneakers, Doc Martens, and stilettos overflowing from the foyer.

"Meow?"

Poetry dropped her gaze to the pitch-black cotton ball staring at her from the floor with his innocent cobalt eyes.

"Hey, Amir," she said. The sight of him always made her swoon. She scooped the kitten up, rubbing her nose against his pink one. "How is my baby? Have you been good?"

Amir responded by purring like a lawnmower while licking her nose.

"Me loves you too," she said. She cradled Amir in one hand, searched for kitty treats with the other. Salmon-flavored Whiskas were his favorite. Making her cat happy made her happy.

She grabbed the remote from the kitchen table and pointed it across the room.

The TV blared to life. "-learned that Frank Fleisher of Grey, Alberta has been granted bail. His lawyer is-"

"Poe, is that you?" Jenny's voice called from her bedroom.

"Nope," Poetry yelled back. "Just the friendly neighborhood burglar come to steal your food." She found the morsels she'd been searching for in the cupboard over the stove. Amir received one for being adorable, plus two more for waiting so patiently for her to come home, before she put him back on the tile. "And to spoil my cat."

She opened the fridge door and basked in the cold air wafting from within as well as the smell of savory leftovers.

“Very funny,” Jenny said. She marched into view, eye shadow compact in one hand, Q-tip in the other. “You need a new joke.”

“Well, who else would it be?” Poetry asked, eyeing a container of pasta. “Hey, can I have some of this?”

Jen nodded. “Have at ‘er. I put Mom’s canned tomatoes in it.”

“Thanks.” Poetry grabbed the bowl of orange and red noodles and loosened the cellophane before popping it in the microwave. She’d had a long day at Vulcan’s Forge, struggling with a pewter ring that just wouldn’t hold its shape. A little comfort food would do the trick. Her stomach growled in agreement.

While her dinner warmed Poetry studied her roommate. Jenny had swept her blonde-streaked hair into a ponytail, emphasizing a long graceful neck and the gold teddy bears on her ears. She wore a new sundress, pale blue with a white floral print. It enhanced her carefully applied cream and coffee tan.

Sometimes Jenny’s vanity seemed over the top, but Poetry kept her comments to herself. Just because Jenny obsessed over her appearance didn’t make her a bad person. Poetry could relate, what with her body issues.

The microwave beeped. “Love the dress,” she said. “It matches your eyes.”

“Thanks.” Jenny smoothed the fabric down slender hips. “I got it on sale. I figured, ‘what the hell?’ It’s just the kind of thing to wear to The Rosemount.”

Poetry was enjoying the creamy sweetness of dairy and tomato when she remembered her promise. She swallowed without enjoyment.

“You forgot.” Jenny’s tone exuded disappointment.

“No, no,” Poetry said. “I just, well…okay, I forgot.” Jenny’s lips tightened and Poetry noted the exasperation in her eyes.

“That doesn’t mean I won’t go,” she said. “Just give me a few minutes.”

Jenny brightened instantly. “Great,” She went back to brushing lavender on her eyelids in the mirror of the compact. “It’ll do you good to meet new people.”

Oh, for the love of God. Poetry tried not to let her irritation show as she stabbed at dinner.

She’d broken up with Kevin two weeks ago and Jenny had been trying to drag her back to the singles scene ever since.

So she’d only been with the guy for four months. That didn’t mean it hurt any less. She wasn’t ready to date, and she definitely didn’t want to go out with anybody Jenny picked for her.

“And The Rosemount is just the place to meet a good quality man,” Jenny said. “You know, guys with jobs.”

“You mean like that line cook you tried to set me up with?” Poetry couldn’t resist, especially when Jenny had the grace to look sheepish.

“Okay, that wasn’t a good idea,” Jenny said.

“You think?” Poetry asked. “He followed me around the dish pit like a trained monkey for a week, asking me to do lines in his car.”

Jenny winced. “Sorry. We’ll do better next time.”

Right. Jenny went for suits. She pushed everybody else in Poetry’s direction.

“Whatever.” Poetry grinned at her, taking the sting from the sarcasm. “I’ll be a few minutes, okay? I need a shower.”

She stopped by her room long enough to pick out a dress, a basic black tank that hugged her curves. She loved the way it made her silhouette a bombshell, not fat and short-waisted. It worked for nearly every occasion. She’d worn it so much she’d already had to re-dye it.

She hung it on the door of the bathroom, with its stacks of teal colored towels and rows of girly products, and shut herself in while scooting the cat out.

Poetry stripped quickly, shedding the odor of hot clay kilns and ovens with her t-shirt and sweats. Sooty streaks covered her arms and darkened the cracks in her hands. She'd have to scrub hard to get that out, couldn't go out wearing the grime of her passions. She adjusted the water and ducked under the showerhead.

Only then did she let the tears flow.

Poetry rinsed them from her face, struggling to swallow the loud sobs she didn't want heard. Jenny wouldn't understand.

Jenny never liked Kevin. Poetry thought she'd judged him by his appearance. Granted bald metal musicians weren't for everybody, and Jenny preferred white collar.

But she could never see past the rock star image to the sweet creative soul beneath. Not like Poetry could. With Kevin she'd found a kindred spirit, a soulmate to share ideas and inspiration with. Him with his music, her with crafting jewelry.

It bothered her how Jenny commented on his tattoos and piercings. Poetry had just as many, if not more. Did Jenny secretly sneer at her looks?

She longed for the smell of Kevin's musk mixed with leather. She remembered his nicotine-stained smile, big as the sun.

But then he started getting weird. Poetry sighed as a pang of regret squeezed her heart. She'd chalked it up to stress; from the band, from losing yet another job. Either of those would've been enough.

Toward the end she'd seen less and less of that smile as he'd become more possessive and his appetites grew strange. He'd changed right before her eyes.

Jenny didn't believe it. "He's finally showing his true colors," she'd said.

Poetry couldn't tell Jenny, but a punch to the gut after too many beers had been the last straw. Now matter how much she loved him, she couldn't stay with an abuser. No smart woman would.

The water cooled, bringing Poetry back to the present. She checked her arms and hands for ash and metal shavings. Puddles from her hair ran clear instead of purplish. Almost done, she had to get the crud out from under her fingernails and then she'd be finished.

The temperature plummeted as Poetry cleansed the eyeliner rivers she knew would leave tracks on her cheeks. Kevin was a jerk. But it didn't make breaking up with him any easier.

Poetry half-assed dried off, the heat outside would evaporate the rest, and shimmied into her outfit. She opened the door to let the steam out and wiped condensation from the mirror before checking her eyes. They were red as coals from crying. Better get the drops.

She opened the vanity to find another reminder of her ex. He always kept at least three bottles of Visine around: one for his place, one for hers, and one in his pocket; for getting rid of the hung over appearance when they'd stayed out too late. Poetry sighed. Now she used it to wash away the tell-tale signs of missing him.

She steeled her resolve. What kind of dweeb hides his nights out so often that he needs more than one bottle of eye drops anyway?

The kind that smacks women around when he drinks.

Bolstering her confidence, Poetry brushed and preened until her hair lay sleek and shiny. She applied her make-up like war paint, with dark eyes and plum lips. Poetry reached for a green bingo dauber, but changed her mind. Red. Today felt like a red day. She gave the bottle a good shake and began striping her bleached bangs with it.

She chose a braided chain with sculpted silver daisies dangling at various lengths with pearly beads to represent baby's breath; one of her most feminine necklaces. After adorning her neck, she owned her style with an appraisal in the mirror.

The familiar padding of tiny paws on the linoleum announced Amir.

“What do you think?” she asked.

“Rowr.”

“I think so too,” Poetry said, placing her hands on her hips and striking a haughty stance. “Kevin who?”

“Ready!” She meandered to the kitchen with Amir trotting behind. “How do I look?”

“That’s what you’re wearing?” Jenny asked. “You have other clothes, you know.”

“You think the guys at the Rosemount won’t like it?”

Jenny shook her head, but her lips betrayed her humor. “More for me.”

Poetry gave Jenny’s arm a swipe. “Nice.”

“Nice, nothing. You can borrow my patent pumps. At least you’ll somewhat resemble a lady that way.”

“Whatever,” Poetry said, covering her cat with kisses. “Give Amir lovins before we go.”

Jenny took him from her arms while Poetry searched for shoes that matched.

Time to have some fun. No more sitting at home feeling sorry for herself. This would be the first night of the rest of her life, and Poetry intended to make it a good one.

CHAPTER THREE

Poetry stifled a groan. She'd envisioned a local hangout where co-workers and friends shared a few quick brews over a game of darts. This place featured a lacquered bar with polished chrome stools and the scent of genuine leather chairs permeated the air. The work of a painter she didn't recognize decorated the walls in black and red.

At least she matched.

How much would a beer cost in a pub like this? She cringed. Maybe she shouldn't order beer. Not fancy enough. The men were strictly suit and tie. Not a hockey jersey in sight. The women…well, needless to say Poetry felt underdressed and over-pierced. People stared. Her favorite little black number suddenly looked too cheap and showed too much ink.

She leaned toward Jenny's ear. "You could have warned me."

"I did," Jenny's tone was insistent. "I told you not to wear that, remember?"

Poetry cursed inwardly. She'd taken the comment as a ribbing.

"Check it out." Jenny motioned to the corner next to the patio with her chin. Bright sunlight poured in from patio doors, showcasing three men and an older woman.

The woman had obviously had more than she could handle. She pawed at a guy with a brown brush cut and biceps that strained the sleeves of his jacket. The lady's voice carried throughout the room, announcing her interest. Poetry was embarrassed, even if she wasn't.

Jenny marched straight for her.

Oh God, what's she going to do?

"Hi, honey," she said with a wave. Who was she talking to? Poetry's jaw dropped when Jenny leaned over to Mr. Biceps and pecked him on the lips. "Sorry I'm late. Is this woman bothering you?"

She didn't.

The cougar glared at Jenny. Her gaze drifted to Poetry with the tattoos crawling down her shoulders and arms. Apparently not liking the looks of them, the woman excused herself in a hiss.

When her rival was out of earshot Jenny flashed a charming smile at Mr. Biceps again.

"I always wondered if that would work. I'm Jenny."

Poetry clenched her teeth in a phony smile. Only Jenny possessed that kind of nerve.

"Well, Jenny." The jock motioned to the now empty spot. "I'm Gary. Why don't you and your friend have a seat? You never know…She might come back, right?"

A barmaid came forward and took their order. Poetry followed Jenny's lead and ordered a vodka-Seven. She squirmed in her creaking chair as introductions were made.

"This is my roommate, Poetry," Jenny said with a vague sweep of her hand. "We work together."

Gary-with-the-beef nodded to his dark friend. "This is Ranjan." He indicated the blonde man closest to Poetry. "That's Adrian. We work at the same law firm."

"Oh, you're lawyers." Jenny beamed while Poetry suppressed a sigh of annoyance.

Lawyers. Great. Should be a fun night.

Intuition told her the guy sitting next to her felt the same way. While Gary and Ranjan devoted their attention to the effervescent Jenny, he slouched and stared at his glass.

What was his name? Adrian. Girl's name. Not bad looking, though. He wore his hair short and spiky. Just enough product to make it sit still.

His face had that sexy chiseled bone structure that makes for pretty men--square jaw and high cheekbones.

But his eyes were the striking part. Such a light shade of blue they were almost grey. Icy. He must be Scandinavian.

Not her type at all.

Especially since he wore a sport coat. No doubt it cost more than your average off-the-rack kind. Were those pink pinstripes in his tie?

She glanced up to see him staring at her. A blush warmed her face as she concentrated on keeping her expression neutral.

# # #

Drinks arrived, and Adrian broke eye contact with the olive skinned girl. He took a long pull from his Guinness and braced himself for a dull evening.

What was he doing here? He'd rather be at home, fixing the splintered board in the hardwood floor he'd installed a few weeks ago. Stupid miscalculation. His head throbbed from dwelling on it. Best think about something else.

As the bitter brew and creamy foam washed over his teeth he appraised the woman, as he'd seen her doing to him.

Not much to look at. She smelled odd, like baby powder and iron. Adrian suspected that if it wasn't for her bubble-puppy friend over there that she'd never set foot in a place like this. Goth girls with rainbow hair and tattoos never did.

And he'd caught the contempt for his tie. Not that he'd do her, either. He liked his women a tad bit thinner. And more conservative.

She fiddled with the rhinestone embedded in her cheek. Why would anyone do that to their face? Bet she had tribal markings across the small of her back like he'd seen on so many hookers and junkies he'd defended. What were they called? Oh yeah, 'Tramp Stamps'.

He spared a glance at his friends. Gary and Ranjan were talking over each other, competing for the other girl's attention. She just sat there, smiling like an airhead.

He glanced at the misfit and experienced a pang of empathy. She sipped and chewed at her straw, obviously uncomfortable.

At least we have that in common. She had intelligence in her eyes, a wariness no doubt borne from others making assumptions about her appearance. Maybe he'd been too critical.

"What's your name again?" he asked.

She took the straw out of her mouth, splashing him with drops of soda. "Poetry."

What kind of hippie names their kid 'Poetry'? A distasteful thought hit him. Maybe it's a stage name.

"Uh huh, and what do you do, Poetry?" Adrian took another pull of his beer. Not like he had anyone else to talk to. Could be interesting.

"I create jewelry," she said with a tilt to her chin that dared him to comment. "I'm an artist."

Adrian almost choked on his Guinness, fizz burned the back of his throat.

An artist. Named Poetry. Lucky him. Who breeds these people?

CHAPTER FOUR

"I choose him," Ares rubbed his greasy hands together. "The blonde man."

Aphrodite rolled her eyes. She expected no less. Ares decided on the one person at the table who found Poetry distasteful. But brutal rogues like Ares could not see the warm hearts of men.

"You lack subtlety," she said. "But it does not matter. I will defeat you."

"You must admit, I have a good start." He planted his dusty sandals on the polished floor and stretched until his joints cracked and popped like autumn leaves.

"The champions have been chosen," Zeus said. Mutterings and whispers quelled and the courtyard fell silent except for the wind.

"Rule number one: aside from your champions, you must not interfere with humankind." Zeus employed a meaningful stare as he pointed to both of them in kind. "I want no repeats of the 'Troy' incident."

Zeus raised another finger. "Rule number two: no outside help. You may use minions and demigods of our community. You may not ask for assistance from the Egyptian, Asian or Indian deities."

"Rule number three," Ares said, glaring at Aphrodite. "No cupid arrows."

"No charmed weapons of any kind, Ares," Zeus said, furrowing his brows at both of them in turn.

Aphrodite smiled her approval as she stood. She did not need her little cherub to do her dirty work. "I do not have issue with your decree, mighty Zeus."

Ares clenched his fists and tightened his jaw. "Nor do I."

“Then it is settled,” Zeus said. “You have two mortal weeks to make them fall in love, Aphrodite. Ares, you must stop her.”

“Let it be known,” Zeus addressed the excited crowd. “The challenge is concluded at the end of July, by the Christian calendar.” A breeze whistled through the hyacinth, saturating the courtyard with its luscious floral scent. “The defeated will be banished from Olympus and must roam the earth as a human for one hundred years.”

Zeus spread both his hands wide creating dancing shadows to dim the golden filigree that accented the furniture and urns. Ares repeated the gesture, pressing one hand against that of Zeus and waited for Aphrodite to comply. She stood, raising her palms and completing the circle.

“We are agreed,” Zeus said, and jagged ribbons of electricity connected them. Aphrodite’s muscles seized as the aching hum coursed through her body. The ritual demonstrated a show of trust and power, like a human handshake. But enduring the physical manifestations of Zeus’ authority left crisp agony in its wake.

She gritted her teeth against the taste of blood, watching Ares grimace as they were honor-bound.

When the lightning faded Aphrodite released the bond. The smell of ozone and charred flesh stung her nose and seared the back of her throat.

“You may begin at your leisure,” Zeus said. “I care not what else you do.” He dissipated without further comment. The hall returned to a loud bustle, ripe with wagers and gossip. Aphrodite leveled her sights at Ares.

“I look forward to your downfall,” she said. Her triumph would be absolute.

His lips crooked upward. “As I do yours.” He spun with a flourish, creating a musky gust with his exit.

The tension left Aphrodite’s shoulders and neck as it always did when Ares vacated Olympus. She breathed easier, in fresher air.

In his stead, a long absent but welcome presence made himself known to her. His arrival could not be more fortunate. Her heart lifted as she faced the newcomer.

Her reason for coming to Earth appeared before her, luminous as sunshine on falling rain. She would never have had Hermes in Eden. Her kind could not procreate there; only in a mortal realm could she give birth.

She smiled her adoration on his perfect tan skin, his flaxen curls. His sea-foam eyes met hers and she saw love reflected there. Whenever Aphrodite worshipped the beauty of him, she forgot the pain of her exile.

"My son," she said, placing a gentle hand on his jaw. "Where have you been?"

"Mother…" He said the word with reverence and deep affection. "… You remember I've been to the southern hemisphere, yeah?" He planted a warm kiss on her cheek. It felt like butter and fireworks to her heart.

"Oh yes, that is correct." She tsked him with sweetness. "You speak in the vulgar dialect of the mortals with their clumsy English." Her child had been chasing waves in Australia, no doubt. "What brings you here, my sweet?"

Hermes held her at arms length and teased her with a grin. Sunlight danced from trellises and twinkled in his eyes. "Can't a man visit his mother on a whim?"

"Surfing season is over?"

Hermes gasped, clutching at his chest in a mockingly disgruntled fashion. "What? You're implying I only came to see you because I'm bored?"

Aphrodite arched her brows and placed her hands on her hips in response, causing Hermes' boisterous laughter to ring off the pillars and shake grapes from the vines. He folded her into his arms and squeezed. She reciprocated, and experienced a comfort she never knew anywhere else.

"You are well timed," she said. "He just left."

"I know." Her son's visage shadowed at the mention of his father as he dropped his arms. "I sensed his anger." He peered into her eyes, concern clashing with his handsome good looks. "He's up to something."

"Absolutely," Aphrodite said. "Did you hear of the competition?"

"Yeah, I was wondering about that. Everyone around here is buzzing like flies on a dead dingo, but I couldn't quite pick up on it. What's going on?"

Aphrodite tried to be brief. "Ares and I are embattled. Losing means departing Olympus."

"Really?" Hermes stroked his smooth chin. Aphrodite could almost see the rivers of thought rambling through his head. She understood how Hermes felt about his father. Their loathing for him was mutual. "So if he fails…"

"He cannot set foot in Olympus for one hundred years. He shall become not unlike a mortal man."

"Sweet," Hermes said. Aphrodite shared the idea of an Ares-free home sifting through his thoughts. But his features crumbled. "Mom, he'll cheat."

"More than likely." She shrugged. "I might need a little assistance, and since you have nothing better to do now that summer is over in Australia…"

He grinned at her, pearly teeth gleaming. "Anything for you, Mom."

#   #   #

Strife relished the bite of a stiff martini as the warble of Circuit Freq thumped through her body and assaulted her ears. She hovered in a dark corner, absorbing the vibe in the air and breathing the dusty odor of dry ice.

The crowd jumped to the beat, their mood giving Strife an extra high that had nothing to do with alcohol.

She delighted in Germany's club scene. The black clothes, the piercings, and dismal dance bars amused her.

She'd called Europe home since the sixteen-hundreds, and Strife enjoyed watching fashion and culture evolve. Just in the last forty years music had gone from Disco, to New Wave, to Electronica. The constant changes thrilled her. Not to mention she'd take Latex and leggings over a toga in any era. And certainly the men were easier to manipulate under the influence of increasingly potent drugs.

Even now, hot sweating bodies writhed together. Lust and artificial pleasure oozed through her veins as though it belonged to her. She leeched it from the crowd like a greedy lover, giving nothing in return.

She became dimly aware of a shift in mood. Strife experienced it first as irritation, an unexpected ache deep within that she tried to brush away. It disturbed her euphoria.

A glance at the thick fog on the dance floor revealed an abrupt scattering of limbs and fists. A brawl broke out.

Strife inched to the edge of it to observe. Dancers fled or became trampled in the melee. Screams overpowered the clash of drum machines and keyboards.

What had set them off? She'd sensed no ill will or anger in this ecstasy-laced bunch before. What happened to the happy haze?

A familiar ghost seeped into her consciousness like poison gas.

By all the realms of life, not him. Not here. Strife recalled the drowning sensation she felt whenever that aura invaded her space. She'd hoped to never experience it again.

Horror twisted her intestines as fighters, victims, and bouncers were tossed like bowling pins from the man marching toward her. A shiver stroked her spine. Strife tried to blink the vision away with no success.

Ares.

"Did you miss me, my pet?" he asked. He looked out of place in formal wear with his wavy black hair slicked back. He'd trimmed his beard to a goatee. Knowing Ares he'd done it purposely, to tempt aggression from those who abhorred the upper class.

She'd run from him more than three hundred years ago and now he stood before her as though time and distance were of no importance. She stood astonished and belittled.

"How did you find me?"

"Dear Strife…" he said, winding her hair between his fingers, and causing her to flinch. His pungent cologne couldn't mask the smell of blood. Strife suspected his sleeves would be warm and sticky to the touch.

I always knew where you were.

The words were unspoken, yet they carved an angry welt in her psyche. Her whereabouts were never a secret; he just hadn't bothered to search for her. Until now.

"You must want something." No need to hide her repugnance, he deserved it. "What makes you think I'll give it to you?"

"Ah, Strife… May I call you Strife? I understand you use your true name these days." He halted a steampunk with a top hat and a soul patch, took the drink from his hand, and claimed it in a swallow. “I imagine it works well with this riff-raff. Makes you sound so interesting.”

“What’s your fucking problem, man?” the kid said, but Ares tamed him with a narrowed glare. Whatever the young man saw, or whatever Ares sent to the boy’s thoughts she missed, but the human went white. He shuffled away, peeking back as he distanced himself.

“I have a task for you,” Ares said.

Strife stood her ground. “No. I like my life here. I have a man that takes care of my needs and gives me anything and everything. Not to mention a lucrative trade.”

“Manufacturing and dealing drugs with your sugar daddy?” Strife wanted to slap that smug expression from his face. “It is beneath you, Strife.”

“You have nothing I want,” she said, crossing her arms in defiance.

“I would not waste your time with petty offers.” A smirk tilted his lips. Strife couldn’t help feeling a twinge of anticipation. Chaos comes when Ares smiles. “How would you like to help me ruin Aphrodite once and for all?”

At the sound of that name Strife’s heart skipped a beat. “I’m listening.”

CHAPTER FIVE

Poetry checked her watch. Jenny was early. And she looked gorgeous as always. Even her spearmint-green pin-striped uniform couldn't spoil her beauty. Poetry smiled anyway. She hadn't seen much of her roommate this weekend and the apartment was quiet without her.

As expected, Gary trailed behind her, followed by Ranjan and Adrian.

"Hey, Poe. I like the matching color," Jenny said, indicating Poetry's emerald bangs. "What section you working?"

Poetry pointed her chin to a row of booths, counted out four menus and grabbed a coffee pot. "I got the wall today. When do you start?"

"Six," she said. "We're not eating, just a quick coffee before my shift." She wrapped her arm around Gary's waist and squeezed. "So we can hang out before I say goodbye to my sweetie."

Poetry made no effort to muffle her gagging while she put the menus away. "Yuck. You two need a room."

"No kidding, eh?" Ranjan said. Poetry grinned in agreement and sat them in the corner. In the light of day she couldn't help but notice Ranjan's distinctive features; prominent nose, dusky eyes, and sienna skin. Pretty exotic. She wondered what part of India he came from.

His eyebrows arched at her scrutiny. She stopped staring and shifted her gaze to the table before making eye contact again.

"Make sure they don't do any funny stuff," she said with a wink. "We just had the seats redone."

She poured coffee for all, acknowledging grunted thanks, including the one Adrian grumbled over his shoulder.

He busied himself inspecting the seams in the fabric, running fingers over the stitching like he expected it to tell him a story. Weird.

Whatever. She made a loop with the coffee pot to other customers.

She let Jenny's entourage hang out undisturbed while she sipped roasted Columbian behind the waitress station. The scent soothed her while Jenny and her new jock canoodled across the room.

Poetry ignored the twang of bitterness in her heart, not her coffee. They were a cute couple. And it wasn't as if Jenny deliberately rubbed Poetry's nose in her new relationship. Just because she'd suffered a nasty break up didn't mean Poetry couldn't be happy for them. Right?

Whatever.

She made another round with her carafe and poured refills for Gary, Ranjan, and Adrian but Jenny put her hand over her mug.

On her return to the dish pit, Poetry heard slurpy smacking behind her. Jenny and Gary were kissing again.

"Gotta go sweetheart," Jenny said. "See you tomorrow?"

"Looking forward to it," Gary replied.

Hidden by the partition, Poetry grinned at Jenny when she emerged to tie her apron.

"Aren't you two cozy," she said.

"Oh God, Poetry," Jenny said. "He is such an awesome guy." Her eyes were bright like Christmas tree lights and she squeezed Poetry's arm with enthusiasm. "He has a condo on Jasper Avenue and he drives a BMW, and you know what? We were talking and he thinks I'd make a great legal secretary. They make decent money, you know?"

Poetry nodded, almost listening. She had a few minutes left to her shift and most of her attention belonged to a table making ready to leave.

"Not a bad idea," she said, and strolled toward the till.

She greeted the regulars with her usual friendly banter, accepting their money and pocketing the tip. She tried to be discreet, but considering they'd only ordered burgers and Cokes, five bucks made her grin.

"Have a great day," the gentleman said.

If everyone else tips like you today, I will.

From her periphery she noted Adrian going for the wallet in his back pocket but waved goodbye to the couple as they opened the glass doors…

...And let her nightmare inside.

Kevin slithered forward, all piercings and attitude. Last night's stubble peppered his face. Poetry could smell the booze, day old and recent, blending with the reek of leather and sweat. She supposed his smile was meant to be charming but it had the opposite effect. Her stomach shrank like crumpled paper.

"Hey, baby," Kevin sauntered to the till as if he belonged there. Arrogant prick. But she was too scared to say the words out loud. "Miss me?"

"What are you doing here?" A tremor betrayed her fear. Poetry straightened her spine in defiance, edging away from the cash register. "You need to leave."

"Aw baby, don't be like that." His sweet tone didn't match the fury in his sun-stung eyes. "I just want to talk."

"There's nothing to say," She started to back away. "It's over." She couldn't do this right now. Time to retreat to the pit until Kevin left or someone called the cops, whichever came first. His dirty fingers fastened on her wrist, preventing her escape. His touch was hot and clammy. Feverish.

"C'mon baby," Kevin said. "Don't I get a second chance?" He squeezed tighter and Poetry cringed in pain.

He wouldn't do anything to her right here in front of the entire restaurant? Would he?

"She told you to leave."

# # #

I must be out of my mind, Adrian thought. Assholes like this were processed through the courtroom, whack-a-mole style. This skinny loser had nothing on him weight-wise, but Adrian never underestimated anyone under the influence. The sour smell of rye alone gave him pause. This creep had the strung-out demeanor of a hardcore drug user, like the twitch in his hollowed cheeks. That upped the ante.

Lucky me.

Adrian arranged his legs in his Kendo stance, feet parallel and his balance forward on the balls of his feet. What he wouldn't give for his shinai right now. This guy could use a bamboo sword cracked against his skull. Still, his training might give him an edge in a scrap. Or maybe he should just let the guy hit him and have his ass thrown in jail.

"What part of 'leave' didn't you understand?" Adrian hoped he sounded braver than he felt.

"What are you, her bodyguard?" the loser asked.

Welcome bulk arrived at Adrian's shoulder. "No, I'm a lawyer." He jerked a thumb behind him where Gary waited for action. "He's the bodyguard."

Ranjan sidled up on his left. "You need to get lost, buddy."

This guy had no balls. "Buddy" let go of the girl's arm and backed off, mumbling something about not being afraid of them. Yeah, sure. The cave dweller wasn't so brave against his own gender. He hated guys like that. He glanced over at Jenny's friend as the Neanderthal made a loud exit, trying in vain to slam a hydraulic door.

Adrian wouldn't admit it, but it felt damn good to go up against one of these guys instead of defending them.

Her face had paled and she shook visibly, obviously terrified. What possessed women to date jackasses like that?

A green blur with blonde highlights flashed past Adrian, nearly toppling him, and Jenny latched onto Gary.

"You're so awesome, sweetie," she said with a squeal. "That was so cool of you to stand up for my roommate."

"It was nothing," Gary said. Adrian snorted and tossed a ten on the counter.

Jenny's friend inched to the register, rubbing her arms. She took his money with twitching fingers.

"You alright?" he asked, taking his change from her unsteady grip.

"Sure," she said. She sounded okay. She'd arranged her face into a mask of indifference, but her color hadn't returned.

"I told you he was an asshole, Poetry," Jenny said. She didn't sound too sympathetic. "Now what if he's waiting for you outside? How are you going to get home?"

The girl, Poetry, placed a shivering hand over her mouth and turned an unflattering shade of pale yellowish-green. Geez, she looked pathetic. Like a Tim Burton movie extra.

"Did you walk here?" he asked. She nodded, swallowing hard.

"Jen's right," Ranjan said. "What if that creep is still out there?"

Adrian sighed. He had a bad feeling about this. In fact, he didn't see how this chick and her dumb choices were any of his business. But when he peered into Poetry's frightened brown eyes, it seemed like the right thing to do.

He sighed heavily. "Where do you live? I'll drive you home."

CHAPTER SIX

Fifteen minutes later, Adrian trudged up the rubberized steps behind Poetry. He hadn't lived in an apartment like this since university. He'd forgotten how the stairways smelled in these cheap buildings, like old mud mixed with a variety of starchy and ethnic foods. He could detect Ichiban on one landing and spicy paprika on the next. Poetry's floor reeked of macaroni and cheese.

If I never eat boxed noodles of any kind ever again I can die a happy man.

When Poetry unlocked her door Adrian got such a lungful he could almost taste it. Nice. Maybe I could die now.

Hot air blasted him like a furnace. No air conditioning either.

"You didn't have to walk me all the way up. But I really appreciate it."

"No problem," Adrian shrugged. "I feel better knowing you're home safe. That guy was an asshole."

Poetry sighed as she kicked her flats across the tile. "So everyone keeps telling me."

A streak of black skittered across the living room and latched pointy teeth into Adrian's toes. "Ow! What the?"

"Amir," Poetry lifted the tiny ball of fur to her chin. "Guests' feet are not for playing with."

"Meow?" The kitten's motor-like purr demonstrated no remorse.

"Bad kitty." And her voice had all the rancor of rainbows and ice cream. She retrieved a stuffed white mouse from the top of the refrigerator. It jingled as she shook it, and the cat's blue eyes riveted to the toy held in her fingers.

Poetry carefully placed the cat back on the floor, tossing the mouse into the living room. “Go play with your friend, Amir.”

“Strange name for a cat,” Adrian said.

Poetry’s eyes never left the tumbling chunk of lint, but she smirked.

“I named him after my favorite rock star, Amir Derakh, lead guitarist of Julien K.” Poetry made eye contact with him. Her grin grew wider still. “He’s Persian-American.”

Adrian snickered. Of course he is. “You’re funny.” His flat tone denied his statement, and she laughed.

An awkward moment passed as she glanced around the small space. “Listen, since you’re here do you mind, uh…”

“You want me to check the rooms?” he asked. “Does your ex have a key?”

“No,” Poetry shook her bangs into her eyes, pushed them back. “I never gave him one, it’s just…”

“Got it.” She thinks he’s dangerous enough to break in. Lucky me.

Adrian took off his sneakers just inside the kitchen area. He didn’t want to lose them in the pile of women’s footwear strewn in the foyer. Women and their frickin’ shoes.

“I wouldn’t put it past the guy to do something stupid.” He grabbed the nearby broom and twisted the bristles off the bottom.

“Exactly,” Poetry stepped aside, letting him pass.

Adrian took a deep breath and went into kamae. He placed his right foot parallel in front of his left, with his improvised weapon held an inch from his belly button.

The stick wasn’t a shinai but it would suffice. A good ‘men’ strike on the head would fix that shithead.

Bright sunlight from the west-facing windows caught floating dust and cat hair as he slid across the dingy carpet. This is why kendokka practiced barefoot on hardwood floors. Maintaining strict form here could put holes in his socks and give him rug burn on the balls of his feet.

He edged to the hall with three doors. Poetry kept her distance.

First stop, Jenny's room, or so the Hello Kitty sign on the door informed him. Adrian wanted to gag. How old was that girl? Twenty-one going on twelve?

The door creaked open with a nudge, and Adrian's eyes were assaulted with unicorns on the walls and stuffed animals on the bed. He didn't quite stifle a groan.

"I know, right?" Poetry said. "If it's sickeningly cute, she collects it."

She punctuated the statement with a quirk of her lips that Adrian returned before poking his head in. Not many places to hide.

"All clear," he said. Poetry sighed, but retreated to the living room.

He prodded the next door open with the broomstick. Must be Poetry's room. No mythological creatures or fluffy bunnies.

A cluttered desk in the corner displayed mason jars of beads and fasteners surrounding a laptop. Haphazard rolls of wires lay next to boxes of Slow-Dry art clay.

Adrian stepped in for closer inspection. Only two things decorated the walls.

One was a certificate from a school called Valentin Yotkov Studio in New York for metal sculpting. Impressive. Adrian developed a bit more respect for Poetry and her claims of artistry. No doubt she took her career seriously. The other picture appeared to be a massive collage, under construction and growing. He hadn't seen one of these since grade five art classes.

Photos of seascapes with quaint villages, Greek if he identified the white buildings and blue domes correctly, mixed with brochures for other art academies. She'd glued in magazine pictures of designs and techniques. The whole vision came together with strategically placed beads and chains to bring them together like a dream.

It hit him. Not a dream. A timeline. This paper tangle represented Poetry's life plan. And she aimed high. She wanted to study and learn her craft before moving to Greece someday.

For a strange moment Adrian shared her hopes. He found himself glad he hadn't brushed her off. Maybe they did have some common ground. The difference between himself and Poetry was she'd taken her hobby and made it her life's work and he'd gone to law school instead.

He hadn't zoned out long, but he realized he stood alone in a stranger's bedroom. Thoughts of forgotten aspirations left him with a gaping emptiness.

And the realization of his mistake. No jackass here either. Good thing too, Adrian had let his guard down.

Bathroom next.

He crept past hair appliances and products on the sink and pulled the shower drape back. The squeal of metal curtain hooks scraping across the rod coaxed a yelp from Poetry somewhere behind him. Nothing and nobody. Outside the bathroom pattering paws and claws made little tears in the rug and the ringing of the mouse's bell continued. Poetry shut both bedroom doors.

"He's not here," Adrian said. He hoped Poetry didn't notice the embarrassing way he let his breath out. He left the cluttered space and headed through the living room to the exit, peeking in the kitchen to be sure. Poetry followed, still trying to act brave.

Adrian handed her the broomstick and retrieved his footwear.

"Thanks so much," she said again. "For coming up here." She kneaded her multi-colored forearms.

He tied his shoes and straightened before meeting her gaze. "Not a big deal. I've seen guys like him come through court all the time." Usually on assault charges.

She scrutinized the kitchen floor as she hugged herself. Her shiver brought another of those annoying pangs of sympathy. She couldn't be cold in this brutal heat. He'd worked up a sweat in the five minutes he'd been there.

You cannot leave her like this.

The thought came like a whispering voice inside his head. Take her away from here. Perhaps for dinner.

Yeah, right. But his stomach rumbled on cue.

"Have you eaten yet?"

Why he was he doing this? He had no interest in this girl. But he could tell by her anxious expression that she's rather be anywhere but here.

She glanced at him sideways, suspicion pinching her lips. "No, I haven't."

"I know this great Cajun place not too far from here."

"Louisiana Purchase?"

"That's the one," he said, and gave her what he hoped was an encouraging grin. "You been?"

"They make a mean shrimp po' boy." Poetry's lips twisted in a good way.

"That's my favorite. Get your shoes and let's go. I could use a beer."

A smile burst across her face. "Me too. Let me get changed."

Adrian's happy face tightened. Wonderful. Should be as much fun as writing the bar exam. Whose dumb idea was this anyway?

# # #

Strife stared at Ares' toes as her aching hips slipped up and down his cock. Her mind focused on his stunning girth, an immense size that Earth girls paid for in tawdry shops with frosted glass windows. It hurt at first, such a long time since she'd had this enormous flesh, but an orgasm was already building.

She could still taste his filth, smell his clammy sweat. It didn't matter. She'd almost unhinged her jaw sucking him stiff and now she would take her pleasure. She rolled her head back while her steady rhythm propelled her to gasping, ferocious joy.

She yielded to it, dimly aware of her squeals echoing off the high ceiling of her loft, of the creaking of her mattress springs as she exploded in ecstasy. She ground her pussy down, savoring the waves of gratification and squeezing every sunburst of intensity from the moment. The black and white prints on her walls dimmed and blurred when her vagina clenched, and she cried herself hoarse.

A final sigh left her lips. Sore but sated, she crawled forward with trembling arms.

She got what she wanted. Ares could jack himself off for all she cared. He wasn't her master. His pleasure wasn't her concern.

She should have known he wouldn't let her go that easily. Even as she attempted to elevate herself off his dick he sat up.

"We are not finished, whore." He shoved her forward, forcing her to her hands and knees. His fingers dug into her hips as he jammed his massive prick in once again.

She screamed. Too hard. Too deep. Too fast.

Ares ploughed her relentlessly, his thickness stretching her as he spread her thighs wider.

"You are nothing but a common slut, Strife," he said through his teeth. "You think you can use men for your own, but you need to be fucked like a rented cunt." He delivered a stinging slap to her ass.

Strife moaned and shut her eyes as her traitorous body pushed against him. Another shockwave of wet desire rippled through her with each pounding stroke. Animal grunts that shouldn't belong to her tore from her throat. Another spanking smarted her skin. She wouldn't let him make her come. He had no power over her. But her body tightened in anticipation.

"Yes, you like it rough, whore." His panting grew louder. "You want it to hurt."

Strife grabbed handfuls of sheet, tried to crawl away. Ares threw his body weight on top of her. Her nipples stung with abrasions from the Egyptian cotton sheets. He pinned her wrists with both hands, ramming her until her pelvis bounced off the bed with each plunge.

She cried into her linens with every wanton pulse as she fought for control. Her heart beat faster as Ares pushed harder against her sweat-slicked ass. His scrotum tapped her clitoris incessantly. His sour breath warmed her ear and his rutting grew more frenzied. He wouldn't stop until she was raw.

"I know how you like it, slut. You will come like the dirty little pig you are."

Strife took the deepest breath her crushed lungs could spare and let go. Another dizzying orgasm took her and she let out a throaty wail as the rush engulfed her.

Spots appeared behind her closed lids, her body alive with sensations of pleasure and pain. She listened to the roar and growl of Ares releasing his seed and lay unresisting as he slammed his prick in for a final thrust and as he pulled out afterwards, dribbling hot semen down to tickle her sensitive folds. She waited patiently while he wiped the stickiness on her buttocks. Only when she felt him leave the bed did she open her eyes again. She glared at him with unabashed hatred. He either didn't notice or didn't care.

He sauntered to his discarded clothing, checking through the pockets of his pants. What was he searching for?

A white rectangle appeared in his hand, which he tossed at Strife.

“Get dressed, bitch.” Strife peeled the envelope from her cheek and opened it. Inside she found a one way ticket to Canada. “You have work to do.”

CHAPTER SEVEN

Poetry tossed her napkin on her plate and grinned in satisfaction. The succulent shrimp and smooth nuttiness of the rice lingered as she sat back to let her food settle.

"That really hit the spot."

"Oh, yeah," Adrian piled the last of his beans onto a crust of bread.

Poetry sipped at her Kokanee, enjoying the subtle breeze that wafted over the patio and whispered through the surrounding hedges. The sun hadn't quite set, but their table sat in shade and the wind raised goosebumps on her skin. Classical music played in the background. The quiet murmurs of other diners added to the ambience.

"So, tell me about your job," Poetry said. Not that she cared really, but it made for small talk. Uncomfortable silences weren't fun at the best of times, but after Kevin's appearance she needed to take her mind elsewhere. "Why did you decide to become a lawyer?"

Adrian smiled. "I don't know, too much TV as a child?" He chuckled and Poetry warmed toward him. He didn't strike her as the kind of kid who parked his behind in front of the tube. "I used to watch a lot of cop shows. Bad boys, bad boys. Whatcha gonna do?"

Poetry grinned into her beer and studied his body language. She liked how he sang with his head tucked down. He had a shyness to him she hadn't expected.

"But you didn't become a cop."

Adrian jerked his head. "No. Not that I didn't want to be part of the justice system. Actually it's the opposite." His lips quirked. "This probably sounds really arrogant, but I thought my intelligence would be wasted on the force."

Poetry opened her mouth to politely protest, but he held up a restraining hand.

"Don't get me wrong. Law enforcement is a noble calling. But in real life perps don't stay behind bars without a good prosecutor."

The beers must be taking effect. That remark should have annoyed her, Poetry didn't like conceited men, but she loved confidence. A fine line separated the two. Those down-turned eyes suggested modesty more than pride.

"And the money's better," he said.

This time she chortled along with him. "So how did you wind up doing defense?"

A shadow darkened Adrian's expression as the waiter came to clear their plates. "The firm placed me according to my talents and compassion. Lucky me." He rolled his bottle on the table between his fingers and ordered them another round.

Had she said something wrong? The jovial mood switched to sour all of a sudden and Poetry didn't understand why. She rubbed the inked-in grape vines trailing down her shoulder.

"Do you want to talk about it?" She kept her tone casual, hoping she didn't hit a nerve or barge into his business.

Adrian sighed. "I shouldn't," he said, and swallowed the rest of his beer in a single gulp. "But sometimes you have to do things you don't like to further your career. Like representing people you think might be better off locked up."

The waiter arrived with two more beer. When he departed, Poetry leaned forward. "What do you mean?"

"Did you hear about that guy who shot two gay men on his property? The rancher from that little hick town west of Stony Plain?"

“I saw that one on the news.” She recalled the footage, remembered the faces on the television screen. “Frank Fleisher, right? You’re representing him?”

“Yep.” He took a smaller pull, regarded the bottle and pushed it a little farther away from himself. “I shouldn’t have ordered this.”

“I won’t tell anyone anything,” Poetry said. It was an easy promise to make--she valued privacy. “Not even Jenny.”

Adrian gave her a genuinely warm smile. She couldn’t put her finger on it, but he seemed different from the first time she’d met him. Even from when he’d been at Denny’s. He’d given her the impression he didn’t like her. But here he sat, eating dinner, confiding in her like a friend. Oddly enough, it made her skin tingle.

Huh. I’d better lay off the beer too.

“Thanks,” he said. “But Gary will probably tell her anyway.”

“Hey, mate. Buy a flower for your girl?” They both jumped as a man appeared next to Adrian carrying a basket of roses.

Poetry’s mouth dropped. If the accent wasn’t hot enough, he had the face and body of a god. His curls shone in the late sun and his enchanting green eyes made her pulse pound in her throat. What a beautiful man.

Adrian shook his head. “Actually, she’s not my girl.”

“She should be,” the tanned Adonis said. “Pretty little Sheila like that?”

Poetry giggled, but groaned inwardly. She sounded like a moron. The only thing worse than feeling fat around good-looking guys was feeling stupid in front of them.

The guy with the rose basket winked at her, driving butterflies around her stomach, slightly unsettling her food. She closed her mouth and sucked in her gut.

Please God, don't give me gas. That's all I need right now is to burp in front of the hottie. Classy.

Adrian made eye contact with rose guy for a hushed tick. "Oh, what the hell," he said. "How about the yellow one?"

The man presented the blossom with a flourish. "Not a bad choice," he said, peering at Adrian sideways. "But…"

"But what? It's the color of friendship, isn't it? That's what I heard."

"Oh, it's true," the stranger said. He glanced over and gave Poetry a wide, knowing twitch of his lips that made Poetry's sensitive stomach flip over. "But I think she'd much prefer this."

He replaced the yellow one. In its stead he retrieved a plum rose so dark it appeared almost black.

Poetry gasped. Her favorite. How did he know? It was a twin to the one tattooed down her thigh.

She glanced at Adrian. He'd seen her reaction, and handed cash to the Aussie rose guy. "Looks like you're right. Thanks, buddy."

Adrian passed the flower across the table. It smelled rich, like summer in heaven.

Poetry found herself so enthralled with its beauty she didn't hear the sexy guy leave, but she didn't much care.

"Thank you, Adrian."

"You're welcome." Adrian shrugged. "You should have seen the way your eyes lit up when you saw it."

Poetry felt her mouth tugging upward until a sad thought dragged it back down. "Kevin never gave me flowers."

Why'd she have to think of him now? He kept popping into her mind like a bad dream. She was sick of it.

"Sorry to hear that." His voice sounded carefully neutral. She didn't look up, but she heard the huffed breath across the tablecloth. She'd ruined the mood.

"Personally, I don't know what you saw in him." Adrian grabbed his beer and took another swig. "Why do girls go out with guys like that?"

Poetry shrugged. "We like to tame bad boys." Wow, what a lame thing to say.

"Guess that's why I'm still single." Adrian said. "The only thing that changes a jackass like that is jail time."

"I know that now," Poetry said and sighed when she caught the edge in her voice. "It's not like I have a lot of practice dealing with guys."

He held his palms up in a placating gesture. "Me neither. I mean, with girls. Practicing." His shoulders slumped. "If only it were that easy, huh? If we could get a trial run or two?"

She pinched her lips shut and kept her eyes to the tablecloth to keep from smiling. That wasn't a half-bad idea.

She heard him shuffling. "How about if we change the subject?"

Poetry released the breath she'd been holding. "Great idea. What do you want to talk about?"

"I'm tired of babbling about myself," Adrian said. "What about you? Tell me about your art. Is that necklace you're wearing one of your pieces?"

Relief washed over her. She never tired of discussing her work. Hopefully it wouldn't bore him. She lifted her fingers beneath the chain so he could see the intricate links, when a shrill beeping interrupted.

"Oh, I'm sorry, that's mine." Adrian yanked his cell phone from his jacket pocket and gawked at the display. "It's Gary."

He pressed a button and placed it on his ear. "Yeah?"

A long pause ensued. Poetry couldn't make out words, but the voice on the other end sounded rushed and garbled.

Adrian's face went from cheerful to alarm in less than a minute. When he glanced her way, she counted the heartbeats in her ears. Whatever it was, it didn't look good.

"She's fine," he said. "In fact, she's here with me. We decided to go for a bite." More squawking erupted from his phone. Why would Gary call Adrian about her? She pulled her own phone from her purse, only to discover she'd shut it off. Right. To avoid any calls from her ex after his cameo appearance. Maybe Jenny was trying to contact her. But why? She wouldn't be off work yet.

"What? Why?" Adrian's mouth dropped. "What?" He said the word so loud, other customers turned to stare.

"We're on our way." He hung up and flagged the waiter. "Check please?"

"What's going on?"

"We have to go to your apartment. Now," he said. "Your ex made it in after all."

Panic set in as Poetry gathered her things. "I'll call a cab." she said, and hurried behind Adrian, dropping the rose to the brick floor in her haste.

CHAPTER EIGHT

Strife dragged her weary bones off the Greyhound and wiped the grime of several time zones from her face. The monotonous trip from Germany hadn't ended at the Toronto Airport. From there, she'd flown to Edmonton, only to take a bus to Grey, Alberta. She'd never been a strong deity. Strife hoarded what little power she had. She couldn't afford to use it on travel.

Despite the fact that Ares could magick her across the world on a whim, he refused. Instead, he made her take human transport the entire way. Something about her mission being secret and conserving his strength to deal with Aphrodite.

Strife sneered. She didn't believe him. He enjoyed making her feel insignificant, like a dog. A lackey. Why did she let him treat her like a slave?

She searched for a distraction to the disturbing thoughts.

A sign in need of a hose down and paint welcomed her to this mangy town. Not much to see. But she understood why they called it Grey. Everything from buildings to lampposts seemed to be covered in a film of neglect. Even the parked vehicles. Apparently this dump had no car wash.

This wasn't a town as such. She hesitated to call it a hamlet. The narrow street boasted a convenience store that doubled as a gas station and a hotel-slash-cafe-slash-bar. Every community it seemed, no matter how small, had one of these.

Strife's spirits lifted as she made her way to the decrepit buildings. She would start there.

#   #   #

The grey-haired woman across the counter scowled. Just as Ares warned, the locals weren't friendly. Strife's appearance didn't help, with her hair the color of pitch and her tilted jade eyes.

The matron pursed her lips, trying not to call her a 'chink' out loud, unaware of Strife's telepathy. Obvious as well was her unwillingness to rent her a room. Granny's disapproval virtually hummed.

Strife cranked her charm; let it ooze from her skin. She batted her lashes in the most sincere manner she could manage and licked caked lipstick from her mouth.

"Please, ma'am," she said. "I really need a place to stay." Somewhere beyond her sight rodents scurried in the walls. She heard the skitter of tiny claws over the wheezing ceiling fan.

"Well…" Granny dropped her gaze to her paperwork, avoiding Strife's pleading gaze.

Strife leaned in, rubbing her wrists together before clasping her hands in a gracious gesture. The crisp sweetness of green apple perfume carried from the fan's draft. She studied the bulbous beak of the old bat across from her, waited for the tell-tale sign of flared nostrils. At last the bitch breathed deep, taking in the chemically altered scent, completing the influence. Strife sensed her mood change.

"Something just opened up." Her dentures gleamed with her phony smile. "I think we could accommodate you after all."

Strife let her open lips spread across her face, aware that her clenched teeth could be interpreted as menacing rather than lovely, but she couldn't help it. Manipulating humans made her giddy.

"That would be nice," she said. "I have a lot of work to do."

CHAPTER NINE

Poetry couldn't get home fast enough. Even as Adrian paid the cab driver she stormed the stairs like a dyslexic lemming.

And came to an abrupt halt when she saw the remains of the doorjamb. Kindling littered the ground. The deadbolt, still in the locked position, lay among the wreckage. Squawking radios chanted from within.

The tall uniform guarding the door held out a hand. "Sorry," he said. "You can't go in there."

"I live here. I need to see Jenny."

Adrian caught up behind her. "What the hell?"

She swallowed. "I have no idea." At least Poetry sounded calmer than she felt. She listened to the strange voices and static for a lengthy moment, trying to pull her head together.

"We should go inside," Adrian said. "The police will want to speak to you. And Jenny needs you right now."

"Go on in," the cop shifted aside. "If you're involved in any way we need your cooperation."

Convincing argument, but now wasn't the time to fall apart. Poetry braved the threshold.

The chaos made her want to spin around and run. She smelled oranges and pungent onions mixed with raw burger. Margarine adorned the walls like abstract art. The word 'slut' and a 'c' word she found too disgusting to say out loud were traced in mustard and ketchup across the refrigerator.

As she inched inside she realized she didn't trip over any shoes. All of them, runners, pumps and boots lay in a charred pile in the center of the living room rug. Soot blackened the ceiling.

Jenny perched awkwardly on the arm of the gutted sofa, Gary's arms secure around her. She hadn't even changed out of her work clothes. She glanced up with her tear-streaked face and a lump of guilt wedged in Poetry's throat.

"We tried phoning you," Jenny said. "The landlord called me home from work. We had no idea where you were."

"I know," Poetry shied away from the aggravated confusion in Jenny's eyes. "It was off. In case Kevin tried to call."

An officer meandered toward Poetry. When she moved to address him, she saw the contents of the cat box spread over the kitchen floor.

Amir.

"Amir?" Panic seized her. All other thoughts washed away as she pushed Adrian aside.

"Where's my cat?"

She stomped to the bathroom, ignoring the cold water seeping into her shoes from the cracked toilet. Shampoo and mousse slimed every surface; the chemical stench teased her nose. Eyeshadow made pretty puddles of pink and blue.

But no Amir.

Her breath came in painful gasps. She circled to her bedroom door.

What bedroom door? It lay in separate pieces on each side of the room.

"Amir!"

"Poetry calm down," Jenny said. But Poetry heard her like a distant shout from another reality. She flicked the light switch and stomped over what remained of her scattered possessions. She slipped and skidded over a lake of beads. "Amir baby, where are you?"

"Mew?" The muffled response came from her end table.

Poetry nearly collapsed with relief. "Where are you, sweetie?"

She clambered over her slashed mattress and pillows, through a cloud of feathers to the dim corner, noting the shattered glass of her reading lamp.

If he hurt my cat, I'll kill him.

Poetry had no doubt in her mind that Kevin had done this. No one else could be capable of so much hatred. And Jenny didn't have any weirdoes in her past.

Why hadn't she seen this coming?

She carefully squeezed her way into the tiny space between her bed and closet, listening for Amir.

"Mew." His call was faint. She strained her vision scanning the shard-strewn carpet.

She hunched, careful not to kneel in the sharp mess or place her hands in the black and gold splinters remaining on the nightstand.

Amir languished in the corner like a discarded stuffed toy, his half-shut blues gazing at nothing.

Joy mingled with intense terror. "Oh my poor angel," she said, picking him up with as much tenderness as she could with shaking hands. "Are you okay, baby?"

But it wasn't her trembling like that. It was Amir. His fluffy body felt feverish and frail. His breathing seemed labored. The taste of regurgitated shrimp and beer hit the back of Poetry's throat.

She'd only had him a few weeks. She'd been stupid to leave Amir so vulnerable. She should have had a neighbor watching him. Or a babysitter. Maybe she was a shitty mommy and shouldn't have brought him home at all.

Fresh tears gushed. That bastard will pay.

“Miss Manousakis?”

Poetry viewed the policeman through the blur of grief. “I need help,” she said, surprised how calm she sounded, despite the whirlwind of emotions flooding her heart. “He hurt my cat. I need to get him to a vet.”

“Yes, but we need to ask you some questions,” he said. “We’ll see to your cat, but-“

“I’m not doing anything until I take care of my fucking cat.”

Another shadow joined the first.

“I’ll take him, Poetry,” Adrian said. “These guys know me. I can take care of Amir and catch up later.” Through the glaze of rage and pain she saw him reaching out. Compassion softened his eyes. “I promise I’ll take good care of him.”

“Roommate says a guy named Kevin Ferris did this. You know him, Olsen?” the cop asked.

“Not really,” Adrian said. “I had a little run in with him today. Didn’t come to anything, but I’ll come by and make a statement later.”

“Works for me,” said the cop. “Miss Manousakis? Give him the cat, alright? Adrian’s a good guy. He’ll take care of it.”

Poetry loathed the idea. She had to go with him. Amir was her cat. She’d failed to protect him and she had to make it better.

“We have your ex in custody on an unrelated charge.” The police man grasped Poetry’s elbow, tried to guide her up. “We need to take you downtown for some paperwork.”

She resisted. Adrian still held his hands out for her kitten.

“Mew.”

The pathetic sound snapped Poetry’s heart in half. Amir needed help. Now. She had no choice. She had to what was best for him.

Poetry relinquished him to Adrian, stroking the soft fur on Amir's head with one finger.

"Take good care of my baby."

Adrian nodded. "I promise I will." He disappeared, leaving Poetry to absorb her misery.

CHAPTER TEN

Poetry couldn't remember a longer night. She ran her hands down tear-dampened cheeks as she stomached the silence inside Gary's BMW. Poetry would have loved to hunker into the buttery cushions, inhale the faint new car-plastic-and-leather scent as streetlamps drifted by tinted windows. Having been in a luxury vehicle only twice in one day, she finally understood the attraction.

But the freakish events of the evening had taken its toll and she couldn't loosen up.

"I told you he was a loser," Jenny commented from the front seat. She'd been using that word to describe Kevin every day for weeks. Months.

"I know. I'm sorry." How many times did she need to apologize? After tonight Jenny would never let it go.

Jenny held her hand at the police station, even though Poetry sensed her hurt, worry, and fear. They clung together for support when asked to identify the man who they believed ransacked their apartment.

Kevin had been bellowing nonsense behind the mirror, saying the war god told him to 'lay waste' to his enemies. Poetry almost didn't recognize the dirty, sweaty gargoyle tipping chairs in the dingy interrogation room. It took four cops to subdue him.

It wasn't until they questioned Poetry about his drug use and criminal record that Jenny's attitude changed.

"We arrested him walking down the middle of the Jasper Avenue, higher than a kite, disrupting traffic. We found used syringes on his person as well as heroin," the officer said. "You had no idea he was using?"

"I didn't," Poetry said. "I guess it explains a lot."

"Then you are unaware he's got a record for possession and a few B&E's."

She'd wanted to vomit. She still tasted the burn at the back of her throat. Who was this guy? Who'd she been dating for four months? How could she be so stupid? And used needles. Thank God for safe sex. At least she'd been smart enough to use condoms. Her dread grew worse when she noticed Jenny's withdrawal. A barrier of seething fury came between them and had remained since. Poetry had no idea how to make amends.

"You're sorry?" Jenny spun around and Poetry flinched at the frenzied gleam in her eyes. "You brought a drug addicted criminal into our lives, Poetry. He wrecked everything."

Poetry winced. She deserved Jenny's rage. And she braced for more.

"I had some of those stuffed animals since I was a kid. Those dishes were the first matching set I'd ever owned. I got them for Christmas." Jenny took a deep breath. "You suck, Poetry."

"That's enough, Jen," Gary said, using one hand to rub her friend's shoulder. "It's been a rough night."

Jenny faced the windshield and ignored Poetry as though she hadn't erupted.

Poetry wished the car didn't have such a quiet engine. She needed something to kill the tension. As much as she wanted to hear the radio, a CD, anything, she figured no one was in the mood for music. And she didn't dare speak. Her voice could crack, and she might start crying again.

"Do I turn left here, Poetry?" Gary asked.

She peered out the window at the teal blue peaks of the Jasper Gates strip mall. "Yeah." She tried not to sound weepy. "Left here and right on ninety-seventh."

Within moments Poetry recognized the dirty-snow colored stucco and green trim of her parents' house. "This is it."

As she expected, theirs was the only one ablaze with light on this sleepy avenue. Not a lot happened on Sunday night in this neighborhood. At least she would be safe.

Gary pulled up to the curb and Poetry clutched her purse. "Thanks for the ride."

She caught a tentative smile lifting his lips through the shadows. "You're welcome."

Poetry gathered her courage. "Jenny? Mom said you're more than welcome to take the guest room."

Jenny stiffened. "Tell your mom thanks, but no. I'm staying with Gary tonight."

"Okay. I'll see you tomorrow?"

Jenny said nothing, so Poetry shut the door and tread lightly over the sidewalk to her childhood home.

Geez, Jenny was pissed. In two and a half years Poetry had never seen her so mad. But it's not as though I did it on purpose, she thought, trying to come to terms with the damage done to their friendship. It scared me too. She didn't think Jenny cared right now. She had to admit, she blamed herself as well.

Before she reached the front step she heard the click of the lock as the deadbolt disengaged. Her mother's thin silhouette blocked the glare of the indoor fixtures, and Poetry experienced a wave of reassurance that transformed her into a little girl again.

"Mama." The screen door creaked open, and Poetry rushed up the concrete stairs into welcoming arms. Behind her the BMW hummed away.

"Sweetie, I'm so sorry," her mother said, stroking her hair and hugging her until she squeezed Poetry's sobs free. "Are you alruh…huh-Achoo!"

Poetry pulled away with a start. Any comfort she'd cherished evaporated with the reminder of her mother's allergies. Poetry gave her clothes a once-over. She must be covered in fur and dander.

"Bless you," she said.

Her mother snuffled. "Sorry. Come inside. I made us some tea."

Poetry followed her mom to the kitchen.

She sat at the wooden table amidst the soothing decor. The blue and white plates and potted ivy crawling up the walls mimicked a Greek restaurant, but she'd always loved it. She decorated her home and body with the same look. Right down to the foliage on her forearms.

"Where's Dad?"

Her mother presented her with a hot beverage. "I let him sleep."

A hush fell as they sipped. Despite the heat outside, Poetry clasped her hands to the ceramic. The warmth soaked into her palms and the flowery chamomile perfume mollified her.

"Are you going to tell him?" Poetry asked.

"Lord knows I should," her mother said, pinching the bridge of her nose. Poetry knew the gesture well. It demonstrated her mother's exasperation. "I don't keep secrets from your father."

Poetry studied her mother's pasty complexion. Too many years behind a desk? Or did her concern wash out her face? Most likely allergies.

"Please Mom. Just this once." Poetry hated upsetting her father. Everything from the downcast expression in his eyes to the heaving sigh as he rubbed his chest produced anxiety and guilt for her.

"Poetry, you can't build trust in a relationship if you don't communicate." Her mother trumpeted her nose through a Kleenex. "If you understood that, you might not be in this situation."

Ouch.

"Thanks, Mom. That was really helpful." Poetry loved her parents, but this was the exact reason she rarely confided in them. She couldn't say or do anything without being judged. From the day she'd had her eyebrow pierced they acted as if she was incapable of thinking for herself. Granted, tonight didn't help matters.

At any rate, she didn't have the energy to fight. With her mother's stinging words ringing through her head, Poetry abandoned her tea and descended the stairs to her old room in the basement.

"Poetry…" Her mother's voice was a stage whisper. "We'll talk in the morning…"

Not if I can help it, Poetry thought. Worse than her father's disappointment was her mother's subtle scolding. But she couldn't find somewhere else to sleep this late.

She let herself into her teenage bedroom and allowed memories to flood back with a flick of the light switch. It hadn't changed since she'd left home. Orgy and Rammstein greeted her without words, their paper faces frozen in a layer of dust. A faded purple comforter on a well-worn mattress invited her to crawl in. She remembered lounging there for hours, listening to headphones and sketching rock stars. Even the scent of hairspray still permeated the walls. She felt so much younger here.

Poetry stripped and slipped beneath the covers. She needed rest, and tonight that meant leaving the lamps on for a small sense of security. Wrapped in the cool sheets, Poetry drifted. She tried not to think about Kevin. Instead she wondered, with an ache in her heart, if Amir would be okay. The skin beneath his fur had been too warm. He'd felt so fragile in her hands and sounded so pitiful when he meowed at her that she…

Poetry bolted upright. All thoughts of slumber vanished.

She'd given her injured baby to a stranger, to take him to God only knows where. She literally didn't have a clue where her cat was or if he lived. Poetry groaned. Why? Why did she let Adrian have him? How could she have been such a bad mommy? Thoughts of inadequacy and self-reproach filled Poetry until her nerves tightened with tension and remorse. There would be no sleep for her tonight.

CHAPTER ELEVEN

Strife swept a hand through her newly blonde hair. She hated it. This tacky shade seemed to be the North American idea of beauty, but Strife couldn't understand it. What a monotonous color. Dreadfully boring. But she would fit in better with these narrow-minded simpletons if she looked more Caucasian.

It took her a long time to find a bleaching agent. Hair dye was not to be found in this backwater town. She'd had to improvise with her personal stash of chemical wonders.

A smile of satisfaction slid up her face as she recalled sneaking the bag through customs. She'd used all her mental abilities and olfactory influence to get the various liquids and powders through.

But the well-meaning and professional staff were exhausted and easily distracted. If anyone discovered what she'd smuggled across the ocean and most of Canada there'd have been widespread panic--terrorism warning levels would reach new heights.

"You're new here."

Strife batted her eyes at the weathered face of a local who'd approached the rickety stools. "I sure am." She sidled closer and spread her palms over the sticky bar. "It's my first day."

"Well, I must say you're a prettier sight than old Max," he said, sizing her up without subtlety. "How'd you get that cheap bastard to hire you anyway?"

Her chiming laughter filled the dank expanse, disturbing the two or three customers huddled at the round tables. It drowned out the country music warbling from the speakers.

Strife's mirth ended in phony nonchalance. This must be her own personal hell. The real question he should ask is why would she want the job?

"I made him a drink he'd never forget," she said with a wink. "It's called an Apple Jack. Want to try it?"

The stranger waved the idea away. "I'm a beer man, m'self. I don't drink that hard shit, pardon my language."

"You know," She poured a shot of Jack Daniels on the rocks, "it would sure make me look good to Max if you had one." She topped it off with apple juice, and her 'spices'. "I'd like to show him that I can sell my…specialties."

She held the frosty glass aloft, letting the caramel color catch the meager sunlight struggling through the windows. "Just try it. For me?"

The bar patron eyed it and licked his lips. The heat of the day had already seeped into the building and the lunch hour wasn't even over yet.

Sweat glittered on his upper lip. "Well…Okay," he said. "But only if you'll have one with me."

"Fair enough." Strife swiped another tumbler and filled it with a scoop of ice. A shot of JD went in along with apple juice. She skipped the cinnamon shaker. No need to muddle her senses.

The man raised his drink. "To your new job."

She lifted hers in response. "To new beginnings."

They toasted and drank deep. Strife savored the sweetness that burned. She heard the audible swallow from her new friend and caught a whiff of his boozy breath as he exhaled.

"Woo!" Strife grinned as he shook off the bite. "That's really something."

"Told you."

"Yep. You were right." He swirled the contents around his jingling glass. "So where is Max anyway?"

Strife pointed to her right where the barrel-chested owner wobbled to a stool. He pumped a fist in the air while he snarled about justice and retribution.

"He's had a few of these," Strife said. "Maybe I shouldn't have let him have so many."

She shrugged. Her customer's beverage needed refreshing. This time she added extra cinnamon-flavored encouragement.

The bar-fly took the refill without question. "What's his problem?"

Funny you should ask.

Strife waved a negligent hand. "He's upset about Frank Fleisher."

She stared at the man across from her, waiting for the desired reaction. His clouded blue eyes refocused and widened. *Perfect.*

"Frank?" He sounded worried. "What happened to Frank?"

"You don't know?" Strife painted her face with innocence. Inwardly, she gloated. Humans were easy. "He's been framed for murder."

His jaw gaped open like a choking victim, disbelief registering in the sudden sallowing of his leathery skin. Shallow gasps emerged from his throat.

"I don't believe it. What happened?"

The man sat primed and ready for her lies and embellishments. Like Max. And she'd just begun.

CHAPTER TWELVE

Depression prevented Poetry from waking any earlier than nine. Tossing and turning for hours hadn't helped. The morning shadows and warmth of her comforter conspired to keep her there.

She'd hidden in her room, pretending to be asleep until her parents left for work at Grant MacEwan College. As soon as she heard the door lock, she snuck up the basement stairs, showered and fixed herself breakfast. Usually she loved bacon and scrambled eggs. Today they sat like salty lard and congealed slime in her mouth.

She didn't have a bingo dauber to color her hair, and leaving her bangs blonde made her feel naked. Wearing last night's outfit made her look grungy. Not a good start.

She called in sick to work, claiming nausea and confessing to a long night of dealing with her ex.

"I'm sorry. I haven't even been back to the apartment yet."

"Not a problem," assured her boss, Carrie. "In fact, I expected this. I heard about it when I got in this morning."

Poetry's gut shrank. "What? From who?"

"It's all over the restaurant that he came in to harass you. Besides, Jenny already called in with the same excuse. We're going to be short today. Good thing it's Monday. Maybe it won't be busy."

Poetry's stomach curdled. "Yeah, um, thanks. I have to go." She hung up without saying goodbye and punched in Jenny's cell number. While she waited for an answer, Poetry grabbed her bus pass, purse, and apartment keys.

"Please pick up, Jen." Jenny was a pain sometimes, but Poetry could count on her. They'd been through rough patches before. Not as bad as this, but they were best friends. They'd work it out somehow.

It would be a long day. She had an apartment to clean, but more importantly, she needed information about Adrian because he had Amir. Not to mention she needed to know what Jenny said to Carrie, and who else she'd told about yesterday's fiasco.

Nothing. An automated voice announced that Jenny Shaw was "not available". Leave a message after the tone. Poetry envisioned Jenny glowering at her phone when she saw Poetry's name pop up on the display screen. Jenny was pretty upset last night. It wouldn't surprise her if Jenny avoided her this morning.

"Hi Jen, I'm on my way back to the apartment. Give me a call when you get this. I know you're mad at me but it's important we talk, okay?"

Poetry made her way to Stony Plain Road. A warm breeze kissed her face, bringing with it the smell of dust and a whiff of clover. Sweat tickled her back and it was only ten o'clock. Gonna be another hot one.

From Jasper Gates she could see that she'd missed the Number 7 bus. No big deal. She'd grab the 121 and walk the rest of the way. It was perfect weather for it.

She quickened her pace. If she wanted to catch any bus she'd better hustle.

# # #

Poetry checked her watch. Quarter to eleven. Time was getting away from her. She glanced up to her apartment windows and braced herself for the mess.

She climbed the stairs to the third floor, thinking how open windows didn't do much to rid the landings of the musty old building odors or the usual lunchtime smells. Nor did it disperse any of the summer heat. Like climbing a mountain in Hell.

Speaking of Hell, Poetry thought as she arrived at her apartment. The door had already been replaced, even if the frame still needed more repairs. That was quick. Her eyes were drawn to a yellow square of paper taped under the eyehole. Breakfast lurched back up to lodge in her throat.

A forty-eight hour eviction notice. Poetry's knees jellied and she grasped the doorjamb to steady herself. She read it again through blurry vision and let her forehead smack the wood. The door creaked open slightly.

This wasn't fair. They'd always been on time with rent. Never brought parties home or disturbed anyone.

She stared at the splintered wood where her ex had kicked his way in. Then she remembered the lake on the bathroom floor. So much for the damage deposit. They'd be lucky if they didn't get charged.

God, I hate you Kevin.

Tears fell hot on her cheeks and she snuffled until she swallowed salty anguish. She'd lost Amir and she had no idea where Jenny could be or if she would ever speak to…

A rustling whispered from within the apartment and Poetry held her breath. Kevin's sorry ass was in jail, right?

It came from the living room, no doubt someone looting through whatever she and Jenny had left.

Enough. So far her week was off to a nasty start and having someone messing with her things rankled her last nerve.

She threw the door open and let it bang like a gunshot against the wall. "Hey! Stop touching our stuff!" The tinkling of Jenny's ruined unicorn lamp followed a loud shriek. Poetry hurried to find her roommate cowering in the corner by the window. "Oh God, Jenny you scared me."

"I scared you?"

Jenny's voice held more anger than fear so Poetry approached with caution. So far this conversation wasn't going well.

"I lived here too, you know," Jenny said through clenched teeth. "Until you got us evicted." She kicked at shards as she glared around the vandalized walls.

Poetry stood next to the shoe fire with her arms folded. Everywhere she looked she saw torn bits of fabric, sofa stuffing, and shattered glass.

"I can't tell you how sorry I am, but I'll make it up…"

Jenny pushed her hand out in a halting gesture. "I don't want to hear it."

Gary appeared from Jen's bedroom. He wouldn't meet Poetry's gaze. "Almost ready, hon?"

Jenny wiped the grit from her hands. "Yeah. There's nothing else worth keeping." She and Gary shouldered past Poetry to the exit.

"Where are you going?" Poetry asked. "Where will you stay?"

"Not that it's any of your business," Jenny said. "but I'm moving in with Gary." Once she got her runners on, Gary settled a knapsack on her back and hoisted a larger hockey bag. He shot Poetry a lame half-smile that didn't match his darting eyes before skulking from the apartment.

"Can't we discuss this? We're friends."

Jenny fetched Poetry a filthy look. "We're finished. I've already blocked you on Facebook and taken you out of my contacts. Stay out of my life."

She spun on her foot and darted through the open door. Her hurried footsteps pounded away before Poetry could get a hold of herself.

For a moment she could only gawk at the light coming from the common hallway as she absorbed the verbal assault. Then it hit her. In all the upset she'd forgotten to ask.

"Wait!" She raced into the echoing corridor and down the stairs. She sprinted all the way to the parking lot in time to see Gary and Jenny pulling out.

"Wait," she said again. Jenny spared her a glance through the open window. "Adrian has Amir. How do I reach him?"

Jenny rolled her eyes. "He works at the same firm Gary does." Gary gunned the engine, and the tires gave a reluctant squeak as they accelerated away.

"Oh, that's just great," Poetry said to no one. "So where the hell does Gary work?"

CHAPTER THIRTEEN

Strife's knees trembled. She wondered if she could make it down the stairs without breaking her neck or vomiting.

What was he doing here?

She would find out soon enough. Her master had issued a summons. Apparently he trusted her very little. She'd arrived in Grey not twenty four hours ago, and already he felt the need to check up on her.

The echo of her heels on the steps couldn't mask the panting she heard around the corner. Strife knew that sound all too well. She would wait until he finished before allowing him to see her. Just in case. She was still tender from her last sexual encounter with him and didn't wish for another.

Her gaze darted around for distraction, something to keep her mind occupied elsewhere, but the ambiance held no loveliness. A fat fly buzzed at the pane of a window that had a decade or more of dirt caked into its corners. Grime trailed down the walls in long, leaky tendrils. The dreariness of the space made Strife long for the grace of Europe and the life she'd enjoyed before the god returned to claim her.

The grunting reached its crescendo, a loud moan. Strife risked a peek. Ares stood stroking his cock over the limp corpse of the hotel clerk. Spurts of white appeared on her face and twisted neck as he jerked his seed. Strife swallowed bile, breathed through her mouth. She could smell his sex.

The woman, whose name she hadn't bothered learning, stared at her in frozen terror. Her expression reminded Strife of what it means to be on Ares' list of victims. She ventured a glance at him now that he'd tucked his spent cock back in his black trousers. Her liver shrank. Smoldering coal eyes betrayed his mood. Despite his orgasm, he wasn't happy.

"M-master?"

"I think you are enjoying your assignment a little too much, wasting precious time socializing and drugging the locals. I should have expected as much."

"No it's not like that." She cowered against the wrought iron railing at his approach. "It takes time to manipulate humans. I can't just march in and say 'Let's storm the city'."

Ares swept his arm behind him, the gesture making Strife flinch in expectation. "You can now. I have given them just cause."

Strife forced herself to examine the woman's dead body. It lay across the faded linoleum like a broken doll some temperamental child had attempted to pull the head from.

"They'll think I did it. I'm the only person staying here."

"Stupidity does not suit you, Strife," Ares said. "Human females do not possess that kind of strength." He zipped up, almost as an afterthought. "Tell these villagers it was in retaliation for Frank Fleisher's murders. Blame it on the gay community."

He strolled to the cadaver and nudged the broken neck with his toe, causing the head to loll back and forth, as if denying its demise. Strife struggled to swallow regurgitated coffee.

"Why do you think I decorated the ugly bitch instead of fucking her?"

That explained why he'd changed his methods. Blame it on the homosexuals and create more discrimination. Strife clamped her mouth shut and nodded her understanding. Ares gave her a condescending smile.

"Do you require more instruction?"

"No, Master."

Ares drew close enough that Strife smelled the wine on his breath and perhaps…mustard gas. It burned her eyes and reeked of hatred.

He stroked her cheek with a gentle touch that put her on edge. He might be tempted to use Strife for his own cruel desires. "The new world is ripe for the taking, Strife. Power beyond imagining can be ours. We will crush Aphrodite and all other gods like insects under our boots." He brought her chin up so that she could meet the ebony pools of his eyes.

"Hurry," he said. "Run and tell them what you have found."

# # #

Please be here. Please be here. Poetry hurried to the huge double doors of Vulcan's Forge, praying her mentor just happened to be around on this sweltering afternoon, however unlikely. Often in the heat of the summer months the shop stayed quiet. Her colleagues had better things to do, like put crafted chainmail to use for mock battles. Some of them travelled with their wares to flea markets and festivals. Poetry didn't have the resources for either. Living on a server's income meant laboring in the dank depths year round to make extra money. Not that she minded the small sacrifice for her art. But today she needed to see the owner of the smithy for reasons that had nothing to do with her work.

She heaved on one handle, using her waning strength to pry the huge door open. The outside heat combined with the stress of the mother-of-all-Mondays had stolen her energy. She let the door slam shut behind her and waited while her eyes adjusted to the darkness. The orange and blue fire of the ovens lent the shop a hellish cast. No windows or cooling systems brought mercy.

"Hugh?" The name reverberated over the roar of the furnaces. "Hugh, are you here?" Poetry risked a few steps. "Hugh?"

She knew this place well enough to find her way in the dark. She eased past the benches of her peers, letting her gaze skip like a stone over half-finished projects. To her right lay George's greaves. He'd yet to properly fit the bindings for his shins. On the table across from his, Shawn's molded pewter goblins waited for their seams to be filed away.

Farther behind the work stations, up a rickety set of stairs, a fluorescent lamp shone like a beacon, drawing Poetry closer. Her heart fluttered.

Hugh's office. She sucked in warm air and dragged herself toward it.

A clammy paw weighed down on her shoulder and she screamed as she spun around.

"Poetry? Aren't you a little early today?"

She craned her neck to meet Hugh's stare.

Sweat flicked off his red goatee as he spoke. This close he smelled like clean sweat and leather. "What are you doing here?"

"I…" Poetry hadn't thought about what she'd tell him once she got here. Didn't know what to say now that his imposing visage peered down at her. Words tumbled out in a frightened babble. "I have no place else to go."

CHAPTER FOURTEEN

Poetry told Hugh everything. About Kevin, the trashed apartment, her missing cat, the fight with Jenny and the eviction.

Hugh took her upstairs where he fixed iced tea. He listened with his bad leg propped on a chair and arms folded while she tried to stop sobbing.

"Damn," he said over and over. "Damn."

Poetry calmed long enough to sip at the sweet beverage that soothed on such a hot day.

"What am I going to do?" She didn't expect an answer. Hugh wasn't much for words, let alone advice. It didn't matter. Just having a sounding board made her problems a little easier to bear.

"I can't live with my parents. Even if I never see Amir again and cat allergies aren't an issue, I can't live with them. They won't ever let me hear the end of this. They treat me like a child."

Hugh ran a burly mitt over the ginger stubble on his skull. The sound cut through the quiet like the whisper of sandpaper. "I know a place you can stay," he said finally. Poetry clasped both hands together. Her mentor always had great ideas. Maybe he knew a way out of her predicament. Hugh shut her enthusiasm down with one finger of condition. "But it's only temporary."

Poetry snuffled. She had to be stronger than this, her hopes were dangling. She peered up at Hugh's stern gaze, knowing how pathetic she must look with her puffy eyes and dripping nose.

"It's pretty small too," he said.

"I don't have a lot of options."

Hugh hesitated for precious seconds. "Grab your stuff and follow me."

He limped to a large closet door near the back of the common room, or at least Poetry had always assumed it was a closet. But when Hugh unlocked it, she saw a set of stairs she didn't know existed.

"Where do these go?"

Hugh smiled wide, soot creating streaks at the corners of his eyes and mouth like ripples. "You're the only other person who knows about this."

The wooden steps groaned under Poetry's feet as she climbed behind Hugh. They were warped, making her unsure of her balance. She waited in the dark, taking note of clicks and clunks as Hugh unlocked the door at the top.

It creaked open and a ray of sunlight bathed the narrow stairwell in pale yellow.

"When I first came to Edmonton this was home," Hugh said, the lopsided thud of his heavy boots nearly drowned out his words. "It was simple, warm, and cheap."

Poetry gawked. The whitewashed trim and moldings along with the decrepit appliances gave away the age of the décor. Poetry experienced a strange timelessness, like she'd walked into the sixties.

Hugh flicked a switch and the overhead light fixture sputtered before providing a better view of the grunge. And the peeling paint. And the dried husks of dead insects on the windowsills.

Drop cloths covered the furniture, but Poetry imagined the table, couch, and chairs to be every bit as ancient as the rest of the place. At least they wouldn't be dusty.

"It's very…" She struggled for the appropriate word while stifling a sneeze. "Nice."

"It isn't much, but it's all yours if you want it."

A smile crept up Poetry's face. Although tiny, it had a kitchen area, a living room, bathroom and bedroom. And she could spend as many hours as she wanted in the forge below. What more would she need? “What’s the rent on this?”

“For you?” Hugh grinned back. It wasn’t something the smithy did often. “Seven hundred.”

Poetry let her jaw drop. Seven hundred dollars a month? She wouldn’t get a better deal anywhere in the city. One bedroom apartments never went for less than nine hundred in Edmonton. She and Jenny had been splitting twelve hundred. Unfurnished.

“Yeah, I can afford that,” she said, trying to sound casual. Her heart thumped faster. So far, so good, but she wasn’t in the clear yet. “What about damage deposit?”

Hugh appeared to consider a price. He stood licking his teeth with his mouth closed for so long, Poetry wondered if he’d forgotten the subject.

Please let it be cheap, Poetry thought. I can’t afford much.

“I’ll tell you what,” he said. “I’ll waive the damage deposit if you take it as is. And you can move in now.”

She could have kissed him. Instead she said, “Deal,” and shook his hand.

What a load off her mind. She could buy groceries this week. Yay.

It occurred to Poetry that she hadn’t eaten since the morning, and she groaned inwardly. She just had to think of food. Her stomach clenched and hunger gnawed like a beast in her belly.

“Great,” Hugh said, cracking his knuckles. “It’s settled. I’ll drive you to the bank, and we’ll settle the paperwork over burgers. My treat. You’ve had a pretty long day.”

“Wow, you’re a mindreader.” Gratitude overwhelmed Poetry. She fluttered her hands to cool her blushing cheeks. She didn’t want to cry again, even if they were tears of joy. “You’re a great friend, Hugh. I can’t tell you how much this means to me.”

Hugh grunted into his chest. "Don't mention it." This time he didn't return Poetry's smile. "To anyone. I don't need anybody thinking I've gone soft."

#   #   #

Strife had to give Ares credit. The war god understood how to stir a hornet's nest like no one else, past or present. Time and time again he proved how the mob ruled.

It seemed the population of the rural town had tripled. Grey's entire police force, all two of them, were joined by a forensics team. Extra RCMP from other counties came in just to control the media. It wasn't a paparazzo's dream, but enough flashbulbs created a menace that left Strife seeing yellow dots behind her eyelids.

It didn't take much for Strife to slip away from the crime scene. She deflected attention away from herself as she always did, expounding on the horrors instead. She pretended to be too distraught to continue.

Part two of the plan involved riling the masses into frenzy.

Strife bathed in the energy of the crowd. Her power grew with the fear, rumors, and speculation. From the minute she'd run screaming into the bar about the murder, chaos had taken hold.

I truly missed this, she thought. Just like old times on Mediterranean battlefields, she could almost smell the blood. But instead of passing apples of discord, she slung Apple Jack from a thermos.

"You folks look like you could use a drink," she said to a middle-aged couple. They'd parked in front of their pick-up with lawn chairs, watching the hotel with unabashed interest.

The man glanced up at her, swallowed the rest of the beer in his mug and held it out to Strife. "Very kind of you."

"My pleasure." Strife poured tainted bourbon into his coffee cup and held the thermos out for his wife.

"Hey, I know you," the man said. "You're Max's new girl, right?"

"That would be me. I'm…" What name should she give? No one had bothered asking her. Not Max, not the old hag in the hotel.

Her ability to influence humans had improved to the point where they did her bidding with blind trust. Interesting.

"I'm sorry about your friend," she said, trying hard to look sympathetic as she poured.

The woman's eyes welled. "Poor Delores. She didn't deserve to die like that. Is it true she was gang-raped and decapitated?"

Strife fought the urge to laugh and struggled to maintain a somber expression. Humans had a unique way of twisting messages for morbid entertainment value. "Yes. It was horrible." She stroked the smooth, cool surface of the thermos. "I think the killers were trying to send a message."

Both people responded with sharp intakes of breath. Strife heard that musical reaction each time she spread gossip.

"A message?" the man asked.

The distraught woman put a hand to her chest. "Who would do such a thing?"

"You know those homosexuals that Frank Fleisher shot on his property?" Strife felt their mounting anger like a swelling river. "I think this was payback."

"Those bastards!" The man's hands shook as he gulped another mouthful of Strife's potion.

"I know," Strife said. "We simply can't let them get away with this."

"Goddamn right," the man said. "We have to do something."

"People have been saying that all day," Strife said, trying to hide her excitement. "But sitting on watch will do nothing to change the situation. We need to take action."

"It's a good idea, but what should we do?" the woman asked.

Strife topped off their drinks as fury elevated under their skins. She could almost hear the blood racing hot through their veins. This was more fun than drugging club kids. "I think you should discuss this with your neighbors. Get a plan together. We can't let this go unanswered, right?" Strife smiled as the couple agreed with shaking fists and mottled faces.

"You're damn right, sweetheart!" The man's face had become ruddy with indignation and alcohol.

"Very good," Strife said. "Now if you'll excuse me, I have to refill my thermos."

She had to mix more Apple Jack and pass it around until everyone came under the influence.

Strife glanced at the late afternoon sky. She had to hurry if she wanted to accomplish all of her chemistry before nightfall. The residents of Grey weren't the only ones who would taste her talents tonight.

CHAPTER FIFTEEN

Poetry ascended the stairs of her new home. Each step grew heavier with fatigue and loneliness. She missed the smell of Ichiban already. Nothing felt familiar anymore. Truth be told, she dreaded sleeping here tonight. She'd never lived alone before, not even during her artistry course in New York.

And she was all alone. She still had no idea what had become of Amir. Jenny wouldn't return her calls and Adrian didn't have her number. Hugh had gone home for the evening after taking her money and handing over a set of keys.

The door protested as she trudged inside. "Home sweet home." Her words bounced back to her along with a violent sneeze.

It wasn't quite twilight yet, but she turned on the lights to chase away shadows.

"Well, it's mine now. I guess I should make myself comfortable," she said to the stove.

Great. Now I'm talking to appliances. I'm so lame.

She tugged on the slipcovers protecting the end table, lamp, dining set, and finally the relatively newer brown sofa. She'd only seen pictures of these textured monstrosities in photos. It seemed that everyone had owned one of them in the seventies. God only knew why.

She entered the bedroom and found a quaint dresser and ordinary double bed with a stained mattress that probably should have been thrown out.

Those lumps must be the size of rats, she thought, and instantly regretted it. Knowing the province of Alberta had a militant rat patrol didn't dismiss the image.

Out loud she said, "Where did I put my bag?"

Right. On the Formica countertop in the kitchen.

Poetry wasn't sure which she found more disturbing, the drone of her lonely footsteps on the linoleum or the dry crackle they caused.

Better get used to it, she thought. Going to hear a lot of it from now on.

She unzipped her luggage and rummaged through her cache of possessions. Kevin didn't leave her much.

A few cups and plates made it, as well as her hodge-podge of Value Village cutlery. Some clothes had escaped his wrath, but most were ripped or too smoke damaged to keep. She still had a few bingo daubers.

She stopped to use the pink one in the bathroom mirror, just to cheer herself up. Some color in her hair always brightened her mood.

Poetry had salvaged most of her fasteners and beads in an empty margarine container. She'd spent over an hour in the old place picking them out of the carpet.

She'd need bedding. And clean underwear. A trip to her parent's house couldn't be avoided. If she didn't she'd have to sleep without pillows or sheets.

Just thinking about it caused Poetry's skin to crawl with an imagined itch.

That decided it. She grabbed her keys and opened the door.

She paused. What was that smell?

A floral scent wrinkled her nose. Roses to be exact. But so much more... The aroma persuaded her to remember shy company, a warm night with a whispering summer breeze. And shrimp po' boys.

Poetry looked down to find a single plum colored rose. She bent to pluck it from the step, ran her fingers along the soft petals as she inhaled the fragrance.

Still fresh. Almost exactly the same as the rose from Louisiana Purchase. Where did it come from?

A chill tingled her spine. More importantly, how did it get there? She hadn't heard footsteps or knocking.

Poetry almost tripped in her rush to reach the bottom landing. She ripped the closet door open and raced through the office.

Nothing.

"Hello? Anyone here?" She listened with strained ears as the words died. Only her thudding heartbeat sounded. Everything appeared to be undisturbed.

"Anybody?" She heard desperation in her voice.

Frightening questions whirled through her mind. Did Kevin get out already? Did he know about her dinner with Adrian?

Was he jealous?

"Ow!" Poetry dropped the rose she'd clenched between her fingers. A drop of crimson appeared on the palm of her hand. She licked the metallic spot of blood and tried to calm down. It wasn't like her to be a scaredy cat. There had to be a logical explanation for this.

Kevin didn't send her the rose, she decided. He'd never given her flowers before, why start now? So who did? How did they find her?

She thought of the golden-haired man with the flower basket. And Adrian. Maybe it was one of them. But if so, how did they know where she lived?

Poetry shook the creepiness off her shoulders. Whoever it was, she felt certain they weren't here now. The atmosphere seemed hollow somehow. But still…

She wanted air. Open spaces. Great idea.

She darted between the tables and forced herself to walk calmly until she found the exit. She would not succumb to paranoia, however justified.

# # #

Rows of taillights flared in the night like demon eyes. Strife traveled in the passenger seat of a pickup truck belonging to the same beer drinker she'd converted yesterday.

Dave, as she'd learned his name to be, became a valuable ally. If Strife believed in unlikely coincidences, this qualified as truly serendipitous. Without the retired city worker's help, she couldn't fully realize the next phase of her plan. Almost the entire population of Grey drove alongside them, a juggernaut of diesel and steel bearing down on an unsuspecting city like a swarm of ants.

She recalled the events of the day. The morning's murder preceded a clumsy investigation. Then she'd poisoned the minds of the locals with Apple Jack and distorted tales. Only when she'd created a hum of anger did she sneak back to her room to mix her potions. She'd recruited Max and other regulars to rally the residents of Grey to her cause. Her memory drifted to a few hours prior in Max's tavern.

She'd balanced high above the throng, sweating in the humidity their crowded bodies created. Even now she could still smell their adrenaline-sharpened body odor.

"The enemy has stolen past us in the night like a wraith. They have taken one of our own, attacked a defenseless woman and violated her body. Do we allow such cowardice go unanswered? Do we stand by and watch while mincing pretenders steal through our ranks like slithering vermin? Who will be next?"

A deafening roar of rage nearly toppled Strife from her pulpit on the rickety table. The power of their angst gave her a rush.

Behind her, various plastered volunteers poured apple juice and whiskey into tumblers. Strife had whipped up a double batch of her special cinnamon and made certain they topped each cocktail with it.

"Do we sit idly by, and let them take us?" she asked.

"No!" The resounding negative bruised her eardrums.

"Do we lay low and allow them to taint our way of life with their filth?"

"No!"

"The justice system punishes the innocent and pacifies the guilty. I say we show them their degradations and blasphemies will not be tolerated."

She focused on the passion and misguided sense of self-entitlement and absorbed its crescendo.

"Who's with me?" She pumped her fist in the air. To her delight, the crowd demonstrated its solidarity, imitating her challenging gesture along with blood-searing screams of hate.

"Citizens of Grey," She hushed her voice until they crowded like livestock to hear. "It is time to load your weapons and gather your courage. Tonight, we bring the battle to them."

The rambunctious cheer that arose swelled her bitter heart. Even now Strife replayed the scene over and over in her mind. Agamemnon would have been proud.

She jerked back to the present as Dave decreased their speed. He signaled a lane change and exchanged friendly waves with the convoy as they zoomed past.

"Is this our turn already?" Strife asked.

“Yep,” Dave nodded. “Just a few miles down.”

“Perfect.” Strife tasted the grit in her teeth as she smiled. Now the real fun would begin.

CHAPTER SIXTEEN

"It stinks here." Strife pinched her nose as her eyes watered. Human feces. Nothing else reminded her so much of filth and disease.

"That would be the sewage treatment facility a click or so away," Dave said. They stood before several massive tanks painted red and white, connected together with a squat metal hut. Dave jerked his head northward.

"What we want is the reservoir." He shifted a full pail to the other arm.

"Don't drop that," she said, anxiety spilling through her voice. "Those are potent chemicals."

A look of annoyance creased Dave's brow. "I got it, I got it. They're also heavy." He punctuated the comment by kneading his bicep. "The stairs are over here."

She held out a compliant hand. "Lead the way."

He eyed her with irritation, which she ignored. He seized his burden and directed his attention to a dirt path.

"This will take us to the back door."

"For which you still have a key, right?"

"Yep." Strife hated the way he used that word. He sounded like a yokel. "They trusted me. I worked here thirty years."

Strife detected pride in his speech, but apparently there wasn't enough of it. Convincing him to use his knowledge for sabotage had been effortless. A little alcoholic persuasion and he quickly betrayed his employer of three decades, not to mention the city itself.

I love my job. This kind of clandestine adventure suited Strife well.

Crickets gossiped in the summer stillness. She followed Dave's footsteps as he swished through long silken grasses that tickled her bare legs, biting down on screams when the long body of an occasional locust bounced against her knee.

How much farther?

She gazed toward the indigo sky, searching for constellations. She longed to see the twinkling symbols of her brethren, but the honeyed glow of the city diluted them to pale dots.

"We're here," Dave said. He pointed to a rickety building pocked with rust. Rivers of brown ran down the sides. "These stairs are a little old, so watch your step."

Strife's mouth was dry. In her zeal she'd forgotten food and drink. Even now, with the clank of Dave's footfalls echoing on steel steps, she dismissed the need. Hatred and pain were sustenance enough, with a feast to come.

She hurried behind him and together their climb rang out like bells in the night.

"Almost there," Dave said between wheezes. "Just a little further."

If you don't collapse first, Strife thought, but kept her remarks to herself, even if it meant biting back her impatience.

From here she could see the highway light up like a Christmas ribbon in gold and red. Strife stretched her lips. No one could see them up here, but they were poised to change lives and disrupt civilization.

"Ahhhh." Dave eased the plastic pail down to the metal grid. He flexed his creaking knuckles, rotating and rubbing his arms.

She gave him her full attention, nearly tripping herself on the last step. Dave hunched over, his shoulders heaving.

"Is this it?" she asked.

“Yep,” Dave huffed oxygen and produced a chunky set of metal fingers from his jacket, choosing an ordinary silver one indistinguishable from the others.

“This is the place.” He jabbed the key in the knob. “The city’s water treatment happens here.” The steel door resisted one moment before jerking open.

“Perfect.” Strife let the old-timer catch his breath while she found the light switch. A loud clunk introduced a fluorescent glare that did nothing to flatter the surroundings.

Water stains striped the walls in the anemic glow. Rust and mold dusted the corners. The odor wasn’t any better than outside. Instead of shit it reeked of rotting vegetation and mildew. Strife could almost taste the decay in the air.

“Reservoir’s over here,” Dave said.

“How did you stand the stench for three whole decades?”

Dave chuckled. “I guess you get use to it.”

“Smells like the Parisian catacombs,” she said. “I never got used to those.”

“The what now?”

“In Paris they have underground tunnels where they kept their dead when they had no more room for them.” Strife couldn’t help but smile when a shudder rippled across Dave’s back even though it brought back bad memories for her.

As an alchemist and a plague survivor Strife did a booming business selling the cure. But when her expensive potions and tinctures did nothing to help them, the villagers rallied against her. Who knew they would survive to prosecute her? They’d accused her of heresy and witchcraft and she’d been reduced to hiding amongst the dead.

Those times would forever haunt her.

Sometimes she dreamed of the endless rows of corpses, still heard the squeaking of the rats and the subtle grind of their tiny teeth against bone.

It angered her. She dealt death. She did not sleep with it.

Irony and bitterness dogged her as she examined the technology that had made that disease a nightmare of the past. It certainly took humans long enough to learn how cleanliness destroys the pathogens that live in sewage and dirty water.

Tonight she would receive a measure of revenge against mankind for those years spent living like a rodent. She would use subtlety and skill to topple first a city, then a nation.

"Here it is."

She barely heard them over the roar of running water but those words snapped Strife back to the present.

"What?" She joined Dave at a railing. "Where?"

"Straight below us."

Strife gripped the slick steel of the banister. Her instrument of vengeance pooled below.

"Could we get closer?"

"Sure, right this way." Dave led her to a bridge. Mist pelted them from the clean churning water and Strife licked it from her dry lips with pleasure.

"Is this close enough?"

"This will do," she said. She popped the lid off the plastic canola oil drum. The bluish-green powder reminded Strife of sea foam…and Aphrodite.

This one's for you, bitch.

She heaved it, and watched as the crystals flowed into the clear pool, causing a ripple of turquoise to fan out like abstract watercolors. The seductive scent of Monkshood drifted.

"It's kind of pretty," Dave said. "What will it do?"

"Not much. It should create a sort of angry paranoia for anyone who drinks it. Destructive behaviors. There'll be other side effects as well, like fever and increased heart rate." She waved a dismissive hand. "I wasn't exact. Didn't have time."

She studied the deepening furrow in Dave's brow. Strife sensed second thoughts. Not her concern. "How do we get down from here?"

"Uh, over here," Dave led her down a different set of stairs. These paralleled the treated water.

Upon reaching the ground floor, he fell in step beside Strife. "Can I ask you something?" His face creased in worry. "What's in that stuff?"

"Some household chemicals, a little belladonna, a little draco leaf, a lot of coca…" She grinned at Dave. "It's the basis of cocaine, believed by ancient Peruvians to inspire humans to go to war."

They prowled along the quieting pools, toward the exit. And Strife gloried in the tension and doubt now emitting from Dave.

"Oh yes," Strife said ticking off an imaginary point in the air with her finger. "And some old-fashioned magick. Can you swim?"

"What? I…"

With a single shove, Strife dumped Dave into the deep water.

He came up sputtering. "What the hell are you doing?" The senior floundered at first, but once he regained his composure he paddled to grip the concrete edge of safety. "Are you out of your mind?"

"Oops, sorry." Strife bent over to reach for him. "That was an accident. I meant to do this."

She grasped the top of Dave's balding head with both hands and plunged him downward. She sighed, counting the seconds as he tore at her arms. He still had some fight left.

Damn. I forgot.

She shifted her grip until she could haul Dave up by his neck. For a brief moment he inhaled with his mouth gaping, coughing like a spent hurricane.

Strife held him aloft with one hand, searched his jacket with the other.

"Keys and wallet, keys and wallet," She let her fingers roam. "Eureka. Thanks, Dave."

She dropped him, pressing him under again when he surfaced. She remained there until he stopped clawing and went still. Strife pocketed his possessions and left. She would have to hurry if she wanted to get a room in the city tonight.

CHAPTER SEVENTEEN

Exhaustion and stress settled between Poetry's shoulder blades, as though her vertebrae were grinding together. Another long shift coming to an end.

She craned her neck side to side, the audible crackle and the relief that came with it induced a sigh of pleasure. The heavy abundance of hard-earned loonies and toonies jingling in her apron lifted her spirits.

After grabbing a coffee from the Bunn burner she plunked down in a teal colored vinyl booth with a phone book and a pen.

She settled her cheek on the surface of the table, just to soak in some of the cool smoothness. But only for a minute. Her nose tingled at the scent of vinegar and other cleaning substances she'd grown sick of. She attempted to blow the odor away from her, but only succeeded in fluffing her pink bangs.

Normally she liked the seven-to-three shift. She earned lots of tips from the breakfast and lunch rush. Better yet, she had her evenings off. But yesterday had been hellish and sleep didn't come easy this week.

Last night she'd bused and transferred for forty-five minutes to pilfer bedding and snacks from her parent's house. The situation went from awkward to tedious.

"What new place?" her father asked. "You and Jenny got a new apartment?"

"No," Poetry said. When she opened the fridge, the fresh scent of homemade tzaziki hit her like a crisp cucumber wave. Yoink. Was there any pita bread? "Jenny isn't living with me."

"Oh? Why? What happened? Did you have a fight?" her father asked.

Poetry locked eyes with her mother. The grim line of her disapproving mouth said it all. Poetry broke contact to search for Tupperware in a nearby cupboard.

"Just boy stuff."

"Not too serious I hope?"

"Oh no, not at all." She brushed him off, determined not to drag daddy into her squabbles with her sensitivity-challenged friend. Dealing with her mother was bad enough, thank you. "We thought maybe we should take a break from each other. That's all."

"Perhaps I should drive you home," Her mother placed half a dozen dolmades into a Ziploc bag, and a small smile perked Poetry's lips. She loved stuffed grape leaves.

"It'll give us a chance to talk things out." her mother said, and Poetry bit down hard in an effort not to groan.

All the way from Stony Plain Road to Fort Road her mother lectured on Poetry's poor choices and lack of responsibility. Whoever said that the prisoners in Guantanamo Bay were tortured and treated unreasonably hadn't sat through one of her mother's condescending speeches about life.

As if she'd know what it meant to have one.

Her academic parents met and married in college, and pretty much stayed there. Existence revolved around work and home. They'd never even been to her father's ancestral home country of Greece. Poetry couldn't bring herself to take advice about her future from a woman who'd compromised hers.

"It's not as though you aren't smart enough. And taking Goldsmithing in New York just isn't practical. What will you use it for? Designing baubles isn't a desirable career for a young lady."

Blah, blah, blah, whatever. If she heard one more word about higher education and how many refined men she could meet in literacy courses, she'd book a one way flight to Tierra del Fuego.

Not a bad idea. She could drink Chilean and Argentinean wine for cheap and sell her wares to tourists.

The fifteen kilometer drive wasn't more than twenty minutes, but it seemed like hours. She didn't get home until sundown, thanks to her mother's inability to talk and drive at anything above a crawl.

Once home, she'd been unable to sleep. Where was Amir? How would she find Adrian? Would Jenny ever return her calls? Would Kevin find her new place?

And where did that rose come from? That part worried her. She couldn't explain it.

The questions and the mystery hadn't left her mind all day. She took another swig of cold coffee and grimaced at the bitterness.

This is what happened when nobody rotates the carafes. The coffee was old enough to vote. Another mouthful. She needed all the caffeine she could get.

She had plans for the afternoon. She couldn't stomach sitting around staring at her belly button piercing. Time to get off her ass and do something.

Poetry dragged the massive tome that was the Yellow Pages over and began scanning its ancient pages. No internet listings for her; Kevin had reduced her computer to shrapnel, and she couldn't afford an iphone yet. She'd just have to do it the old-fashioned way.

"L is for lawyer," she said under her breath, and did a quick glance around. The restaurant appeared nearly empty with only a few java junkies. The occasional student from the college across the street studied and did their homework. Nobody paid her any attention. No one stared as she muttered so she returned her attention to the task at hand.

Whoa. Poetry counted the pages and shook her head in disbelief. Did Edmonton actually need forty-eight pages of lawyers? True, a few of them were full page ads, but forty-eight pages?

"Mel?" she said in the direction of the service area. "Can I get another coffee?"

This would take days. Poetry's sigh ended in a yawn. It sucked, but if she had to call every damn lawyer in town she'd find the guy who had Amir.

The chunky bass line from 'Message from Opticon' growled from her pocket, startling her. She grabbed the vibrating phone and checked the display. She hadn't heard her ringtone for two days. Not since her neanderthal ex had-

Whose number was that? Local, but unknown to her. Not a cell number either.

Hope blossomed. What if it's him? What if it's that Adrian guy who has Amir?

Poetry snapped open the device. "Hello?" She heard the slightest sound from the other end, a gentle sob. "Who is this?"

"Poetry?"

"Oh my God, Jenny?" Poetry's heart began to pound. "What's wrong?"

"I need to see you. Can you meet me somewhere?"

Niggling doubts teased Poetry but she squashed them. Now was not the time to bring up hurt feelings, not when a friend needed help.

"I'm coming. Where are you?"

#   #   #

Aphrodite hugged herself. She knew the ice surrounding her to be god-made illusion…just like the rainbow bridge she crossed to get here. But the effect was overwhelming. The high walls soared into nothingness, the endless gray blended all corners of the room together in a disconcerting wash of solemn neutrality and the dead flickered like shadows. It must inspire a great deal of fear and awe in mortals.

A brawny Siamese and a petite snowy cat paced in front of Aphrodite. Both glared up at her with contempt as pure as the blue of their eyes. She hoped Freya's love of felines did not include anything larger than the domestic species. These animals clearly had no love for her.

By the Energy's mercy, I want to go home.

"Aphrodite, Goddess of Love." The feminine voice purred from a stone chair before her. The cats ceased their haughty scrutiny to curl in their mistress's lap. "You are a long way from Olympus, brave girl."

Aphrodite flinched. No one called her 'girl', but she held her tongue. Here in Sessrumnir, with the menacing presence of a mournful army of spirits, it would be foolish to challenge the woman.

For on this throne sat the Norse goddess of lust, love, and fertility and she housed her hall with her share of Odin's slain warriors. Not a being to be taken lightly.

It was not just her intimidating appearance. With her white hair flowing down her cloak of falcon feathers and her eyes like frozen ponds she resembled the frost that permeated this country for much of the year. It was the aura of menace about her. The Norse were not a friendly lot.

Aphrodite licked chapped lips. No food or drink had been offered. Apparently they were not known for their hospitality either.

"Freya," she said. "I am honored that you would see me on such short notice."

The other goddess cocked her head. "You have been busy."

Aphrodite tensed, but tried to keep calm. Freya's knowledge of her business caught her unawares, but she suspected the Norse deity would be sensitive to any weakness she might betray.

"Do not be surprised." Freya fluttered her fingers at her before stroking the Siamese. The throaty sound of its pleasure dispelled the quiet. "News travels fast. Everyone has heard of the challenge you face. Odin's crows brought word to Asgard days ago."

"Then you understand my need. Ares will use unethical methods against me."

"As you are now," Freya's colorless eyes narrowed. "If you come to me for help is this not also cheating?"

Aphrodite took a gulp of the chill air and ran her hands down her naked midriff.

Perhaps she should have worn something more respectful and less revealing than her usual garb. From the disdainful vibe she felt, her choice of clothing gained her no favor with her Nordic counterpart.

"I am not breaking the rules," she said. "Merely bending them to suit my needs."

Freya sat back, toying with her exalted amber necklace. Aphrodite coveted the glittering jewels.

Legend said the goddess had slept with four dwarven smiths to own them. Aphrodite could understand why. They represented an opulent masterpiece of light and sorcery she could detect from across the room.

I would have done the same to own that treasure.

"From what I hear, the rule is 'no outside help'."

"Zeus allows no outside help from the Egyptians, Asians, or Indian deities," Aphrodite said. "He mentioned nothing about Teutonic."

“I see.” Aphrodite sensed a sort of amused respect from her. In fact, the Norse beauty wore a subtle smirk. “And you chose me because…?”

Aphrodite met Freya’s cold glare. “You and I want the same things. We draw our power from the pleasures of human interaction.”

“Surely you understand that if Ares wins, your own power would dwindle. And besides,” Aphrodite said, straightening and stretching as tall as she dared before Freya. “The male is of Norwegian descent.”

The twitter of Freya’s laughter caused ghosts to rush in frenzy to all corners of the cavernous space. The white cat appeared to smile as it blinked.

“And you think because your target has Scandinavian blood that I hold some sway over him?” Her mirth might have sounded pretty had it not been so mocking. “And this is why I should help you?”

Aphrodite took two courageous steps forward. “It is to your benefit. Together we could become even stronger, transform this world into a haven of pleasure and joy not unlike Eden. We could restore your influence to that of-“

Aphrodite realized the arrogance of her statement only as the cats darted from sight in a flurry of scampering claws. Freya arose abruptly and stormed toward her, her hair and cloak streaming behind her like wispy clouds. Aphrodite cowered.

“How dare you insinuate my power is lesser than yours.” Even with her eyes shut tight Aphrodite felt the goddess towering over her. Freya’s breath rustled the top of Aphrodite’s hair. The musty odor of feathers and rawhide filled her nostrils.

“I may not be revered in the classic artwork of man, or gloried in literature, but I am the goddess of lust and fertility, little one. Humans do not require love when they are controlled by their genitals.” Aphrodite recognized sarcasm in Freya’s tone. “They need no romance or tenderness to procreate.”

To procreate, the chamber echoed. In her rage she reminded Aphrodite of Ares. But she would not taunt Freya as she did him.

A rustling of cloth and retreating footsteps allowed Aphrodite to peek. She saw only Freya's ivory hair and the striking black and grey of her cape.

"It is not me who should worry about the balance of magick," Freya said over her shoulder. "Regardless of who wins this contest, I will remain strong."

Freya's left hand shot out and she snapped her fingers.

Aphrodite found herself shivering on the rainbow bridge.

CHAPTER EIGHTEEN

Poetry found Jenny hunched like a broken doll over tea in the far corner of Second Cup.

Poetry looped her purse over the chair across from her and parked. She uncapped her bottled water--no more caffeine on an empty stomach---and took a long swig.

It eased her tightened throat, but for a moment Poetry couldn't speak.

Jenny had abandoned her, ditched her when she needed her the most. Yet here Poetry sat, prepared to shove their disagreement under the rug once again in the name of friendship.

Poetry wondered if maybe she deserved Jenny's anger. She had a point about her bringing that thug around. And what would have happened if they'd been home when Kevin went on the rampage? Guilt brought Poetry here.

Jenny picked her head up and peered at her with crimson-rimmed eyes.

"You look awful."

Jenny stared her down. "Thanks."

Suddenly Poetry's ragged cuticles and peeling cobalt nail polish became the focus of her attention. She bit down a terse response. Meeting Jenny had been a mistake.

"Sorry," Jenny said. "It was a long night."

"I bet." I had the worst week of my life, thanks for asking.

Poetry waited for Jenny to quit rubbing at mascara tracks, tapping an impatient beat on the plastic water bottle.

"Listen, I'm sorry for the way things ended. I shouldn't have yelled at you like that."

"We both made mistakes," Poetry said, feeling some tension seep away. "You were right. Kevin was a jerk and I couldn't see it. I should have listened to you."

"You're a really good friend for coming here after the way I acted." Jenny looked down again and picked up her tea. The fresh green grass smell of it wafted over to Poetry, reminding her of old times hanging out, watching movies, and talking about guys. She could almost taste buttered popcorn.

What I am is a sentimental mush.

A variety of comforting platitudes came to mind but Poetry couldn't push any of them past her teeth. She didn't want to tell Jenny it didn't matter now, that all was forgiven. Jenny would not do the same for her.

Instead she said, "Tell me what happened."

Jenny put her cup down, pressed her tissue back to her cheek as fresh tears pooled at the corners of her eyes.

"It's Gary." A dramatic torrent of sobs and moisture gushed forth, and Poetry peered around to see if anyone gawked.

Other than a young woman on a laptop, they were the only customers. A furrow appeared between the girl's brows as she typed.

"Whoa, whoa," Poetry said, her hands going out to squeeze Jenny's. "What did he do?"

Terrible thoughts surfaced. She pictured the biceps on Gary, what they could do to a woman of Jenny's petite stature. "He didn't hurt you did he?"

"What?" Jenny stopped wheezing long enough to scowl at Poetry. "No. It's not like that."

“Then what is it?” Poetry asked as she took her hand back. What else could a new boyfriend do to upset her so much?

Jenny exhaled, a weary sound that suggested reluctance. “We got into an argument about money.”

Poetry’s shoulders slumped. Of course. What else would it be?

“Wow, that was quick,” Poetry said. “Don’t waste any time, do you? Most people don’t fight about money until they’re married.”

“He wanted me to help pay rent,” Jenny said. Her gaze drifted away from Poetry, past the parking lot to the traffic along Jasper Avenue. Her lips tightened into a stiff line of resentment.

“Oh, is that all?” Poetry couldn’t help the sarcasm that oozed from her lips. “How dare he.”

“Why should I pay rent?” Jenny’s slicing glare prevented Poetry from smiling. “Gary makes four times as much as I do.”

Poetry fumbled for words. “That’s not the point.”

“The point is I can’t afford a place like that on my wage,” Jenny said. “Why should I pay for it when he can?”

“Because it’s the right thing to do. Because you don’t want him to think you’re with him for his wallet. Besides, I’m sure he doesn’t expect you to cough up half.”

“Hello?” Jenny smacked herself in the forehead. “I’m a waitress? He’s a lawyer? He drives a BMW? He can afford his own rent.”

“Whatever.” Poetry wanted to smack Jenny in the forehead too. Not everything was about money. “So what happened?”

Jenny drained her mug. “I left. Then I called you.”

“I see,” Poetry said. She sipped at her water, wishing for a stiff drink. “So what are you going to do?”

“Well, I’ve been thinking.” Jenny began wringing her hands.

Not a good sign. Whenever Jenny did that it meant she was working up to something.

“I don’t have anywhere else to go…”

Oh no. No.

Poetry’s stomach rolled.

Not that.

“Could I stay with you?”

Hell no. “Jenny, my new place is way too small.”

“I could sleep on the couch.”

“No, you don’t understand…”

“No, you don’t understand.” Jenny’s fingers knotted over and over themselves, squirming like vipers in a nest. “I have no place else to go. And besides,” she peered at Poetry from under her eyelashes, “you did get me evicted.”

Poetry swallowed her anger. It didn’t want to stay down.

I can’t believe I’m hearing this. Of all the obnoxious…

“Please?” Poetry made the mistake of making eye contact.

Jenny had changed tactics. She leaned forward, resorting to the doe-eyes Poetry had seen her use on countless people. “It’ll be fun.”

Fun? I’m going to puke. That would be more fun.

An ear-shredding blast cracked the windows of the coffee shop, chasing the thought from Poetry’s head and replacing it with confusion.

“What the hell?” Poetry could hear screeching brakes and car alarms. The girl with the laptop stood with one hand covering her open mouth.

“Oh my God!” She jabbed a finger eastward. “Buddy’s is on fire!”

“What?”

“Where? What’s going on?”

Poetry shot to her feet and pressed against the spider-webbed glass. Jenny did the same, mashing her nose into it as though it would help her see.

A barista abandoned the counter and ran outside. Poetry followed. She needed a better view.

“Poetry?” Behind her, Jenny shuffled around chairs. “Where are you going?”

Poetry ignored her and bolted for the parking lot, nearly bowling into an employee with the nametag labeled ‘James’. He halted near the corner and stared wide-eyed at the charred remains of the bar across the street.

Blackened bits of plastic and rainbow-colored cloth floated through the air. Pepper lights dangled. Shards of glass and broken stools littered the street. The air smelled like smoke; noxious with the taint of fertilizer. When it burned her senses, Poetry slapped a hand over her mouth and nose.

“Oh shit, Poetry.” She became aware of Jenny standing next to her, as well as the odor of scorched flesh. “What’s going on?”

“I don’t know,” she said, squinting her eyes. Through the smoke she could make out the gaping holes where a row of windows used to be. Flames clawed for the sky, blocking the entrance. Screams of the dying grew fainter by the minute.

A crowd had gathered and they were…cheering? For what? The destruction of the well known gay hang out wasn’t something to be happy about. She'd thought Edmontonians were more enlightened than that.

Fire engines appeared, their sirens drowning out the conflicted noise.

Neon yellow coats leaped from the massive vehicle. Poetry watched in horror as bystanders dragged the firemen away from the explosion, kicking and pummeling. Others scattered the hoses, or used them to vandalize the grocery store across the street. Looters charged through broken glass.

A chant reached Poetry's ears. Burn. Burn. Burn. It churned her stomach.

Poetry heard a shriek from behind. The other customer hugged her laptop like a security blanket. "What are they doing?"

"They're attacking the firefighters," James said. His voice held incredulous anger. "They're attacking the fucking firefighters. Hey!" He broke into a run, straight for the melee. "Leave them alone!"

Another howl, this time from the other patron. She raced to join him, brandishing her computer over her head with lethal intent.

Poetry turned toward Jenny. "This is surreal, I…" Jenny had her dilated gaze fixated on the violence. She tried to pass Poetry with a lunge but they both tumbled to the asphalt.

"Ow! Jenny, what's wrong with you?"

Jenny rolled off, tearing her hands across the ground in her struggle to rise. She growled and grunted, snarling like a beast as she tried to break Poetry's grip.

"Has everyone gone insane?" Poetry had to stop Jenny. Even as she fought with her friend she heard running footsteps and shouts.

The only thing missing is the din of swordplay, she thought.

Gunshots rang out.

“Jenny, we gotta go,” she said. Jenny didn’t seem to hear her. With singular intent she groped the ground, trying to free herself.

“Let me go!” The frightening snarls coming from Jenny’s throat made Poetry tighten her grip. . “I want…I need to…”

“Need to what?” Poetry asked. She managed to crawl over Jenny, turning her over and straddling her.

“I have to…”

“Get a hold of yourself!” Poetry delivered a slap so hard it stung her palm. Jenny went still. Her body unwound beneath Poetry, her pupils shrank to their normal size.

“That hurt,” she said, raising a hand to the welt on her cheek. “Thanks. I don’t know what I was thinking.”

Poetry got off Jenny and helped her stand. “Me neither, but it seems to be affecting everyone.”

They glanced around. People were tearing at each other. Or racing aimlessly in full-blown hysteria. Bellowing intermingled with screeching tires and crunching metal as cars plowed into buildings, parked vehicles, and pedestrians.

“We have to get away from here,” Jenny said.

“Yeah,” Poetry nodded. “But where?” They began to back away from the riot. More men and women were swarming to the vortex of frenzied humanity in front of the damaged drinking establishment.

“Can we go to Gary’s? Doesn’t he live on Jasper Ave?”

Jenny shook her head. “No. I’m not going there. It’s too far to run anyway.” She bit her lip and glanced around at the skyscrapers. “But you gave me an idea.”

Jenny pointed northwest, to a tall building with red balconies. “We need to go there.”

A second explosion rocked the block, superheating the already sweltering air and frightening situation. Poetry guessed it came from the basement dance bar, Woody's.

"Let's go. Now," Poetry shoved Jenny in the opposite direction. "Run."

CHAPTER NINETEEN

"Alright, alright." Adrian hurried at the sound of insistent knocking. "I'm coming." So much for coming home early to get some practice in. What did he have to do to get some time to himself these days?

He disengaged the deadbolts and the alarm system with quick fingers. Adrian yanked the door open and Jenny tumbled into his arms.

"Oh God, thanks so much for letting us in, Adrian," she said, squeezing him tight. "You're a lifesaver."

Us?

When he'd buzzed the intercom, Jenny hadn't mentioned company. Adrian glanced past the tangle of Jenny's hair to the other woman waiting in the hall.

The one with the crazy ex. She looked frazzled. He could smell fear and the city's smog radiating from her, even over Jenny's fruity perfume.

Shit. Now what? Was the boyfriend back or something? Why were they here?

Instead of voicing those thoughts he said, "No problem. Come in." He released Jenny and swept his arm wide in welcome. "Me casa, es su casa."

Jenny flounced in as though she lived there, the other girl…Pamela? No, that wasn't right… entered with obvious reluctance.

"What's going on?" Adrian asked. He inclined his head toward… Patricia? "Hi."

"Hi." She wrapped her arms around herself and stood perfectly still inside the foyer. Her discomfort and wariness reminded him of a city rabbit; perhaps she thought she might be safe if she didn't move. Of course, Edmonton rabbits bolted when you looked directly at them.

“Where’s your ‘mote?” Jenny asked. “Maybe it’s on the news already. Geez, if I had a TV this size, I’d actually use it.”

“What? I like it off when I practice.”

“Is that why you’re wearing pajamas?”Jenny busied herself by pawing through the issues of Home Builder and Canadian Homes and Cottages on the coffee table. He fumed inwardly when she knocked his shinai to the floor without even noticing.

Adrian’s face flushed in irritation. “This is my gi. It’s a uniform for martial arts.”

Jenny ignored him. “I can’t find the remote.”

Adrian strolled past her, snatched up the bamboo sword and leaned it against a corner of the room far away from her, biting down a snarling comment about disrespect. He plucked the controller off the plasma television stand.

“Right here,” he said, and pressed the power button.

“…Aren’t sure what motivated the attack, but it is believed to be an act of violence directed at the gay community specifically…”

Adrian squinted at the screen as images of smoke and fire danced with a throbbing crowd. He couldn’t make out the ranting but he recognized a riot when he saw one.

“Police are saying little at this time, except to stay indoors.“

He became aware of the dark-haired girl beside him. “It was so weird,” she said. “Everyone lost their minds all at once.”

“What do you mean?” Adrian asked.

“Like someone threw a switch. One minute everyone’s normal and going on with their day, and suddenly Buddy’s blows up and they’re all intent on maiming each other.” Her voice dropped to a near whisper. “Even Jenny went kind of insane.”

They studied her back as she sat riveted to the broadcast. Jenny showed no outward signs to suggest violence.

"She seems normal now," Adrian said.

She pushed her garish bangs from her forehead. "Well, as normal as Jenny ever is."

"Do you think she's a danger to us?" he asked. "Or herself?"

The goth girl shook her head. "No. I think the worst is over."

"Mew."

The girl's head snapped toward the sound in the kitchen.

"Amir?" She nearly shoved Adrian over in her desperation to get to the adjacent room. "Amir!"

Speaking of losing your mind.

Not that he could blame her. Cat had grown on him as well. Even if he did have a chewing fetish. And he couldn't deny that the expression of joy radiating from her face warmed him in a way he didn't see coming.

"Oops." Jenny palmed her forehead and gave Adrian an absent-minded smile. "I didn't know you still had Poe's kitty."

He watched an angry shadow pass over tattooed girl's face before she bent to collect her cat. Poetry…That was her name. No wonder he couldn't remember it.

"Careful, little guy's got some deep bruising." Even as he said it Adrian judged the warning to be unnecessary.

Poetry gathered the purring ball of fur in slow motion it seemed, tender as a mother.

"Hey, sweetie." Loving coos accompanied a nose nuzzle that made Adrian want to retch. "I missed you so much. Did you miss me?"

Chicks and their animals. But he had to admit, it was kind of cute in an Ihazcheezeburger kind of way. Yuck.

Poetry turned and Adrian's heart lurched. Her eyes gleamed. He couldn't mistake the gratitude shining there. It poured straight from her soul to her face. He wouldn't be surprised to hear harps in the background.

He couldn't help thinking how striking she looked. Vibrant. Alive.

Sexy. Whoa. Where did that come from?

"I don't know how to thank you," she said. "I am just so grateful for everything…"

No, no. Don't cry.

"Yeah." That was smooth. But he didn't know what to say. He'd just done what was right. Anyone else would have done the same…"Hey, I need a beer. You girls want one?"

He slid past Poetry, stopping to rub a finger along Amir's silky jaw. The lethargic cat mustered the energy to bite the tip with his pointy little fangs. Again.

Adrian shook off the sting and retreated to the fridge. Cool air seeped past his nose to his feet as he groped for the cold ones at the back. He popped all three before taking a swig.

Poetry still had her hands full of black Persian so Adrian left hers on the edge of the counter before heading back to the living room with a brew for Jenny.

"Oh my God!" Jenny's squeaky voice brought him back to the situation at hand "Would you look at this?"

She cranked the volume and Vinesh Pratap's voice boomed through the speakers. "We have since learned the fire was caused by two bombs…"

“That explains the bangs I heard,” Adrian said, gulping another mouthful as he passed her a bottle. “Thought I had new neighbors coming in.” Stupid. How could he mistake explosions for clumsy movers?

“…Buddy’s, a known gay club. It is believed to be the work of a protest group in support of Frank Fleisher…”

The lager went skunky in Adrian’s mouth. This wasn’t good. He tried to calculate the impact this information would have on his case, but rational thought eluded him.

As if on cue, the phone rang. The news hounds had descended. Lucky him.

CHAPTER TWENTY

"Pretty please?" For the second time in one day Aphrodite found herself submissive in the presence of another god…in their territory. She did not enjoy it. Especially since this particular deity was once her mate.

Hephaestus tapped out a chest plate. His measured strikes shaped space for a man's pectorals. The insistent clanging drummed a painful rhythm in Aphrodite's temples. She had loved him long ago. Until Ares stole her away. She left Hephaestus behind in Eden to dominate this realm.

But he pursued her, sacrificing everything he knew and loved to come for her. His journey through a dimensional portal had ended with a long fall from the heavens that permanently maimed him. And still Aphrodite had shown no sympathy. She shunned him in favor of her lover.

Now, like her, he remained a prisoner of this world.

It was a mistake, breaking the ancient and sacred bond. She had scarred him deeply, but it was too late to heal ancient wounds now. Perhaps she could beseech him for old time's sake.

"No. I won't help you."

Or perhaps not.

"In fact, I hope you lose. I relish the thought of you wallowing among the humans without your powers or indulgences." He returned to hammering the metal, every beat a dagger to Aphrodite's ears.

"Like you?" She made no effort to hide her contempt. "You are nothing more than a Nephilim."

"I chose this," Hephaestus said. He spread his arms to encompass the huge forge in which they stood. "I embraced this planet and made the best of my situation. I certainly don't spend my days mincing around, playing at false godliness."

Aphrodite swallowed angry remarks and pursed her lips. This was not going well. Hephaestus's resentment oozed from his pores like a sickness. No doubt he blamed her for his physical hurts as well as his emotional ones. She could almost sense his ill will on her skin. His love for her was long gone, withered and decayed from neglect.

She attempted another angle. "She is one of yours."

"Who is?"

"The girl. My champion is one of your protégés."

Hephaestus abruptly ceased his labors. For a moment Aphrodite wondered if she had gone deaf. Neither breathed. The stillness gave the monstrous room an ominous bearing. She jerked when the woof of a gas flame burst to life in an oven somewhere behind her.

"Poetry." Hephaestus spat the name of the only female under his tutelage. "Why would you choose my favorite smith? Was it not enough for you to destroy our union?" His face reddened, his eyes blazed. "After all these years you dare interfere with my humans?" Her former partner advanced.

"I apologize. I did not know she was yours. Her parents revere me as classical art." She retreated, knocking a pair of pliers and a ball peen hammer off someone's work space as she groped her way. "She wears my likeness on her back."

Hephaestus stopped, putting his weight on his good foot. He dropped his chin and rubbed a calloused hand over the bristles on his head. Quiet returned, less profound than before.

"I hate that tattoo."

"I had no knowledge that she toiled beside you," Aphrodite said, clasping her hands together in a mockery of prayer. "I swear. I only learned of it when I followed her here."

She experienced his exasperation, saw it in the way he tugged at his beard.

"I am sorry."

"I almost believe you mean that."

"I do." Almost. She poured softness into her voice as she approached. "There is a human saying 'great minds think alike'."

He peered at her from beneath his feathery eyebrows. "I am aware of the phrase."

Aphrodite smiled. His roar had become a mere growl.

"It seems we have the same taste in mortals." Aphrodite traced her hand along his sooty chin, delighting in how it tickled her palm.

"Would you permit Ares's victory simply to spite me?" She twisted a subtle hip forward, unleashing her charm. Her nipples hardened; she aroused herself with her own seduction.

She crushed them against Hephaestus's naked chest, inhaled his masculinity.

"Would you really let the war god hurt me?" She fluttered her lashes in a way that manipulated males of any age or profession. "Would you let him break Poetry's heart? Destroy her spirit? You understand his cruelty. Once he finishes with her, she may never create again."

A tremor passed through Hephaestus. Aphrodite felt it rumble through her body as though it belonged to her.

"You win," he said, a heavy sigh slumping his massive shoulders. "I will come to your aid if I am able."

Aphrodite rejoiced and clutched him closer. "I knew I could count on you."

Hephaestus removed her arms from his torso. "I'm not doing this for you. Poetry doesn't need you playing games with her life, her craft is too important."

“Yes, of course.” Aphrodite straightened the folds of her toga, noting with irritation how her touch created black streaks. The fact that her femininity had little effect on him heightened her ire, but she willed herself calm. “I understand.”

She had nothing more to say. Now that she had his assistance she would depart. She took a last look around Vulcan’s Forge, with its towering ceilings and boxy ovens. The sooner she made her exit from this ugly place the better.

“I appreciate this, my husband.”

His face contorted from hate and pain. “Do not call me that.” He resumed pounding a curve into the breastplate.

Aphrodite nodded, more to herself. They would never be together again. She ought to remember that if she wished to avoid upsetting her new ally.

She pivoted toward the exit, keeping eyes open for a certain spot before she went.

She almost missed Poetry’s corner tucked out of view. Aphrodite recognized the carved petals waiting on the table.

She approached them, noting how only some were glazed and polished. Certainly they would become another necklace. They reminded her of the daisies Poetry frequently wore only these appeared to be roses. Such a dark color she chose, purplish-black. Aphrodite mused vaguely if her son had anything to do with the strange choice. He had a love of roses, and a way of seducing women with them.

Aphrodite fingered through tools, molds and a dusty pile of photos. Pitch flew into the air, tickling her nose. She repressed her sneeze, sniffling instead and in doing so noting how the residue stank of iron.

A quick flip through the pictures demonstrated a common theme with Poetry’s work. Did this woman do anything other than flowers? How dull. Beautiful work, yes, but time for something new.

Something a man might wear.

She caught sight of a spool of wire and a spark of an idea formed. She did not have Apollo's power of inspiration, but no matter. If love could not move a woman to greater heights, it was because she did not live.

Aphrodite picked the roll from the shelf and kissed it. A whispering mist passed from her lips to the shining silver thread.

With her work done and her plans in place, Aphrodite disappeared. She very much enjoyed when things went her way.

CHAPTER TWENTY ONE

Adrian drew a deep shaking breath of metal and dust. But he wasn't complaining. Anything to get away from the chaos on Jasper Avenue and his landline. He had a bad feeling this would be the nearest thing to peace and quiet he'd get for a long time.

"Thanks for the ride," Poetry said. "You keep doing me all these favors…" She shook her head. "…I don't know how I'll ever repay you."

"It's no big deal." He gawked at his surroundings; sky-high ceilings, wall-to-wall kilns, ovens and fire pits. Uncomfortable warmth settled on his skin. "Do you live or work here?"

"Yes." Poetry shot him a smirk over her shoulder. "I moved into an upstairs apartment after…after…you know, 'The Kevin Incident'."

Jenny ran her fingers over a work bench as she strolled. "Ew. This place is gritty."

"If it really bothers you that much you don't have to stay here," Poetry said. Adrian heard the edge in her voice and saw the tension in her shoulders as she led them to a staircase. "Besides, it was your idea."

"Rowr."

"See. Amir likes it already." Adrian's lip curled at the loud smacking-kissing noises. Obviously Poetry had a closer friendship with that fluffball than she did with her roommate.

In the hour she'd been reunited with Amir he'd shown signs of improvement. She literally had him eating out of her hand, Seafood Medley treats to be exact. His Bentley reeked of them. He hoped to God the stench was temporary.

He hated to admit it, but watching them relieved a lot of tension on the drive over. The streets were creepishly hushed in some areas and overrun with raging motorists and crazy pedestrians in others. Broken glass covered the roads. They'd taken a few detours. The radio blared nothing but disturbing updates and violent arguments between DJs. Not a pleasant trip. Even the music they played became progressively Megadeth.

But when Adrian thought of his incessantly ringing home phone and the multitude of messages that were building up on his cell, he'd prefer to hang out with the girls in this sweat box.

They climbed the stairs, and Adrian peered out across the field of equipment and metalwork. If he saw Poetry's station would he recognize it? He tried to picture it. Would it have a feminine touch? Would it reflect her gothic style?

"Right through here," Poetry said.

"Oh, thank God," Jenny said, her shoulders dropping with relief. "I thought this was it."

"No, this is the common room," Poetry said. "But the apartment isn't much bigger." She approached a closet. Adrian checked again. Yes, it was a closet door.

Poetry opened it and bent to crawl inside. Adrian glanced at Jenny, her expression uncertain.

Poetry popped her head out. "Are you two coming?"

Adrian grinned at Jenny, gestured toward the small space. "After you."

Once his turn came, he saw another narrow staircase. Unlike Poetry's last apartment, these didn't smell like cheap, starchy food. Instead, he detected the mildew and mustiness common to architectural relics. It tickled his nose and he discretely covered it.

"Oh my God, Poetry," Jenny said. "This place stinks."

"And here we are," Poetry said, her voice too cheery, too loud. No doubt trying to gloss over Jenny's rude comments. What did Gary see in her? Besides the tight ass... "Home sweet home."

Poetry flicked a switch, and the true grime of the suite became apparent.

The walls needed washing and painting. The linoleum had wrinkles and cracks. Everything, the appliances, fixtures and cupboards, begged to be updated.

"I love it," Adrian said.

Both women gaped at him.

"Really?" Poetry asked.

"Really." He envisioned stainless steel faucets and cork floor tiles. New storm windows and weather stripping. Cut glass light fixtures. DIY heaven. "It has character and potential."

Poetry peered around as though seeing the suite from his perspective. "I guess it does."

Jenny rolled her eyes but said nothing. For once.

Poetry placed her sleeping cat on the floor next to the refrigerator beside his food and water dish, fashioning the towel into a makeshift bed.

Jenny paced the floor, grimacing and touching various surfaces.

"Can I get you guys something?" she asked. "Perhaps some..." She opened the door and stared inside for a long pause. "Water?"

She sighed and went to the cupboard for glasses. "I need to do some grocery shopping."

A shrill beeping interrupted. Jenny checked her purse and yanked out her cell phone. A grunt of satisfaction puffed from Jenny's lips as she viewed the screen and accepted the call.

“Gary…” Jenny transformed from obnoxious houseguest to instant sweetheart. “I’m so glad you called.”

Trepidation crept down Adrian’s spine. He’d talked to Gary that morning and knew about their blowout. He’d made plans to go for beers with him and Ranjan so they could get ‘the bitch’ out of his system. That was before she rang his intercom. So that’s why Jenny was staying here. Duh.

“No, I’m safe,” Jenny was saying, “thanks to Poetry and Adrian.” Adrian heard a muffled version of his friend’s voice over the crack of an ice cube tray. “Yeah, we were less than a block away. It was like that thing in L.A. with the black guy. It was so frightening.”

Adrian detected a hint of artificial tears in the end of her sentence and bit his lip to hide his exasperation.

Poetry didn’t bother. She glared at the ceiling and blew her bangs into the air. She handed both of them a glass of water.

“Aw, you’re so sweet,” Jenny said. “I’m just fine.” Another long moment passed between Adrian and Poetry while Jenny continued her conversation without them.

Poetry peered around at everything except him as they sipped. “Well, I’d give you the grand tour, but this is really it.” She motioned at the few walls. “Not much to see.”

Jenny shot a visual snarl and gave them a wide-handed shushing gesture. “I’m at Poetry’s place.”

Adrian crammed his hands in his pockets. "How about your work?” he asked. “Would you show me?”

“Really?” Poetry’s face lit up. “You actually want to see my art?”

“Sure.” Great way to get away from Jenny’s manipulative sweet-girl voice…which got louder with every sentence.

“I missed you too.”

"If I have to listen to another cutesy squeal from her, I'll be sick," he said.

Poetry guffawed, and received another filthy glare from her friend. She leaned close to speak in a whisper. "Jenny has that effect on people."

He motioned toward the exit as Jenny gave them her back and put a finger in her free ear.

"Lead the way."

Poetry brought him to the main floor. "Watch your step," she said.

They meandered past tables littered with metal parts, half-finished projects, and tools he couldn't guess what function they served.

Adrian's skin began to bead from the heat of the ovens. In the dim lighting he noticed the sheen of sweat on Poetry's neck and breathed in her iron musk. Over the collar of her uniform he could make out shades of sunrise pink and blue. He stared so intently that when she stopped he nearly buried the back of her head in his chest.

"This is my bench. This is where I work."

"Interesting." It looked clean enough, no shaving piles or scraps like the others, but it had an organized chaos that Adrian figured only Poetry would understand. Boxes of beads jammed next to spools of leather and wire, stacks of papers and photos stuffed in cubbies.

"What's this?" he asked.

"What? This?" Poetry picked up the chain and held it up for Adrian to see. "It's a necklace I'm working on."

The metal appeared to be darker, like pewter, and half the decorations were almost black. They resembled roses.

"May I?" he asked as he pulled the unfinished piece from her fingers and brought them to his eyes. Yes, they were roses, and well crafted ones at that. It almost appeared as though she'd placed the petals individually. "Nice work."

"Thanks. Do you recognize them?"

"Yeah, they're roses."

She smiled. "They're modeled after the ones you gave me."

He handed her project back. "You mean the one I gave you at Louisiana Purchase."

"Yeah, and the one you sent here."

What?

"Say that again?"

"You know," Poetry seemed to shrink as she balled the jewelry in one hand. "The other one you left here. At my door."

"No…" Adrian cringed as the blood drained from her face. "That wasn't me. I've never even heard of this place before today."

Adrian had no clue who sent it, and obviously neither did she. Her ex was probably out of the clink by now. The asshole couldn't have found her yet, could he?

"Sorry." He realized how dumb that sounded. He never knew what to say to this girl.

"Don't be." She deposited the necklace on the counter with distinct and abrupt loathing, and curled away from him. "It's not your fault."

Adrian licked the salt from his lips. Between the lack of noise and the unnatural temperature, his comfort level bottomed out.

"It's very nice," he said.

Poetry shrugged as she picked a roll of silver wire from a ledge. "Thanks." She pivoted to face him but her eyes were on the shining thread in her grip.

“I’m thinking of trying something different,” she said. “I don’t know exactly what…”

She peered up at him, and even with the dim lighting Adrian didn’t miss the dilation of her pupils. Big as dimes. Her breath stirred gooseflesh on his neck as she strode forward; her scrutiny awakened long quiet sensations and tickled nerves in his gut.

He watched her gaze as they wandered over his features. First his eyes, then his lips. It lingered along his jaw as though she longed to touch it. Her mouth parted, and Adrian became aware of her reaching hand…

A door slammed, jarring Adrian from his trance. He heard Poetry inhale as he spun toward the sound.

“Poetry, come up here and get changed,” Jenny said. “Time to go.”

“What?” Poetry asked.

Jenny skipped toward them, at risk of cracking her skin with her smile. “Gary and I are going to work things out.” She faced Adrian. “You don’t mind driving us, do you Adrian? Seeing as how you’re meeting him too?”

“Wait.” Poetry tossed the spool and waved her reluctance. “Why do I have to come with you?”

“Because you’re my best friend, silly. If he has his buddies with him I’m taking mine. I need someone on my side.”

“Oh, no…” Poetry said. Adrian gave her a pleading stare and cleared his throat. He did not want to spend the night listening to Jenny pout.

Poetry got the hint. A smirk crept up her cheek.

“Okay. Since you put it that way,” she said, her twinkling eyes never leaving his. “Just let me wash up.”

Adrian released the air in his lungs. Thank God. He’d have something else to do other than referee for Gary and Jenny. If he knew Ranjan, he’d find ways to excuse himself from the drama, leaving Adrian to endure it. At least Poetry had some personality. They might actually find something to talk about.

Stranger things have happened.

CHAPTER TWENTY TWO

This beer is going down way too good.

Poetry tried to savor a mouthful, to take pleasure in the subtle hint of hops before gulping it. Why did she agree to come? Oh right. *Because I'm Jenny's best friend.* Another swallow and another nasty thought wormed into her mind.

Best friends don't abandon you at the first sign of trouble.

She reflected on that. Of course, Jenny had tried to warn her. Several times. And she'd been right. Kevin was the worst thing to ever happen to her. Beside her, Jenny and Gary alternated between words of adoration and biting criticisms and blame.

Poetry was getting drunk but refused to feel bad about it. She deserved alcoholic tranquilizing after her terrifying run from Jasper Ave. She had a tendency to think of Edmonton as a really big small town. Riots didn't happen here. Not like say, Vancouver. It freaked her out to see it firsthand.

She glanced at Jenny. What had happened to her? Did she even remember it? She'd been like a beast, snarling and scratching to join the violence. Yet here she sat, the same old Jenny, crazy only for guys in pricey suits and stepping into a relationship at breakneck speed.

Adrian looked worse, and he hadn't even been there. He kept fiddling with his cell, nervousness etched creases between his brows. She couldn't figure out why. He'd shut his phone off.

He caught her staring. "Are we having fun yet?"

Poetry smiled as she took another sip of her lager. "Sure. Who needs reality TV when the drama's right here?"

Adrian chuckled and she caught a whiff of his beer breath.

“I think Ran’s got the right idea,” he said, pointing his chin toward a dark corner. “Looks like he’s having a good time by himself.”

“What’s he playing?”

“Arkanoid.”

“Are you serious?” Poetry could picture the grainy screen from the mother of all ping-pong games with its rolling capsules of goodies. “I didn’t know any of those were still kickin’ around.” As though to emphasize her point, a series of loud pops resounded accompanied by grunts of frustration from Ranjan.

“Uh-oh,” Adrian said. “That sounds like the one with the extra balls.”

“The light blue?”

“Can’t remember, but it always kills him. I don’t know why he picked it up.”

Ranjan let out a loud groan and the game buzzed in triumph. He glowered at the screen before downing the rest of his drink. He spared their table a nod and retreated to the bar.

Poetry heard him order an ‘Apple Jack’ from an exotic beauty Poetry hadn’t noticed last time she’d come to the Rosemount.

“What’s an Apple Jack?” Adrian asked. Apparently he’d overheard as well.

“I don’t know,” Poetry said with a shrug.

“It’s Jack Daniels and apple juice and I think maybe cinnamon,” Jenny said.

Nice of you to acknowledge us, Poetry thought.

She held her tumbler toward Poetry. “Wanna try it?”

“No, thanks.” Poetry eyed the unpleasant shade of Jenny’s brownish cocktail. Gut instinct told her she wouldn’t like it. “I’ll stick to beer.”

"They're good," Gary said. "They kind of have this sweet and sour thing going on." He drained his glass and signaled the waitress with a spin of his finger, ordering another round.

"But as I was saying, honey," Gary said, focusing on Jenny. "It's the principal of the thing-"

"Is that all you care about?" Jenny asked, her voice reaching shrill levels.

Poetry went back to gazing into the bottom of her mug, tuning out the circular bickering. It sounded too much like high school.

The Rosemount seemed quiet tonight. Either Tuesday's weren't busy here or the loving couple's side show chased away the rest of the customers. Their group remained the only people in the place.

Gary and Jenny barely paused to breath between subjects and moods and Ranjan chatted with the woman behind the counter.

"You want to play?"

Poetry faced Adrian. His eyes were on the corner Ranjan vacated.

"What? Arkanoid?"

"Sure. Why not?"

The server arrived with two Apple Jacks and two Kokanee.

Poetry couldn't help but stare. The girl's eyes had the upward tilt of a cat and shone like the purest jade. The waves of her silken hair made Poetry finger her dry strands self-consciously. She wondered if the girl was part Asian. She had pale luminescent skin. Stunning.

No wonder Ranjan gave up Arkanoid to sit with her. Even Adrian, who struck Poetry as being too cool for ogling, sat with his mouth hanging open until the super model sauntered away.

Poetry sucked in her gut. "You ready to get your butt kicked?" she asked, stealing his attention. Not that she was jealous or anything.

“I don’t think so,” he said, pushing back his chair. “I’ll be doing the butt-kicking.”

“Whatever.”

She pawed through her purse for quarters on her way to the low video box. She found handfuls; she’d get more for laundry later.

“My quarters,” she said as she scooted her chair to the glass top. “So I get to go first.”

“No problem,” Adrian agreed, awkwardly rolling his seat to the other side. “I like to know what I’m up against.”

Arkanoid twittered to life and Poetry got comfortable. She cracked her knuckles just for show and positioned her hands on the wand and the red button like a pro gamer. Time to make the ball sing.

Sure enough, the controls in her skilled hands did their thing as she spun the knob and sent her silver bar across the screen. Another pill tumbled toward it, and Poetry chose the navy-colored oval. A hum sounded and her ark grew in size.

“Good one,” Adrian said, sipping his beer. “Did you play this a lot?”

“Some. I used to play it in the Wizard’s Castle at West Ed.”

“Me too. I hung out there when I was a kid. Funny we never ran into each other.”

“Nah. I only went when my dad gave me his change.” They shared a silence that Poetry found surprisingly nice, listening to the beep and chime of the game. Poetry blinked against the dryness of her eyes while piano music played in the background and Jenny’s voice had returned to a melodic metronome.

“Is that where you met Jenny?”

“At the mall? No.” Poetry’s brow tensed. The game sped up. “I met her at work. We’ve both been at Denny’s for two years.”

"Oh, yeah." He maintained his nonchalance.

"You and your posse seem inseparable," she said with a toss of her head. "Where did you meet them?"

"We went to U of A together."

"Same fraternity?"

"No. Fraternities are for sheep."

Poetry grinned, unsuccessful at squelching her approval. "I agree."

The incessant chime of the computer ball couldn't compete with the crescendo of Jenny's whining. Like a dentist drill. Poetry darted a glance over her shoulder to check on her…

…Only to hear the deep zipping noise of her loss. "Damn."

"Too bad." Adrian straightened his spine and positioned his hands. "My turn."

Poetry settled in, her eyes on the screen and her ears trained to hear Jenny and Gary's repetitive griping.

"They sound like they're already married," Adrian said.

"At the rate they're going, it wouldn't be a shock if they did run off to Vegas."

He smirked. "The two of them kind of dove in head first, didn't they?"

"They definitely should've taken things slower."

"Relationships are like Kendo," Adrian said.

Poetry frowned into her mug. The foamy head of her beer bubbled against her upper lip. "How so?"

“Everyone’s quick to learn the basics, but you spend years practicing to master them. It looks simpler than it really is.”

Poetry knew nothing about Kendo. But she remembered the stance he’d used at her apartment, the graceful fluidity as he slid on the balls of his feet. His posture remained perfect and the hands holding the improvised weapon never shook or wavered. He did it so naturally it made her forget he’d wielded a broomstick. He obviously understood more than just the basics of his sport.

Another dull zoom and a sigh from Adrian when his ball crashed.

“Wouldn’t it be easier if we could practice our romances before we got into them?” Poetry said.

“You mean just going over it, from the same level until we got it right?”

The mostly empty lounge echoed with their laughter and it gave Poetry’s heart a lift. She’d needed that and her stomach ached with a pang of wistfulness. How long had it been since she’d shared a joke? Just appreciated the moment?

She and Adrian let their chuckles subside while wiping mirth from their eyes. Poetry expelled a happy sigh as she shifted in her chair. Quiet had fallen between them again. The game waited with lights flashing for the next play.

“Poetry.”

His sudden seriousness made her look up. His baby blues held no trace of humor.

“That’s not such a bad idea.”

“What? Dating drills and mock affairs?

“Precisely,” he said, and Poetry felt her smile fall. “We could see each other as procedure and give feedback and critiques.”

Poetry sat back, dumbfounded. "Adrian, how many beers have you had?"

CHAPTER TWENTY THREE

Strife ran a hand through her back-to-black hair. Her stomach churned. Confidence returned with natural beauty, but things weren't going quite as well as planned. She could call her chemically induced riot a success. With the city's water system compromised, violence would continue. But the civil upheaval chased new recruits away from the taverns. Things were stagnant all over Edmonton. Mass hysteria buzzed in her blood, but most people were frightened into remaining at home. At least she'd made the right decision in coming to this establishment to apply her trade. Ares was correct about their chosen haunt and would be pleased to learn Strife had acquired the targets.

Still, she glanced around warily. Her hands shook a little. Perhaps he lurked in the shadows, spying on her and would appear when everyone left, just to remind her he owned her. The expensive art on the walls stared back. No manifestation tickled her senses. She was not ready for her master yet. Not only were the chosen humans avoiding her potion in favor of beer, but Adrian and Poetry appeared to be getting along quite well.

The other couple was clearly influenced by the drink. Their constant waves of lust, happiness, and pettiness created a nausea rivaled by a bad day at sea.

"I'll have another if you don't mind." The Eastern Indian perched in front of her shot a flirtatious grin in her direction.

"Sure thing," she said, gifting him with a dazzling smile. "Glad you like these so much." Better put in extra spice. After three Apple Jacks he was a little drunk, nothing more. His aura remained calm, his face personable.

"How's it going?" The other female approached from behind him with Aphrodite's champion, clapping both hands on his shoulders affectionately. "You loaded yet, Ran?"

"Working on it," he said. The women strolled past, apparently for a 'girl trip' to the washroom.

The handsome brown-skinned man turned his attention back to Strife and flashed another glimpse of perfect white teeth. "Friends of my friends."

"I see." Her heightened hearing picked up on the girls' conversation, not that she could make out much more than echoes. The one with the streaked hair did most of the talking. Or rather, whining. That must be Poetry's stupid friend, Jenny. Not that Strife cared. Not unless she could use her. She considered that option and dismissed it. Too self-absorbed to be serviceable.

Right this instant she must pretend she worked here, to feign interest in the human sitting at the bar. His eyes mooned at her like a puppy begging for scraps. Pathetic.

Strife tilted her lips in a friendly expression as she engaged him. Being human bored her sometimes but she had to play along. Good thing he was attractive.

"So I haven't seen you around here before. When did you start?"

"Yesterday. I'm new to the city."

"Really?" His chocolate eyes twinkled, reminding her of Ares. And just like Ares, he had sex on his mind. Desire oozed from his pores like the sandalwood cologne and curry scent of him.

Her master never exuded such warmth.

"I know Edmonton like the back of my hand," he said. "I'd love to show you around."

To Strife's left, the washroom door squealed, announcing the women's return. They spoke in hushed and urgent tones as they approached her. The usual guy stuff: Gary's a jerk and Adrian is good-looking. Meaningless chatter.

“Another round, ladies?” Strife asked. Maybe she could smuggle some spice into Poetry’s beer. They muttered their approval, but before she could fill the order another presence arrived.

Strife whirled toward the glass door on her right. An overbearing essence wafted in like the subtle kiss of a forest fire’s flare. A beautiful man entered the tavern, raising her hackles. She recognized those foppish curls. She longed to scalp them from his tanned forehead.

“You.”

The word came from not only from her lips, but Poetry’s as well.

Hermes spared Strife a haughty glance before sauntering towards the human females with his noxious basket of roses.

“Hello, love,” he said, and Poetry’s tattoos leapt out in contrast to her paling skin. “Did you get your flower back alright?”

Strife didn’t need to see her stricken face. Rank terror rolled from her pores like a gush of blood.

“How did you find out where I live?”

“I have my ways. I…” Hermes’s eyes narrowed at the unexpected reaction. It seemed Poetry did not succumb to his charms. Her friend hugged her protectively. The Indian stood in front of them, a noble gesture from a man who had no clue what he truly faced.

You screwed up, pretty boy.

Out loud Strife said, “She does not like you.”

His irises shrank to pinpoints. “This isn’t your concern.”

He extended his hand toward the girl in a placating matter. “Listen, I was just…”

“I’m afraid this is my concern,” Strife said. “My pub, my customers.” My territory.

She crossed her arms, lifting her chin to glare down her nose at Hermes. Try me.

Aphrodite's favorite son peered from Poetry to Strife and back again.

"Please," Poetry pressed her fingers to her mouth. "I've had enough of this kind of attention for a lifetime. Just leave me alone."

Hermes appeared to consider his options.

"Don't make me phone the police," Strife said. Her widening lips hinted dangerously. He would not challenge her here. Not in front of the mortals.

He stared her down, even as he pivoted away. "This isn't over."

"Leave."

The four of them watched him depart. The only sounds were his unhurried footsteps and the tasteful notes of contemporary jazz. Adrian and Gary held quiet conversation, unaware of the confrontation.

At the thud of the door, Poetry exhaled audibly.

"Thank you so much," she said, her eyes bright with gratitude.

"No problem." Strife resumed the task of opening a beer and mixing another Apple Jack. "That is not my first run in with him." She constructed lies about him hassling and stalking customers. "Consider him barred."

"Thank you. Thank you." The girl babbled while hugging her friend and glowing at Strife.

The brown man gazed at her with renewed respect and appreciation.

"What's your name again?" he asked.

She opened her mouth but stilled her tongue. She'd almost given them her true identity, the hiss forming on her lips.

What was she going to call herself? Something beginning with 'S', since it was halfway out of her mouth.

"Sarah," she said.

"Nice to meet you, Sarah. I'm Ranjan."

Strife's lips twitched. Ranjan. "Delight to his parents," if she understood correctly. It had been hundreds of years since she'd been in that part of the world.

"That's Poetry and Jenny. Over there are Gary and Adrian." He indicated his cohorts with vague hand gestures. His eyes never left her face.

"That was a cool thing you did for me," Poetry said.

Strife performed a demure lift of her shoulder. "Glad I could help."

Poetry and Jenny took their drinks back to their seats, their humor returned.

She'd gained acceptance. Even if their glances and grins had not said so, their resonance spoke for them. How she hated 'sweet and fuzzy', but that's what she must work with.

Then it occurred to her, perhaps she could use this to her advantage. A plan began to fester. If she entertained this mortal, her proximity to the prey would increase. If she treaded carefully.

"Where were we?" she asked.

Ranjan drained his Jack Daniels and apple juice. "Excuse me?"

"You were saying you could show me around?"

Happiness encompassed his entire face. "Absolutely."

"That would be nice." Step One. "Throw in lunch and we have a deal."

CHAPTER TWENTY FOUR

Hephaestus allowed himself a leisurely perusal of Freya's throne room. Not what he expected.

All of Asgard lacked opulence and color, but Sessrumnir's grey stone walls lent the cavernous space an intimidating iciness. The ghostly wisps that drifted in and out of view did nothing to enhance the place, nor did the smell of mildew and old meat.

"You waste your time and mine," Freya said. Her only movement since his arrival was to pet the black and white cat perched on the arm of her chair. Hephaestus stared into the feline's green eyes and instantly thought of margaritas. He could use a drink right now. "Your bitch will not receive my assistance."

Hephaestus shook his head. "She is not my bitch." She is a bitch unto herself. "I am not here on her behalf." He hoped the goddess experienced the purity of his distain. Otherwise this visit was pointless.

He retrieved a bauble from his vest, letting it twinkle in the meager light.

"She does not understand her place," he said. He twisted the bracelet over his fingers and smiled as the diamonds dazzled rainbow colors. "She knows not the charm and strength you possess, my white queen. Nor did she show the proper respect."

Hephaestus glanced at the Norse goddess. Her wide eyes stayed transfixed to the gold and gem encrusted masterpiece. He had no doubt they would be. Pretty trinkets were her legendary weakness. Even mortals knew how she'd 'entertained' dwarves to own the trademark necklace she wore.

"In Canada, in a province named Alberta…"

"I know where Alberta is," Freya said, the edge in her voice ringing off the slate.

“But did you know there are endless tunnels where vast wealth still lies hidden?” The wonder and curiosity in her expression lent her youthfulness. “They are the Cadomin mines, once bursting with coal.”

He extracted an ordinary lump of the inky rock from his other pocket and held it before her.

It amused Hephaestus how she leapt from her seat for a better view. Her hide-bound footsteps skittered and echoed across the silent hall as several felines scurried from her path. Her falcon feather cape gave her the illusion of flight.

When her slender fingers ventured to the fossil, Hephaestus closed his hand, denying her.

Anger and disappointment drifted across Freya’s features, but her emotions remained unspoken.

Hephaestus smiled. “Allow me.”

He tightened the fist holding the ebony stone, grunting with the effort to squeeze it. Sharp edges began to shift inside his grip. He concentrated on the body heat he generated, on the brawn required to transform this humble chunk.

“What are you doing?” Freya asked. “Surely you can’t…”

Hephaestus released the pressure with a gasp and opened his hand. “But I have.” In the center of his palm sat a rough diamond the size of a milky grape.

“For you, my raw wonder.” He placed the unfinished jewel in her hand.

Freya’s face brightened. “You are so strong.” She caressed his twitching muscles as she stared at his offering. Her mouth curved in a lopsided quirk of lascivious intention.

“It is true,” he said. “Indeed, I employ my power to make these treasures of the Earth into pretty things.”

He brought the bracelet forward to encircle her wrist.

"I made this for you. You are a goddess worthy of my finest." His eyes met hers. "Had I met you before Aphrodite, my life might have been different."

That much might have been true. Freya spent her existence pursuing lust, whereas Aphrodite believed in love.

But his lost lover proved herself to be a betrayer, and Freya knew her own heart; she never denied it. What could have been had he met this volcano of passion before he'd known Aphrodite? Or the smoldering simplicity that was Poetry?

Freya caressed his stubbly cheek, causing him to twitch. "It matters not," Her breath tickling his ear. "You and I can be together here. Now."

Freya heard his thoughts and desires as though he'd spoken them. And she had not judged.

Her touch wandered downward. She stroked his hardening length and his heart lodged in his throat. She drew nearer, her breasts brushing against him to create an electric shock that spread to his curling fingers and toes. With a quick flutter of fingers, her cape and clothing ceased to exist and she stood naked before him. Once again she eased inside his personal space, brushing her taut nipples against his chest as the environment shifted around him.

Before he could find his balance, Hephaestus found himself sprawled on a bed of furs, Freya straddling him like a determined wrangler. The softness of the pelts against his buttocks reminded Hephaestus of Freya's will. He had no idea how or when his garments had disappeared, but he was more than willing to give her whatever she wanted.

She would take without hesitation.

Freya lowered her body to meet his throbbing cock and sighed. Her rhythm started slow, her groans subtle. He gripped her hips, squeezing them as he dragged her deeper. Ragged breathing puffed from his lips. He wanted to fuck her harder.

He growled and thrashed, fantasizing that the pale nipples bobbing before his eyes were dark like Athenian olives. In his mind's eye her shoulders were decorated with tribal markings, lilies and satyrs…like Poetry's. He savored the woman on top of him, gloried in her shouts and her tightening spasms as she came. Spurting sex streamed warm down his loins.

Freya went limp, but Hephaestus knew the Norse goddess of lust and fertility wasn't done yet. He sat up, gently pushing her back as he got to his knees. Her skin, soft and yielding as he parted her thighs, reminded him of flower petals. Her sparse ivory curls opened to reveal the tender pink meat he needed to taste.

He teased at first, darting his inquisitive tongue in and around her flesh until she whimpered. His powerful grip held her legs apart as he dove in, smearing his face with her creamy heat. She bucked into his mouth. He obliged by licking faster, lapping at her sweet nectar.

He continued this dance until his jaw ached and her howling grew hoarse.

He sat back on his heels, watching the perspiration beading on Freya's abdomen like tiny stars. A wicked smirk crept across his face with her desperate panting.

The scent of her drove him mad: a combination of sweat, sex and Reinroses. Like a rutting beast, he plunged his cock inside.

More.

His pulsing need ached. He collapsed on her torso, grinding against her clitoris. His relentless, eager movements would make her orgasm with him. He wouldn't stop until she did.

He rutted with her for what seemed like hours, growling and biting until Freya's screams joined with his in ecstasy. Hephaestus sucked the sweat off her collarbone as they climaxed together, sliding at last to a joyous conclusion. He roared his release, snarling with his final thrusts while fireworks erupted throughout his being.

The rush ended. Hephaestus could not move. He relished the sensation of his spent cock spilling from Freya along with his seed. How it would feel to have Poetry tremble beneath him like this?

Freya planted both palms on his chest and nudged him off. With some effort he crawled off the bed and got wearily to his feet. He sensed her delighted exhaustion, shared it.

He extended both his hands to assist her, careful to keep his head respectfully bowed and eyes lowered. This magnificent woman he accepted as his superior. He would not risk offending her, not when he'd come this far.

He felt a flicker of respect from her before her delicate hands took his calloused ones. He pulled her from the mess of sex-stained wolf and rabbit hides.

Freya's wet tongue darted across his cheek and Hephaestus raised his head to draw her into a kiss. Her mouth still tasted fresh and sweet; he drank her in like a dying man until she struggled for oxygen.

"I enjoyed your visit, Hephaestus," she said, her gaze sleepy and dazed. "Come to my hall anytime you wish."

She crushed his knuckles and yanked him to her chest, the movement so sudden that he stumbled. The eyes that had twinkled with pleasure were now secretive slits.

"The magick will activate only when the piece is complete. When they are worn for the first time, the wearer will yearn for the first person she sees. Be certain it is you, or your quest is for naught."

His eardrums popped and Hephaestus found himself alone in his Edmonton condominium. He shivered from head to foot as his sweat slicked skin chilled in the summer heat. He opened his clenched fists and grinned. In pleasing her he'd received his prize. Two round beads of amber, each the size of his thumbnail nested in his palms, dazzling in their refinement.

Hephaestus peered through the balcony doors of his living room to the setting sun. The sky matched the stones exactly. He limped to the veranda and took in the view. To his left, the River Valley flowed with streams of headlights along Groat Road. To his right, new apartment towers clawed the sky.

He felt like a true god for the first time in decades. Invincible. His heightened awareness presented him with the human vibe he once shunned. Petty squabbles reached his ears, but their amplified outrage and heartbreak failed to move him.

Though unlikely anyone saw his statuesque nudity, Hephaestus cared not. Not if they could see him, nor how it might offend them. Modesty and emotions were for mortals.

Never again would Hephaestus permit his feelings to get the better of him. But inevitably, he felt rage sneaking into his soul. He'd long ago disposed of his hurts in the face of Aphrodite's and Ares's duplicity. He would never surrender to love again.

A breeze caressed him, bringing with it the odor of mutual gratification that clung to his flesh.

He pushed his fury aside and grinned.

What a woman. Perhaps he would return to her hall someday.

But he must give Poetry the amber. Between Freya's magick, his limited abilities, and Poetry's talent, Hephaestus would have what he coveted. The human female would belong to him.

CHAPTER TWENTY-FIVE

The best thing about living above Vulcan's Forge, Poetry decided, had to be the immediate access to the tools she required to create.

Her black roses lay unfinished in a heap, but they gave her the heebie-jeebies now. She'd already moved onto something new.

She crouched over a wooden dowel, coiling wire through precise loops two centimeters apart. She paused long enough to assure straight lines by making marks with a pencil. She'd only been at it for two hours but her hands cramped from the strain.

So far the pattern seemed tight enough, a testament to Poetry's patience. The links were forming a snake-like chain the width of her finger.

She'd woken early and set to work before breakfast or showering.

Her stomach complained, but Poetry didn't dare stop now. She might lose her rhythm. Third loop, pull, turn the peg. Fourth loop, little tug, shift again.

"What are you working on?"

Poetry gave a yip of surprise, spinning to face her mentor. How did a man with such a pronounced limp manage to sneak up on people like that? He'd told her it was from a long drop from the sky, but never gave her details about the parachuting accident. Sometimes she wondered if it was the truth. He was pretty stealthy for a guy with a crippled leg.

"You scared the crap out of me." Poetry placed her project on the counter with a trembling hand.

"Sorry," Hugh said, not that he looked apologetic with his lazy grin.

Poetry rubbed her face, using the unexpected break to unwind muscles she hadn't realized were so tense. Her shoulders, back, and feet began a throbbing chorus, and she did the hokey pokey to relieve it.

Hugh glimpsed over Poetry's shoulder at the intricate metal weave she'd been working on.

"Interesting," he said. "What's it going to be?"

"It's a torque."

Hugh grimaced, an expression Poetry knew to be disapproval or irritation. "Since when do you create Viking art?"

She shrugged. "I thought I'd try something else."

Poetry glanced over her shoulder at the sleek ribbon of interlocking wires. For someone who didn't do this kind of metal work often, she'd done a pretty good job, she thought.

"It's a far cry from flowers," Hugh said.

"An artist should strive to grow and experiment with new things."

She caressed the ridges she'd so lovingly crafted and the sharp slopes of Adrian's face appeared in her mind.

Along with their odd agreement.

Hugh cleared his throat, and Poetry realized a conspiring smile had crept up her face. Her cheeks burned in embarrassment and she dropped her gaze.

Poetry zeroed in on Hugh's meaty paw. "What do you have in your hand?"

He brought his fist into the light and opened it.

Poetry caught her breath. Among the lines and cracks of Hugh's palm lay two exquisite orbs the color of tangerines. Inclusions bubbled within them like champagne frozen in time.

"Are those real?"

“Sure are.” He pushed them toward her. Poetry could smell the warm metal heat of iron on him. “Here. Take them.”

“What?”

“You heard me. Take them. I got them from a friend, and I figure the person who could do the most with them is you. They’d make a great pair of earrings, wouldn’t you say?”

Poetry plucked the stones from his hand, trying to contain her excitement. Her reverent sigh betrayed her. “Stones this gorgeous,” Poetry choked on her heart, “are so rare. They must have been expensive. Are they Baltic?”

The breeze from Hugh’s chuckle tickled her ear and Poetry glanced up to find him sharing her space as they leered over the gems like a pair of pirates. The visual seemed so absurd she almost burst into a Spongebob Squarepants sea shanty but Poetry squelched her laughter. She didn’t want to come across as immature or ungrateful.

“I have connections in high places near Sweden,” Hugh said with a wink. “Mutual back scratching, that kind of thing.”

The semi-precious spheres glittered, even under the harsh fluorescent lights. They reminded Poetry of their ancient beauty and future potential. An unwelcome thought occurred to her. “Why give them to me?” Was it a gift or was she working on commission? Poetry caught his startled expression before he could replace his mask of grim cynicism.

“No reason. You’ve had a hard time of it lately and I thought you could use some cheering up.” He grasped one of the jewels between his fingers and brought it next to Poetry’s head. “They’d make lovely earrings.”

“You mentioned that. Not a bad idea.”

Suddenly, Hugh’s intimacy lost its appeal, and Poetry couldn’t explain why. She took a subtle step away.

Hugh seemed to detect the change and also moved for greater distance. His features never changed from their brooding stoicism.

"Thank you," she said. "I don't know what to say."

"Just make something great with them. Something for yourself." He pivoted on his good foot and hobbled away.

Alone once again, Poetry slumped. The strain in her muscles no longer had anything to do with how hard she'd worked. Since when did she react like that to Hugh? Shame warmed her cheeks. After all, they were friends and he was just trying to help.

But the expression on his face suggested something she didn't want to think about. He didn't expect me to ask that. He had to think up a lie. Poetry pushed the thought from her mind. Hugh was like a father to her. Why would he lie to her about anything? She gave her head a shake and returned to her bench, rolling the amber around in her palm.

Her silver rope waited to be completed. She had a lot of work left to do before she went to visit Adrian.

Poetry placed the round stones on the surface next to it, careful not to let them spill to the floor. As she lifted the dowel, she noticed the circumference and an idea struck her. Grasping one of the jewels, she placed it on the end of the stick where the daisy anchor began.

A perfect fit.

Didn't it make sense to use Scandinavian stones on Viking necklaces? Nothing else would do. These glistening fossils would never become the earrings Hugh hoped for, but once he saw how she'd used them, Poetry knew he'd understand.

CHAPTER TWENTY-SIX

Adrian suppressed a grimace as Frank Fleisher used a toothpick to flick gunk from his teeth to the charcoal carpet.

His client slouched in a chair with one knee crossed and an arm draped along the back. The arrogant body language brought Adrian's hackles up.

Why had he taken the case again? Right. To further his career.

At first he'd been flattered when chosen for the high profile case. Especially with him being one of the youngest at Bailey, Bailey & Wallace. It was a credit to his knowledge of law and quick thinking. Or so he thought.

But when he got to know the rancher from Grey, Adrian realized he got the job solely based upon his appearance. Frank Fleisher had probably hand picked him from a sea of Indian, African, and Asian faces. In a quilt of diverse cultures, he had the whitest skin in the firm. Pure Caucasian.

The idea left the rot of resentment in his mouth. Adrian believed racism to be an idea for the uneducated, uninformed, and close-minded; a refuge for those who flatly refuse to think for themselves in favor of antiquated dogma.

"So you had no prior knowledge of the bombings?" Adrian's head hurt, but not from the previous night's beer. The bright white walls seemed to close in; the relentless clacking of keyboards outside his office tapped at his temples. Reporters had harassed him all night. After a few terse 'no comment' statements he'd turned off every ringer. Still, he'd dreamed of hounds that bayed for blood. He awoke to sheets damp with sweat and a throbbing brain.

And here he sat, cooped up in the air-conditioned chill of his office on a beautiful day trading lies with the man whose bail he'd negotiated, while reporters camped outside his building.

"I give you my word," Frank said, "I can assure you I didn't put the folks of my town up to this."

That didn't mean much to Adrian.

"There have been arrests, police interviews," Adrian pointed out. "Suspects have openly admitted to doing this in protest of your charges."

Frank shrugged, dipping his head so Adrian couldn't see his eyes under the cowboy hat.

"There you have it. But I can swear on a stack of bibles that I knew nothing about it. I was in custody at the time, as you might remember."

Adrian dignified Frank's answer with a snort. It was most likely the truth. Leading a mob took more organization than could be done over the phone from a jail cell. But Adrian couldn't dismiss the itch telling him Frank Fleisher took pride in the savagery his community performed.

Adrian's first impression of the man had been fine. Frank's no-nonsense attitude and rugged quality reminded him of Rick Simon from Simon and Simon. And he wore Brut 33, just like Adrian's dad.

But after weeks alone with him, listening to his racial and homophobic slurs while he proclaimed his innocence, Adrian had his doubts.

"Fucking faggots were there to siphon gas and God knows what the hell else," Frank had ranted. "Not enough for them doin' each other up their assholes. No telling what other perversions they had in mind. Man's gotta protect his property and livestock."

The prosecution disagreed. A Toyota Camry registered to one of the victims had been located not two miles from Fleisher's property with an empty gas tank. One of the men had been carrying a jerry can, but there wasn't any evidence to prove Fleisher's claims. No cutting instruments or makeshift tools were found on the bodies. Since that area was a cellular dead zone, it seemed more likely they'd approached the ranch for help.

Thinking about his client murdering innocent people for seeking assistance made Adrian's stomach curdle. He no longer liked Frank. He loathed him. Representing Frank Fleisher made him feel unclean.

"Fine, I believe you," Adrian said. "But this is going to make the jury less sympathetic."

He rubbed his aching eyes. This is stupid. I can't work like this.

"Look, why don't we call it a day? It's almost lunch time anyway."

"If you think that's best," Frank said.

"For now. I'll escort you to the door and we'll see to it you get to your truck without being eaten alive." He stood and forced himself to shake Frank's calloused hand. "We'll talk tomorrow."

The walk to the main desk was awkward. Staff stared openly and the hum of cooler talk ceased. Even the keyboard clatter tapered off. Some gave Adrian sympathetic looks. Other sneered and whispered, glaring at Frank, who clomped along in his shit kickers without shame. No one envied Adrian the plum case anymore.

Once in the lobby, flashbulbs blinded them and the din of shouted questions built to a crescendo, driving new spikes of pain into Adrian's head.

As soon as I get home I'm taking a twelve hour nap.

A displaced patch of blue moved at the corner of his eye.

"Adrian. Adrian." Poetry jostled her way to the front of the surging crowd, using her ivy-covered elbow on other people's chests. Adrian shook his head. He didn't want to meet her in a mosh pit. "Let me in."

What was she doing here? Poetry squeezed inside.

"Hi," she said, her teeth gleaming in a smile meant to sweeten the unexpected surprise, no doubt. "Are you busy?"

“I wasn’t really expecting you,” Adrian said, trying not to grind his teeth. Her timing sucked.

“I came to bring you treats.” She hefted a Kokanee beer bag that bulged and clinked, then directed her attention to Frank. “There’s enough food and beer for three.”

“Well, aren’t you sweet,” Frank said. Poetry didn’t notice, but Adrian had enough experience with Frank to recognize condescension coming from his client.

“I’m Poetry.” She extended her hand.

Adrian stole her away before Frank could soil her with his touch. “Poetry, can I talk to you for a second?”

“Sure, what’s up?”

He took her by the arm and led her back to reception. He dragged her around the corner away from the curious staff before hissing in her face.

“What are you doing here?”

“It’s noon. I thought it would be fun to have lunch together. You know, sort of like a date.”

“Couldn’t you have let me know ahead of time?” he asked.

“It’s supposed to be unexpected,” she said. “A real girlfriend would do that kind of thing. And maybe you should tell me I look nice. That’s an appropriate boyfriend response.”

Adrian wiped a hand down his face in exasperation. He took a quick glance at her sapphire bangs and Wal-mart sundress with her personal ink poking out from under the straps. It wasn’t the kind of outfit he imagined her wearing, and it didn’t suit her. Maybe she’d borrowed it from her roommate trying to be something she wasn’t in order to be pretty. Adrian didn’t know if he should be flattered or embarrassed for her.

“You look nice,” he said, and changed the subject. “You know, I haven’t even drawn up the paperwork for this project yet.”

"Paperwork? Oh my God, you are such a lawyer." Her robust laughter echoed down the corridor, drawing attention. "You're so lame."

"I'm not kidding. We need to set boundaries and establish rules. It's not just for my protection but..." The pungent perfume of garlic slapped him in the nostrils. It smelled so delicious his stomach ached with longing. "What is that?" he asked.

"Homemade hummus. And pita bread, some salad. Oh, and some cold chicken. I thought we could find a park somewhere."

Adrian's stomach agreed so audibly he placed a hand on his torso as if to shush it.

"Fine. You win." He didn't want to be there anyway. "Just wait here, and let me finish up."

"Rule number one, Adrian." Poetry grinned and batted her eyelashes. "I'm a girl. That means I always win."

Adrian didn't bother answering. Why did women always assume they were in charge?

He'd work that out later. First, he had to get rid of Fleisher. Summers in Edmonton were too short to spend indoors. Besides, he loved hummus.

The rancher hadn't moved. He waited with that same smug posture Adrian had grown to loathe.

"Listen, our security guys will escort you out. I'll call you later."

Frank tossed his head in Poetry's direction. "Got plans with the lady?"

Not that it's any of your business. "Just a quick lunch." Adrian checked his watch, demonstrating his impatience. Go home already, buddy.

Frank made no attempt to hurry, even though a security staff member huffed behind him. "You're not seeing that girl, are you?"

“Poetry?” Adrian tugged at his silk tie. It seemed he tied it too tight this morning. “No. We’re working on a…project together.”

“Well, that’s fine. Just you make sure to be careful,” he said.

Adrian paused to make eye contact. “Careful of what?”

“Her kind, you know.” The rancher crumpled his face into a maze of distasteful crevices. “Spics. They’re dirty. Just look at her, she’s got more tattoos than a whore.”

Adrian swallowed a lump of rage. With measured words he said, “She’s not Spanish, she’s Greek.”

“Spic, Greek.” Fleisher waved a dismissive hand, seemingly unaware how his offensive words carried. Or Adrian’s flinching. “Pretty much the same if you ask me. Point is they have no sense of hygiene, if you know what I mean. Dirty.”

Adrian’s stomach did a slow, hot, roll and his appetite waned. He only thought of Poetry as an acquaintance, but a sense of honor burned in his ears. Someone needed to tune this asshole in to reality. Lucky for Frank nobody here was dumb enough to try it.

Instead, Adrian kept his composure. “It’s not that kind of relationship.”

“Didn’t think so,” Fleisher said. “You’re a smart lad.” He clapped Adrian on the shoulder and meandered out of the building with two guards in tow.

Adrian eyed the sanitizer on the front desk. He resisted the urge to slather it over the tainted body parts Fleisher touched, and instead stormed away.

Poetry waited where he’d left her.

“Your client seems very nice,” she said.

Adrian thanked God she didn't catch that exchange, but when anger burbled to the surface, he tempered it yet again. He shook with the effort, hiding his hands behind his back. "Can we just get out of here?"

"Sure." From the corner of his eye Adrian noticed her studying him while they walked. "How's Hawryluk Park sound?"

"Don't be ridiculous." He straightened and softened his tone. It wasn't her fault his client was a slime ball and the media wouldn't leave him alone. "I mean, there's nowhere we can go that they won't follow us." He gestured to the dense throng of men and women packed outside the entrance.

"Aw, that sucks." She slumped until her arms went slack but her dejection didn't last. "Guess we'll have to go with Plan 'B'."

CHAPTER TWENTY-SEVEN

Poetry congratulated herself. Thanks to quick thinking, she'd saved their lunch plans.

As Adrian predicted, the press dogged them at every twist throughout downtown, into alleys and one way lanes. Now she knew how Princess Diana must've felt; freaked out and cornered. No green peace in a park today.

At Poetry's suggestion, Adrian drove to his condominium. They darted inside before anyone could catch up and barge their way through, pulling the security door shut and racing for the elevators. They made a quick pit stop so Adrian could shed his suit for a tank and shorts, grabbed a spare blanket and sound dock, and headed for the rooftop.

Now they basked in the unrelenting heat of the sun.

"This was a good idea," Adrian said. "I never would have thought of this." He sounded much calmer.

Poetry surveyed thc tar-striped concrete surrounding them. Nothing interrupted the vista but wide expanses of blue sky beyond.

"It's not the best view," she said. "But it's private."

"I'll take it."

Poetry popped open two beer and handed one to Adrian. She took a greedy pull of the crisp lager before assembling their lunch.

"Ahhhhh…"

Adrian nodded. "This is much better than wasting the day in an office." He shot a grateful smile in Poetry's direction.

"You're welcome," she said. "But I'm just getting started."

She placed foil-wrapped chicken on a paper plate, along with homemade pita bread, still soft and fresh. She fanned the lid to the hummus at Adrian's dilating nostrils with a flourish.

"Oh, wow." He blinked in pleasure.

"And," Poetry plucked two small Tupperware containers from the bottom of the bag, "Greek salad."

Adrian gave her a goofy smirk. "I love Greek salad." It looked and sounded so unlike him Poetry giggled.

She straightened self-consciously and covered her mouth with a plastic fork. "It's the genuine thing too." She unfastened her container and scooped a forkful of tomato, feta, and olive into her mouth. The salty tang of the Mediterranean exploded in her mouth and she sighed.

"No fake ingredients."

Adrian opened his and dipped his nose close to inhale the food. "Smells like fresh basil and oregano."

"It's how my dad does it."

Adrian took a bite that made his eyelids flutter. She laughed and almost spat on her knee.

"This is the best salad I've ever tasted."

"That's nothing. Try the hummus and pita bread."

#   #   #

"Son of a bitch."

Frank Fleisher got tired of holding binoculars up to his lawyer's balcony. He could smell his own stink so he let his arms drop. He couldn't see shit anyway.

He'd seen Olsen go in with that tramp, and he ain't been out yet. That meant only one thing.

Adrian Olsen was balling that dirty spic and he'd lied about it. Come to think of it, that meant two things. Frank had seen the mean in Olsen's eye when he'd tried to set him straight. Offended in that way a man gets when somebody puts his woman down. He was surprised the boy didn't jump him. Had to see it for himself though. Ditched the press first and found his lawyer's fancy building with his fancy loft and his fancy balcony.

Sure as shit. Olsen ran through those doors like a jackrabbit with his harlot trotting behind. No movement by the windows or veranda meant they weren't standing. Playing hide the salami, that's what they were doing.

Frank's bowels curled like a coiled snake ready to strike. He tuned out the din of traffic surrounding him as rage simmered like all-day stew. He'd thought Adrian Olsen was different, not like these bleeding-heart Liberal types. The boy was smart but soft.

But that was just fine. He knew how to deal with guys like him. He'd play it cool for now. Frank put the truck in gear. He had an errand to run.

Frank sucked hard on his dentures until he tasted breakfast. No, he hadn't planned that bombing, but he sure wanted to shake the hand of the guy who'd done it.

# # #

Strife couldn't remember when she'd had such a good time. Playing human had advantages.

Like the simple pleasure of exploring a new city with a learned escort. Ranjan treated her with respect: opening doors and paying for lunch at Tony Roma's.

He almost charmed her into forgetting her true intentions. She should have absorbed the rich history of the Aviation Museum or the splendid decadence of West Edmonton Mall. Instead, she took stock of the military impracticality of the airport and the casualty potential of the world's largest mall.

Standing over the performing sea lions, Strife surveyed the mortal throng. So many people from all over the world. And she'd kill them all. The thought of work almost spoiled her date.

But she'd already chosen her target. In the T & T supermarket, where her senses were overwhelmed with the abrasive shouting of Cantonese and the briny odor of live seafood, she placed her ammonium nitrate surprise. Feigning a strap adjustment on her sandal, she'd been sure to tuck it below a busy sushi counter, knowing it wouldn't be discovered before noon tomorrow.

"Are you alright, Sarah?"

Strife almost didn't respond to the name. It took a moment to register that Ranjan addressed her.

"Me?" She focused on his warm mahogany eyes. "I'm fine. Maybe just a little tired."

"How about we take a break?" he asked, lightly rubbing her back. "We've been walking around all day. Have you ever heard of Marble Slab?"

Her brow furrowing in curiosity. “No. What is it?”

“Only the best ice cream in the entire city,” Ranjan said, grasping her hand. “And you can have any topping you could ever imagine. Cookies, candy, fruit. Trust me, you’ll love it.”

Despite her depressing bone weariness, Strife relented. Finally, a delight she could enjoy. There were no tactical strategies to be had from frozen treats.

CHAPTER TWENTY-EIGHT

Aphrodite smiled at the sleeping pair on the rooftop. Cold lager on a hot day and a satisfying meal invited a siesta in the sunshine.

It pleased her how relaxed they were with each other, discussing the mundane such as contracts and veterinary bills along with hopes and current events. Like friends.

At rest, they resembled little ones caught counting clouds when Morpheus closed their eyes and made them dream.

The bottles were warm to the touch. Traces of hummus and gnawed chicken bones attracted flies but the low, buzzing hum could not disturb their slumber.

Poetry and Adrian lay side by side, not touching, but not at an uncomfortable distance. Adrian's nose wrinkled like that of a dog even as he dozed, and Aphrodite stifled laughter.

But sleep would not bring them together. How fortunate the weather in this land changed so abruptly.

Aphrodite stirred billowing moisture from the azure expanse overhead and gathered them in a cottony mass. It grew heavy and dark in the circumference of her immortal hands. Winds changed direction at her command until a whining gale whipped dust and paper in cyclones around her feet. She smelled the ozone, almost tasted oncoming rain.

"Come alive, my beauties," she said to the howling elements. "It is time to play."

Aphrodite clapped her hands.

\#   \#   \#

A thunderous boom startled Poetry awake. Cold rain needled her skin, drenching her.

"Oh, shit!" She hustled to her feet, noting that Adrian shoved garbage and leftovers into her Kokanee tote while the deluge weighted the clothes to his body. He grabbed the sound dock.

"I got the stuff!" He yelled to be heard over the storm. "You get the door!"

Easier said than done.

Her flip-flops slid on the slick surface and she floundered in the effort to keep her footing.

"I gotcha…" Adrian appeared next to her, lunch bag slung over his shoulder, sound dock in hand. He grabbed her elbow, but they fell to the cement in a heap of laughter.

"No, here." Poetry got to one knee and pushed his arm upward. A gust shoved them toward the door. Once on their feet, they shuffled with heads ducked low, giggling and huddling.

"I got it," Poetry said. She turned the knob and the metal slab caught the wind and slammed against the opposite wall.

"Get inside," Adrian said.

Poetry ran down a small set of stairs and waited while he juggled his burden and dragged the exit shut. The snarling weather continued to demand entrance, but it no longer hurt Poetry's ears or tugged at her dress. Shivering, she endured the frigid bite of soaked skin and clothing.

"Shit, it's cold," Adrian said, echoing her sentiments.

"We need towels."

He shook droplets from his hair. “Right. The elevator’s this way.” He marched toward the inside door. Poetry followed.

“I can’t believe it got so chilly so fast. How long were we out?”

“No idea.” Adrian glanced her way. “You have goose bumps.”

“So do you.”

The elevator bell dinged and they hurried in. Adrian pressed number fourteen.

“Here,” Poetry said through clattering teeth. “I’ll do you if you do me.” She placed her hands on Adrian’s bare arms and rubbed vigorously.

“Oh yeah, that feels so good.” He dumped the cooler bag and sound dock on the floor and returned the favor.

She jogged in place while the elevator descended. It made her stomach lurch in a butterfly kind of way, causing her to crack up.

“What?”

“I’m freezing! Brrrr!” She said, burrowing into his arms.

To her amazement, he folded her into an embrace and stroked her back. She got a whiff of his cologne; one of the new Old Spice blends if she wasn’t mistaken. Romantic puppy surprise?

“Me too.”

The delicate moment brought Poetry back to reality and she backed away.

I’d best keep my hands to myself. Can’t believe I just snuggled a ‘suit’. Poetry eyed his lean physique. But he’s not wearing a suit…

Adrian cleared his throat and concentrated on the descending numbers on the digital display. Poetry quit gawking and shifted her gaze to the carpet. Fourteen couldn’t show up fast enough. At least she felt warmer.

“It was a great lunch. Thank you.”

“My pleasure,” Poetry said, bewildered that she meant it.

And why not? He’d taken care of her cat even though she’d been sure he didn’t even like her. He’d agreed to let her pay him back in small amounts for the vet. He’d driven her home after the ‘Kevin Incident’ and checked her apartment over. Dinner at Louisiana Purchase. She shrugged. Lunch was the least she could do.

Another bell. Wordlessly, they departed the elevator. Adrian grabbed his sound dock and Poetry carried the cooler bag.

They strolled to his apartment in mute respect for each other. Or so it seemed to Poetry.

As the rasp of Adrian’s key in the lock reverberated down the hall she remembered how shivery she felt. And how dripping, sopping drenched she was.

She allowed her chin and voice to rattle in the universal song of those in need of heat.

“Yes, I’m hurrying,” Adrian said. The door swept open, creating a breeze that raised new prickles on Poetry’s arms and legs. “I’ll get you that towel.” He disappeared around the corner.

Poetry huffed in relief, making herself at home in the kitchen. She’d be dry soon. “Thanks.”

She busied herself tossing rain-soaked bits of cellophane and squishy pita bread into the garbage.

Poetry emptied the rest of the bag’s contents into the sink, including the beer bottles.

A Ziploc bag at the very bottom of her insulated carry case caught her eye. How could she forget about that? Her entire reason for seeing Adrian lay neglected in a pool of rainwater and melted ice cubes.

She fished it out, tossing the cooler aside.

"Here we are," Adrian said from behind her. She accepted a large charcoal-colored towel from him, still staring at the shiny object encased in plastic.

"I forgot to give you this," Poetry said, drying her head with the terry cloth. She left it there like a shroud so she could use both hands. "I worked so hard on it too."

"Give me what?" He peered forward as she popped open the seal.

"This…" Poetry held it aloft, allowing the amber to sparkle in the light of the ceiling fan.

"What is it?"

"It's a Viking torque. This isn't something I normally do. I prefer more feminine designs, bracelets and necklaces. Stuff like that." She tested the flex of the braid, pulling it apart gently to see how far it would stretch before she risked breakage.

"I wanted to give you something that would tell you how much I appreciate what you've done for me." Satisfied with of the strength of her work, Poetry faced Adrian. The rippling spasms of her body no longer had a connection with her damp clothing. The metal tingled in her hands as though it had life of its own. For reasons she couldn't explain, she need to do this. It was too important. Everything faded from her vision. She saw only Adrian.

Poetry tiptoed to encircle his neck. He obliged by bending so she could place the jewelry around his Adam's apple, spinning it so the amber came to rest on his collarbone. The stones seemed to wink at her, like they knew something she didn't. She dismissed it as silly, all in her head. Maybe if she chanted that to herself, she'd believe it.

"Do you like it?" Adrian hadn't said a word. It made her nervous.

Poetry became acutely aware of her appearance. She shed the towel, conscious of the streaks of blue bingo dauber staining her face and clothes. She mustered the courage to meet his gaze.

And found fire. His azure-gold eyes immobilized her.

“Adrian?” The tremor in her voice made her cringe.

This whole thing, practice dating, eating together, giving gifts, was trouble. What had she been thinking?

He advanced. She couldn’t move. To her left, the exit seemed too far.

Poetry cowered under his scrutiny. She wouldn’t resist. No, she saw the reflection of her eagerness. Excitement, not fear.

This wasn’t like her.

She chanced a pace back, and her spine bumped the granite countertop. Adrian closed in, one hand cupping her cheek.

“Adrian, I don’t think…” Thunder drowned out her protests.

His lips were silky, his tongue teasing. He kissed her reluctance away until she responded. Her knees went weak and he lifted her onto the smooth surface.

“Adrian, we haven’t…” She meant to remind him they hadn’t signed anything. After all, he did everything by legal standards, right? But the words wouldn’t come.

Adrian’s touch created unexpected desires. He caressed her chin, squeezed her breasts, and fondled the curves beneath her panties. He waited, poised with calloused thumbs tracing her hips. Her thighs quivered beneath his fingers, the heat of his lust hot between her legs.

Her hands traveled the taut muscles of his chest of their own accord, much to her embarrassment. She gazed at the neckpiece she’d given him. It seemed to glow in the pulses of lightning like a living entity.

I shouldn’t be doing this.

“Adrian.” Poetry searched the lines in his features. “Are you sure this is alright?”

"I am," he said, his voice low and husky. "Isn't this what a real lover would do?" His lips grazed her throat along her jaw line to her ear. "Say yes."

She couldn't let it go this far. Sleeping with Adrian wouldn't work out. They came from different worlds and could never be more than friends, and even that seemed unlikely. No matter how good it felt right now she had to say no.

"Yes."

Even in the shade of the late day and the overcast sky Poetry could see the mischief Adrian intended as he peeled her underwear off and pulled the dress over her head. He smiled like a predatory cat before trailing hot kisses along her neck. She trembled as he branded her nipples, her belly button, the tribal tattoos on her abdomen and…

Oh. Oh God.

Her other piercing. The most private one.

He draped her legs over his shoulders, fully exposing her. He explored with his fingers, playing with the golden circle.

"Hmm…"

What an odd sound, one of wonder. Poetry guessed he'd never seen a labia ring before. She forgot her self-conscious body issues. She forgot to think of anything at all. She squirmed as he learned how to make her whimper and sigh.

Poetry's senses faded until she knew only Adrian's touch. She tried to steady herself. The rising tide of pleasure had her grasping for something, anything, to hold on to. Canisters and spices toppled and clattered. The reek of dill saturated her nostrils.

But oblivion approached. She vibrated with anticipation. Her entire body clenched in expectation.

Adrian stopped. He rose to his feet, face glistening with her stickiness. He held her gaze, licking her cream from his fingertips.

"Tell me you want this, Poetry," he said. He leaned in and she tasted her saltiness in his kiss. "Say you want me."

I can't, she thought. Not with him. But she couldn't stop. Every nerve ached.

"I…" She wrapped her calves around Adrian's damp shorts and put her arms around him. "I want…you."

He wasted no time carrying her to his room. He navigated by memory; his gaze never wavered from her. His smile didn't fade, not even when he dropped her to the edge of the bed. Shorts and shirt hit the hardwood floor with a wet plop. His sleek muscles flexed in the gloom. His thick penis bobbed toward her, proudly erect.

Adrian produced a condom from a dresser and eased the lubricated latex over his cock with care and attention. It thrilled her even more. She looked forward to that kind of sensual consideration, something she hadn't had for a long time.

He didn't disappoint.

He spread her knees and mounted her. She shuddered when he entered, but not from pain. A shockwave of rapture raced through her limbs with each slow stroke until he filled her.

He paused. Poetry listened to the sound of her ragged breathing mingling with the drumming of the rain. She couldn't bear anymore. Why was he making her wait? Why didn't he just…

"Adrian." Was that her? She'd lost control of her words. "Please, Adrian."

He smiled down at her. "Yes."

He coaxed her into a sitting position, and she opened to him like a morning bloom.

Her body responded quickly. She cried out as his thrusts elevated her to new levels of intensity. They rocked together in endless gratification, voiced in grunts and murmurs.

She delighted in this sweating dance that made her float dangerously, always gracing the edge of the abyss.

He rolled her over. Poetry braced against the mattress, galvanized as Adrian quickened the pace. The music of flesh smacking on flesh heightening her need. He reached beneath her, massaging her sex until primal, graceless shouts filled the room.

She dropped to her elbows, unable to stabilize herself any longer. She clawed the covers, wriggled into each tap of his scrotum against her clean-shaven folds.

So close. She wanted to feel him all over her. Wanted to watch him come. She switched to her back and pulled him inside.

Poetry bucked with every plunge, desperate to take his entire length. The pungent smell of sweat saturated every struggling breath until her head swam.

Finally her senses exploded and a raw shriek tore from her throat. She arched her back, pressing her nipples into his chest. She cried. She moaned. She gasped for air, and Adrian pushed deeper as her body throbbed.

Poetry squeezed her eyes shut, savoring the sliding weight of Adrian's groin and the after burn of giddiness as he collapsed on top of her. But only for a moment.

He climbed off with a self-satisfied laugh. His sudden absence made Poetry long for his return, but she didn't have the energy to reach for him.

They lounged in the quiet. Poetry inhaled the scent of sex and rain, counting seconds as thunder roared miles away. In spite of her fulfillment, she wasn't complete. Poetry studied Adrian's profile.

"You didn't come," she said.

"I need a break." Adrian seemed winded. "But you had an orgasm, right? That's the important thing, isn't it?"

Adrian's erection remained unspent. His breathing slowed. Poetry smiled, feeling passion and purpose return.

"It's not the only thing. Now it's your turn."

She shimmied down his torso, planting kisses down his sternum to his stomach until she nuzzled the golden hair surrounding his cock.

Time to show him what her tongue piercing could do.

CHAPTER TWENTY-NINE

Adrian awoke with his neck stinging. He raked at his collarbone as he shot up in bed. Something fell and hit his closet door, metal against wood. Late morning light splashed across rumpled sheets and the odor of sex wafted past his nose.

It took a moment for his head to clear. Then the awful truth of what he'd done revealed itself like a lifting fog. He shot a glance to his left. Poetry lay blissfully sleeping, unaware of his turmoil.

Last night's acrobatics resurfaced, causing his cock to stir.

How could I be so stupid?

A one night stand was one thing; bedding an acquaintance that owes you money was an altogether different beast with possible legal repercussions. He hadn't even started the paperwork for the 'practice dating', never mind any intimacy clause.

Feelings of lust warred with ethics inside his head. He wanted to run to the bathroom and hide.

His dick had other ideas. This was more than ordinary morning wood. Adrian wanted to rouse Poetry and play with her piercings, make her scream his name again. He wanted to lick those tribal markings on her abdomen until she begged him to…

"Fuck." He forced himself to retreat from the bedroom. He didn't need to make matters worse.

His reflection in the bathroom mirror looked disheveled. Like a perp. His pale skin only emphasized the dark pockets under his eyes. Worse were the mosquito bites at the base of his throat. He bent forward for closer inspection.

No, not bites, burns. How the hell did he get those?

"Hey."

Adrian jumped at the sound of Poetry's voice, and he bit down a yelp.

"Don't do that." His heart thumped like Japanese taiko drums.

"Come back to bed," she said. "We've barely slept." Her grin suggested she didn't plan on sleeping. She eyed his erection, ran her tongue piercing along her bottom lip.

"I know, but I…" He wanted to. His balls twitched just thinking about her lips swallowing his length.

But slumming wasn't his style. He didn't do her type and it baffled him that he'd even found her attractive last night. Maybe the heat got to him.

"…I have work to do at the office." Perfect excuse.

Poetry crinkled her indigo-stained forehead. "It's already kind of late in the day."

"True." Adrian drew the shower curtain and stepped inside the tub. "But you know, high profile case." He shut it behind himself, hoping she got the message. "I'll give you a ride home."

"Sure."

He hated himself for the sadness in her voice, but they'd never work out. They were from different sides of the street. About as compatible as North-South magnets. Better to let her down now before any real damage occurred.

"I left extra food for Amir…" Poetry said, her footsteps retreating. "But maybe he's hungry by now. Or lonely."

Adrian winced when the icy water pelted him in the face. He deserved it.

#   #   #

Kevin wanted to vomit. The stench of armpits and shit churned an already upset stomach, and he had to swallow the pastiness of his dry mouth a couple of times. He'd been in jail for days without anything to cook his brain. No weed. No coke. Nothing. They even took his hash pipes.

Kevin rolled on the cot, moaning when his joints flared in pain. That skanky bitch did this. He wouldn't be here if she hadn't left him. What was her fucking problem anyway? He hadn't done anything wrong. Well, trashing her pad probably wasn't a good idea. But she'd made him do it. After she sicced that 'suit' on him, Kevin had gone to get something for his nerves. He'd have to have a word with his dealer. That powder had some wicked shit cut in or something. Not a fun trip.

He pictured the dark man who claimed to be Ares, god of war, who commanded him to 'lay waste' to his ex-girlfriend's apartment. Not the usual hallucinations for sure.

The footsteps approaching his cell drove spikes of agony into his temples.

"Ferris." Kevin didn't bother facing the newcomer. It hurt too much to move. "It's your lucky day. You're getting out of here."

He bolted up so fast his stomach contents sloshed to the back of his teeth. Every tendon in his body screamed, causing the room to lurch. The tinkling of keys and the metallic clang of the cage door pounded at his ears.

"How?" He wasn't getting out for good behavior, someone had posted bail. But who?

The chunky uniform scowled. "Your dad."

Kevin sneered. No fucking way. Nothing would move that limp old prick to help him. That bridge had been torched years ago with a lighter and a spoon.

Well, it didn't matter. Kevin couldn't score if he stayed in jail.

He allowed the pig to lead him to the effects room to get his shit. An empty wallet and a couple of smokes. He already knew they'd taken his stash.

Fucking procedure took forever. Kevin loathed it. But he'd behave and slog through it. Anything to get out. Just when he thought his fingers would fall off from signing shit they brought him to the front desk.

"Mr. Ferris?" The cop addressed a distinguished gentleman wearing an expensive black suit. He looked out of place in the dinginess of the room around him; a gold tooth in a rotten mouth.

Kevin swooned on his feet like a girl. This asshole wasn't his father but he sure as hell recognized him. His bowels churned so bad Kevin thought he'd shit right there on the linoleum.

"Thanks so much, Officer."

That voice. It wasn't delirium. It really was the war god standing there. Beads of sweat formed on Kevin's forehead and upper lip. His hands began to shake.

"I appreciate your help," Ares said. "Did my son trouble you much?"

The police man gave him a genuine smile. "Not too much, Mr. Ferris. He mostly kept to himself."

"Good to know." The oily grin Ares gave the cop made Kevin's skin dance with goosebumps. And when he fixed him with his cruel scowl, Kevin wanted to slink back to the safety of his cell.

"Stop staring, stupid boy," Ares harsh voice rang throughout the room. "Have you no manners left at all?"

Kevin averted his eyes and swallowed. "S-sorry."

“Not as sorry as you will be,” Ares hateful glare turned Kevin’s intestines to squirming maggots.

“Okay, you’re free to go,” the guard said. “For now.”

# # #

The intense pressure of the man’s grip on his elbow added to Kevin’s discomfort as they left the station. Better make nice.

“That was cool shit. I can’t believe those dumb pigs thought you were my dad.”

The war god said nothing, just smiled that freaky fake grin as he led Kevin toward a black Porsche.

The lack of conversation unnerved Kevin. He wasn’t stupid. This asshole wanted something. Possession had heavy bail bonds attached to it, and nobody did nothing for free.

“Get in.” Ares jabbed a finger toward the passenger side.

Kevin did it, even though he hated fancy cars. He had a feeling this guy got pissed easily. Most people thought the Porsche was a wicked ride. Not Kevin. They smelled like clean leather, but that’s where the cool factor ended. They made him feel cramped, like his ass was too low to the ground and his knees were gonna hit him in the nose.

Besides, what kind of dickless corporate nerd did you have to be to drive something worth that much cash?

Kevin pushed the thought out of his head when Ares took the driver’s seat. This guy had a nasty vibe, like he could make him have an aneurism just for thinking shit. Even his cologne smelled evil, like embalmed fruit or something.

“Here.” Kevin didn’t want to make eye contact. Instead, he concentrated on the packet that magically appeared between the man’s fingers. White powder glittered like fresh snow in a tiny Ziploc bag. It made Kevin’s nose itch and his mouth water. “What is it?” he asked, trying to mask his eagerness. Everything had a price.

“A little something a friend of mine conjured. She creates pleasurable substances; has done so for ages. Go ahead.”

Kevin willed his shaking hands to pry open the red seal. He didn’t want to appear desperate, but kind of figured Ares knew anyway.

“Looks good.” The drug twinkled at him, seducing Kevin with imagined promises.

“Only the best,” Ares said. “You must be suffering. Try some.”

The words smacked of kindness and generosity, but Kevin wasn’t new to this game. This would cost him.

“What do you want? “ he asked.

“I want to be friends,” Ares said, his voice smooth.

Sure he did. But Kevin needed the fix. He dipped his pinky nail for a generous scoop, and an intense snort launched it to his brain. “Ahhhhh.”

“What did I tell you? My girl does fine work.”

Kevin barely heard him, didn’t care either. He tasted acrid chemistry before his face went numb.

His body seemed to liquefy, slumping while everything he saw turned to gold.

It was all so…shiny. He’d never had anything this good. What few coherent ideas he still had in the back of his skull worried that it could be too good. Anything this awesome had to be pretty expensive.

“You can have as much as you like,” Ares said. The grin on his face seemed genuine….but that could just be the drugs making him look human.

“Uh-huh…” Even in his haze of beautiful giddiness Kevin wondered, “So what do you want?”

“I need you to do a few odd jobs for me.” Another pouch appeared in the palm of his hand, this one a sandwich sized Ziploc bag full of glorious white excellence.

“You want me to sell it?”

“If you wish. But this is all for you.”

Kevin’s mouth hung open. He could make a lot of money on this shit. It got him higher than anything he’d ever done in his life, even heroin.

Maybe he’d hoover it all himself. Didn’t matter. He had to have it.

“What I gotta do?” he asked.

“Nothing too perilous.” Ares’s smile seemed pointy, like a shark. “Do you like Bentleys, Kevin?”

“Hate ‘em. Hate the guys who drive them too.”

“Good,” Ares said, passing Kevin a new stiletto dagger. “Then you will enjoy this.”

CHAPTER THIRTY

"Sarah?" At the sound of a booming knock, Strife checked the motel's clock radio. Twelve thirty. Ranjan arrived sooner than expected. He must have sacrificed his lunch hour and surpassed speed limits to get here. How sweet. "Are you there, Sarah?"

Strife arranged her silk robe off a creamy shoulder and strolled to the door. She spared a moment for the mirror. She'd spent an hour styling her tresses to this sleep-tousled look. It flowed like a restless night.

The things I do for men.

She spritzed spicy green apple perfume on her throat and wrists, placing an appropriately scared expression over her features.

"Sarah?"

Three, two, one…

In a well-practiced move, Strife flung the door open and leapt into Ranjan's arms.

"Oh, Ranjan! I'm so glad you're here."

Strife articulated a loud sob, squeezing close. She willed moisture to spill from her eyes until they tracked itchy trails down her cheeks.

"I was so frightened." She nuzzled into his sandalwood-curry scented neck as Ranjan led her away from the hot sidewalk, back into the air-conditioned shadows indoors. "We could have been killed."

"Sarah," His voice held tenderness. "You sounded so scared on the phone. We are perfectly safe, I promise."

He settled her on the orange bedspread, his demeanor that of concern. Until the television stole his attention.

"Is that it on the news now?"

"Hold me." Her words dripped with damsel in distress drama, but her hero fixated on the broadcast.

"Police are not saying whether the attack was the work of Frank Fleisher's vigilante group," the newscaster said. "Or perhaps retaliation for the bombing of Buddy's earlier this week."

"Pure speculation," Ranjan said, his brow crinkling. "But it's still not good."

Strife placed her hands on Ranjan's jaw, pulling her aromatic body parts in line with his nostrils. "I'm so scared," She put as much tremor in her voice as possible. "I can't believe this is happening."

She eased into his lap and wrapped her arms around his shoulders…

…And felt him stiffen in all the wrong places.

She glanced upward. Instead of the dull, adoring glaze she'd become accustomed to, his narrowed stare defied her. How could this be?

Her olfactory spells and seduction had failed. Surely he must have consumed the tainted city water at least?

But when she searched his coffee-colored gaze, she found no madness, no drug induced haze, and no evidence of magick.

If anything, he seemed suspicious. She searched his mind and feelings.

Apprehension crept up Strife's spine. She'd gone too far. He found her attempts to bed him reprehensible. Cheap and manipulative. His thoughts stung her.

"I am sorry," she said, sliding to the corner of the mattress. "I don't know what came over me." An unrehearsed shiver raised prickles on her skin. He hasn't succumbed to my will. "I'm alone in a city that's had two bombings in one week."

Kindness returned to his expression. "Edmonton isn't usually like this." He reached out to stroke her back. "We don't have explosions or riots. Okay, maybe when the Eskimos or Oilers win cups." Ranjan shrugged. "This is the City of Champions."

Strife relaxed somewhat. Perhaps she could salvage this fiasco. She didn't need alchemy to control this man, just old-fashioned feminine wiles.

"Can you get me out of here?" she asked. "I don't want to be alone in this ugly place."

Ranjan's sense of chivalry returned with puffing chest and a resolved stance.

"Absolutely. I'm here for you, Sarah."

"That makes me so happy." Strife clenched her teeth in what she hoped resembled a lovely smile. "You're such a good friend. I'll get dressed."

Ranjan beamed as she clutched modestly at her robe, backing into the bathroom. Strife nudged damp, faded tangerine towels away with her toes and shut the creaking door. She locked it, just to demonstrate shyness. The human should believe she hadn't been serious about her intentions.

Musty fingers locked on her face. Another arm slithered around her midriff in a constrictor's embrace from behind.

Despite her closing airways, Strife smelled old wine on the breath of her assailant.

Did you miss me, Strife?

Ares words hissed through her brain like rushing blood. Vomit burned the back of her throat.

You've been slacking off, Strife. Going on pleasant excursions instead of fostering war. I am not pleased.

The hand on her waist crawled to envelop her breast. He crushed it, pinching the nipple until Strife whimpered and fought against his pitiless groping.

You know what happens when I am not pleased.

Strife understood all too well, but her efforts to break free were meaningless. Still, she writhed from the heat of Ares's lengthening member.

He crushed her against the wall with his chest. Even with her mouth now free she lacked the ability to scream.

So you want some dark meat, do you Strife?

He pushed her ankles apart with his foot and shoved his calloused fingers inside her, scraping and jerking them in a mockery of foreplay before wedging his cock against her anus. Panic fluttered in her chest.

Please, master. Not that. Not again. Strife heaved sideways from the wall with all the strength she had left. She took a sparse, noisy gulp of air and shrieked as Ares gripped a fistful of her hair and dragged her down. Her vision blurred with the pain of a tortured scalp and bruised knees but she couldn't shirk from the mottled prick before her.

Take it in your mouth, bitch.

"Sarah?" Ranjan's muffled voice gave Ares pause. "Sarah, are you alright?" The sharp rapping of knuckles on wood startled Ares into releasing her.

Strife sank to the floor, grateful for the timely interruption and oxygen flooded her lungs.

The lock on the doorknob jiggled, echoing in the cramped space. "Sarah? Please open up."

Strife sensed rage draining from Ares, watched his cock diminish in size. He snarled in contempt, not bloodlust.

This isn't over, Strife. Ares faded like a bad dream. His essence left an odor of blood Strife nearly tasted.

"Sarah!"

Strife fumbled with the doorknob until she heard the clunk of disengaging tumblers. Ranjan spilled inside to drop to the floor.

"Are you alright?" He tucked strands of wayward locks away from her temple.

"I'm fine," she said while the precious gesture, coupled with his worried expression ruined her practiced stoicism.

Strife coughed forth a broken dam of relief. True tears gushed hot and salty down her nose and mouth.

"Oh, hey..." Ranjan said, venturing closer to cradle her. She allowed it, and he massaged her back again in that soothing way she'd grown to appreciate.

Strife nuzzled into him, listening to the babble of some North American soap opera on the television, as he rocked her shuddering body. She preferred their perils over her own.

"Did you faint? I should get you to a hospital. The stress of this city has really gotten to..."

"No!" Strife smeared sorrow from her face. "No hospitals. I'm fine. Just...get me out of here. Take me someplace safe."

She beseeched him with her eyes, knowing his immunity to chemical charms. A war of indecision clashed in his mind.

His shoulders slumped. Fortunately his virtue won out.

"Alright," he said, lifting her to her feet. "I'll take a sick day. Where's your luggage?"

#   #   #

"Adrian? Earth to Adrian." He jerked to attention, sitting up so fast his paperwork scattered.

"My, aren't we jumpy today."

Adrian rubbed grit from his eyes. He must have dozed off. He squinted through the sleepy haze to see the slim silhouette of his boss looming.

"Mrs. Bailey," he said, rushing to his feet. More important documents hit the floor. "I'm sorry. What time is it?"

Mary or 'Bones', as many called her behind soundproofed doors, Bailey checked her watch. "Quarter after one. I tried to call you, but your messages are full."

"I'm sorry," he said, repeating his apology like an idiot. What else could he say? He tucked his wrinkled shirt and tightened his tie. Caught snoozing when he had files to process.

He pawed at the odd sensation on his mouth to find a stuck paperclip covered in drool. Nice.

"Poor thing." Behind her thick spectacles, Mrs. Bailey's gaze drooped as though tired herself. "Didn't get much sleep last night, did you?"

"No…I didn't." His reluctance came from the truth. He didn't have a decent excuse for slacking. He shouldn't have taken yesterday afternoon off. If he hadn't he wouldn't be in this awkward situation.

"It's understandable that you're burnt out," she said.

"I'm not. I just…"

Mrs. Bailey raised skeletal fingers to shush him. "Don't argue with me, please." She positioned both hands on the maple desk and leaned in. She hovered close enough for Adrian to smell tuna on her breath. So she does actually eat, Adrian thought, suppressing a gag. "We need you in top form, Adrian. I understand that the Frank Fleisher case is important to your status in the firm."

Not so much anymore, Adrian thought, but he wasn't about to correct her. Mary Bailey had no respect for anyone who wasn't a team player. Hints of resentment would cost him.

"But you're no good to us if you're sleeping on the job. Go home and get some rest. None of these files are going anywhere." She straightened and adjusted her glasses before fetching him a nicotine grin. "We'll see you tomorrow, bright and early."

"Yes, ma'am."

Mrs. Bailey departed without further comment, leaving Adrian to collect his wits. Lucky him.

He gathered photocopies and triplicates as fast as his groggy state permitted. Old Bones wasn't a moron. Sooner or later she'd catch on. He'd take her advice and get the hell out of here before she figured out he'd been dipping his wick instead of working.

Adrian's groan echoed in the empty office. Poetry. She'd been on his mind all day.

He'd been a jerk this morning.

The drive to her loft had been worse than uncomfortable, without small talk or eye contact. Adrian hadn't missed how her body language went from the bowed shoulders of brooding acceptance to the rigid posture of indignation. He didn't need a criminal profiler to know she'd written him off as a creep. Poetry's terse goodbye as she slammed the car door rang in his memory. Adrian cringed, feeling the cold breeze of manufactured air on his gums. It sucked to be an asshole.

At the time, he'd worried about how her temper affected his wheels. You don't just wing the door shut like a Ford truck, for God's sake.

But right now he cared more about her mood than his precious machine.

He stood and stretched until his back cracked. Adrian surveyed his clean but cluttered surroundings. His sigh came back to him in a tinny vibration.

Just yesterday Poetry came to see him, looking like Little Blue Riding Hood with beer and other goodies. An unexpected smile stretched his face. He could almost smell garlic.

If this were a movie, she'd stroll in right about now with forgiveness in her eyes and an unseen orchestra would play something cheesy and romantic. He shook his head. She wouldn't be out there today. He'd seen to that.

He put the image out of his mind. Since when did he think like a paperback romance? He must be wrecked.

He began straightening his paperwork, but decided against it. He'd be back in the morning. Time to disappear. He grabbed his cell phone and headed for the underground parking. This way he'd steer clear of any ambitious reporters.

It wasn't a long walk, just a contemplative one. He twirled his keys, pondering his case.

Frank Fleisher was a jackass, for sure. He admitted to racism and shooting the trespassers because of some misguided ideas. Would he lie about the bombings? Truth be told, Adrian probably wasted time worrying. It wouldn't hurt his case, they couldn't link his client. Frank had been in jail.

Cool basement air enveloped Adrian. He was grateful for the deep chill; it kept him alert. Nothing disturbed the hush, save his footsteps. He pointed his remote starter, reassured by the eager tweeting response and instant ignition. The Bentley purred to life. Damn, he loved his beautiful beast.

Adrian couldn't wait to get home. His pillow called to him.

Headlights illuminated the gloom, and Adrian's weariness evaporated in a moment of rage. His keys clanged to the concrete.

His heart lodged in his throat when he caught sight of the scarred remains before him. Glass littered the ground. A can of spray paint lay discarded next to a pillar.

"What the fuck happened to my Bentley?"

CHAPTER THIRTY-ONE

Poetry reached for her kitten with trembling fingers. She wanted his soft warmth and rumbling purr, a comfort during emotional rough patches. Her hand found nothing but emptiness on the pillow where Amir slept. The spot still held his body heat. He must have just left.

She'd probably stolen a couple of hours of slumber, not that it helped. Her eyes remained puffy and sore from crying, tracks crusted her face. She still wore yesterday's dress and it bound her thighs uncomfortably. Her mouth tasted gritty.

After she'd checked Amir's food and water to assure that he'd eaten something, she'd brought him to bed, hoping for a nap before the evening shift. Collapsing in a shaking, sobbing pile of sex-stinking misery, Poetry slept fitfully.

How could she have been so stupid? Humiliation and regret threatened to overwhelm her again as Poetry rehashed the recent memory.

Seduced by a suit.

What was I thinking?

She'd let her guard down and he'd boarded her like a pirate. No wonder people hated lawyers. The hard part? She was fond of Adrian, thought he might be different.

Wrong… As Lemmy Kilmister would say, "The chase is better than the catch".

She didn't know which felt worse, the fact that he'd tricked her into sex or that she'd enjoyed it so much.

Her heart ached as she remembered the way he'd touched her, how his fingers feathered over her skin. Poetry let her hand slide down her stomach. She could almost feel him between her legs as he pumped inside her over and over.

The tears started again, much to Poetry's frustration. Poetry jerked her hand away and willed herself to stop fantasizing. She thought back to Amir's absence.

Amir stayed close and meowed when he wanted down, especially now with his injured ribs. Where would he go?

Sorrow forgotten, Poetry sat up. "Amir?" Nothing disturbed the stillness. "Where are you, baby?"

A presence caused her to jerk her head toward the shadowed door. Something…no, someone waited there. Just staring. Not moving. A sense of dread crept from her gut to her throat.

"You," she said. "What are you doing here?"

No answer. Poetry drew a sharp breath as the shadow manifested to the solid form and a fist to her temple killed the scream before it could leave her lips.

# # #

The officer handling the scene didn't like Adrian. He wore the distain on his face as if it were part of the uniform. Not that Adrian really blamed him. As defense lawyer and cop, they were sometimes at odds. This guy brought criminals in and Adrian got them off. Plus, Adrian got paid a lot more without as much personal risk. Sometimes knowing that embarrassed him.

"So whatdaya think?" The policeman took a pen and notepad from his pocket, keeping his tone carefully neutral. "Former client, maybe?"

Adrian bit down his rising anger. “Not exactly.”

Adrian had a pretty good idea who’d done this. All four tires were slashed, every window smashed. His leather seats were punctured in a dry parody of a murder victim, like a warning. The noxious smell of spray paint, gloss red to be exact, stung his nose.

After the police arrived to bag evidence and take photos he made some inquiries. Sure enough, Kevin Ferris was out on bail.

How did that asshole find out where he worked and which car belonged to him? How’d he get past the parkade guard?

It had to be him. Adrian couldn’t think of anyone else who might hold a grudge.

Adrian ground his teeth so hard his jaw ached. Innocent until proven guilty, he reminded himself. Resentment seethed inside his chest and he swallowed it like half-chewed meat.

Watching as fingerprints were lifted from a wheelwell put his mind at ease.

No problem. Forensics would prove it. When they did, Adrian would pull a few strings to lobby for a six-figure bail.

“Are we done?” he asked. “I’d really like to get out of here.”

“Suit yourself.” The pen and blank paper disappeared. “You think of anything, you know where we are.”

“Thanks.” I’m sure you’re right on it. For the umpteenth time Adrian wished he could clock that jackass junkie. But he’d have to drop it and let the system work.

And he genuinely hoped it would this time.

Adrian snuck out a side door and checked both ways before making his exit. Police interceptors were parked on the other side of the building. Lucky him. That should keep reporters engrossed long enough for his escape. He walked west a few blocks until he crossed 109th. He should grab a bite to eat.

Adrian absentmindedly pressed Ranjan's number on his cell. His cases were wrapping up. Maybe he could spare an hour.

Half a ring. "Adrian, where have you been?"

Why? What was that about? He should have checked his messages.

"Sorry, Ran," he said. "I'm having a shitty day."

"So you heard about the bombing? Not Buddy's, the one at West Ed."

The sidewalk wobbled beneath Adrian's feet, bringing him to a halt.

"Where exactly?" Not that it mattered. An explosion anywhere in a mall that size spelled disaster, but Adrian had an ugly hunch.

Please tell me it wasn't Frank's buddies. Please tell me it wasn't another tavern.

"The Asian grocery."

T&T Supermarket. An entire store dedicated to imported foods; fresh, frozen, dried, and cooked. It catered to Chinese, Vietnamese, Filipinos, and more.

"Racially motivated." Adrian groped for a nearby bus stop, wincing as his palm found the hot plastic window of the shelter. Dizziness nearly claimed him before he found the tiny metal slab that served as a seat inside.

"That's what it looks like." Adrian hadn't even realized what he'd said until Ranjan agreed. "Do you know where your client is?"

Adrian didn't need to ask which one.

"Come to think of it, no." He hadn't thought about the bastard all day. "I've been kinda occupied filing police reports for vandalism."

"Why? What happened?"

"I was calling you for a sympathetic ear," he said. "Somebody trashed the Bentley."

Adrian's eardrum rattled with the noise of a loud exhalation on Ranjan's end. "Shit."

"Yeah. This day just keeps getting better and better."

"Where are you?"

"I'm on Jasper and 109th." Adrian rubbed the bridge of his nose, desperate to drive away the ache burrowing into his eye sockets.

"Where should I meet you?"

"I could really use food and beer." Adrian checked his surroundings. "Kyoto is right behind me. Make that sake and a bento box."

"Sounds good. I'll be there in a half hour. Oh…" Ranjan spoke away from the phone. A feminine voice answered but he couldn't make out words. "I'm bringing Sarah, okay? She's had a rough day too, and I don't want to leave her alone."

"Sure, whatever." Right now Adrian didn't care who Ranjan invited. He just wanted some miso soup and a shot of alcohol. "See you in a bit."

He ended the connection and took a deep, humid breath. The tiny structure made it unpleasant, like breathing steam, so Adrian stepped back into the sunshine. Kyoto's front entrance was on the other side of the mini mall.

He took note of the new store on the corner. Adrian didn't spend a lot of time in this square, but he couldn't recall a florist being there.

Poetry.

She popped into his head for the first time in an hour and a fresh wave of guilt hit him. He'd need more than a single rose to make up for his earlier attitude. He found himself trudging to the door. All women liked flowers…Right?

The name 'Herrold's' flowed across the windows in black and yellow paint. Pink blooms decorated the glass along with chubby cherubs playing horns and harps. Adrian recognized the work. Several pubs and retail establishments used the same cartoonist who painted in a washable medium.

A tinkling chime announced his entrance in the dim shop. The chill of air conditioning relieved him instantly. The welcome sight of wall-to-wall carnations and baby's breath lifted his mood.

"Can I help you?" asked the man behind the counter.

"I remember you. You're the guy who sold me the black rose."

The golden-haired man emerged into the light and flashed a winning smile. "Told you the little Sheila would like it." He winked as if they'd shared a dirty joke. "Back for more, then?"

"Yeah." Adrian studied his shoes and rubbed the back of his neck, suddenly uneasy in the Australian's presence.

"What did you do?" His tone suggested Adrian had committed some crime of the heart. Which he had.

"I, uh…left her. After…" Why was he telling this guy his personal business? "I had to go to work."

"You didn't…" Adrian wanted to shrink into a corner. As if he didn't feel bad enough without this guy's two cents. "You're going to need a huge bouquet."

"I know." How big would it have to be to make Poetry absolve him? Maybe he should just buy her a tree.

The owner, Herrold, Adrian assumed, poised a pencil above notepaper.

"I'm thinking something soft and romantic," he said. "And apologetic. We better break out the red roses."

Adrian shuffled uncomfortably while Herrold muttered and sketched. A peek at the picture prompted Adrian to dig out his Visa. Forgiveness looked expensive.

"There we are." Herrold presented the doodle like an easel, pointing out highlights. "Red, white, and yellow roses with a spray of baby's breath and forget-me-nots. Beautiful and symbolic."

"Looks good." Adrian handed him the credit card. "I don't suppose I can get that delivered?"

"Of course."

"Today?"

Herrold shook his mop of golden curls. "Not a problem."

Adrian checked the time on his cell phone. Maybe he didn't understand just how badly he'd screwed up. The sooner Poetry got it, the better he'd feel.

"Can you put a rush on it? I'm in a bit of a hurry."

Herrold gave him a slow easy smile. "Dude, I've been doing this a long time. Trust me, I'm fast."

Herrold seemed to reach inside Adrian's to skull with that stare, exposing him.

"You're gonna think I have wings on my feet."

CHAPTER THIRTY-TWO

Strife jumped at the unexpected chance. Joining Adrian for a meal offered her an opportunity to get back on task. Ares might forgive her if she at least re-established contact with his pawn.

Perhaps he'd be easier to manipulate than Ranjan.

Her current prey seemed amicable. Strangely enough, she liked him. His manners were refined by proper rearing and education. His confidence had not yet aged to arrogance.

But her affections wouldn't complete the mission. She still had no idea why he seemed immune to her spells. And she needed a plan.

Adrian sat hunched over a ceramic flask and matching cup when they arrived. He greeted them wearily.

"Thanks for coming," he said. He bear hugged Ranjan, nodding politely to her before they sat.

"You work at the Rosemount, right?" He eyed her curiously.

"Yes, good to see you again. I wish it were under better circumstances. Ranjan says someone vandalized your car."

"It's been one hell of a day." He waved down a waitress in a navy blue kimono covered in cherry blossoms. "More tea please, and…" Adrian gestured with an open hand.

"I'll have sake as well. Sarah?" Ranjan looked at her, questioning. "What about you?"

"Tea is fine," she said. Despite the dim lighting and the delicious scents of cilantro and chicken broth, Strife felt ill at ease.

Something wasn't right. She scanned for the cause of the twitch between her shoulders, but she couldn't see beyond the L-shaped alcove.

“Where’s the ladies room?”

Adrian waved back the way they’d come. “To the right of the sushi bar.”

“Thanks.” She examined faces as she strolled. She recognized no one.

Not that she expected to sense anyone from her past. After all, this was the New World. The only other gods she’d been in contact with were Ares and…

…And that candy-assed hippie, Hermes.

She glanced back to Adrian’s table before quickening her pace. Both men were ignoring her in favor of secretive chatter, judging by their hunched shoulders. Her nemesis must be here somewhere.

She rounded the corner. Neither man would notice she’d left the restaurant so Strife slipped away to investigate.

Once outside the vibe became stronger. Where did it come from? She surveyed her surroundings, peering across the parking lot to the Save-On-Foods and Quiznos. Too far away.

She moved her small purse over her shoulder and opened the zipper. She had backup weapons inside she might need.

If I were the pretty-boy offspring of a prissy, naïve love-goddess-whore where would I be?

To her left were more businesses: a dental office, nail salon, and a florist on the end. Her head throbbed with his presence.

She remembered Hermes carrying his basket of roses, not to mention the golden logo seen around the world representing flower delivery bore a strong resemblance.

Eureka. Some people never changed tactics. Predictability will get you killed, Hermes.

Strife yanked the door open, nearly tearing it from the hinges. Chimes jangled in protest.

A pair of scissors flew past her head. She heard the loud chunk as they embedded themselves in the wall.

"Is that so, Strife?" Hermes crouched behind the till. He'd recognized her as well, now he had her at a disadvantage. "So will barging into a man's domain when he knows you're coming."

"This ends here." She pried the blades from the wooden frame with a tortured squeal. "You've interfered with my work long enough."

"Are you sure that's wise?" A small paring knife sliced the air, but Strife dodged before it could strike her left eye. "I am Ares's son, after all."

Strife snorted. She aimed the scissors for Hermes' face but missed. "He donated his seed, nothing more. You are a disappointment to him. He won't protect you from me."

"I don't need protection from you." Hermes edged backward, and Strife made ready to strike. "You're just his whipping-bitch underling, begging at his feet for scraps and cock. Ares only kept you because my mother had more respect for herself than to tolerate his abuse."

Strife shrieked, vaulting onto the counter in a single leap. She perched like a gargoyle, hissing her rage as Hermes fled.

She pounced on his back before he could escape.

"I'll kill you," Strings of spittle flew from Strife's mouth. "I'm going to snap your neck."

Hermes struggled beneath her weight. She gripped his hair with one hand and groped his jaw with the other, but he wriggled free and tossed her before springing to his feet.

"Nice try. But you'll have to do better." He hurled a computer monitor from the desk.

She scuttled to one side and the equipment slammed into the wall. Glass and plastic showered Strife. She ducked and shielded her face.

The rumblings of wood rolling against tile alerted Strife and she stood in time to avoid decapitation. Hermes pinned her with the oak desk, grinding it into her hips with bone-crushing intent. Hot agony raced up Strife's spine and Hermes increased the pressure, grunting with the effort like a wild beast.

She struggled, both hands prying at the solid edge in vain. Her thumb brushed her purse, and Strife wriggled her fingers inside, searching for anything that might assist her. They closed over a vial. She popped the top and dashed the contents in Hermes's eyes.

Talcum clouded the air, instantly filling the small space with delicate sweetness, blinding them both. The painful tension ceased. Hermes bellowed in anguish. Strife collapsed to the floor, retching with the soapy taste of perfume in her mouth.

From the corner of her watering vision, Strife saw Hermes lurch toward the entrance. You will not get away this time.

She gave chase, determined to finish him.

But he'd almost made it to the door. She had to do something.

Hermes made a critical error in judgment, shuffling left of the exit. Strife once again leapt on the service counter.

A cooler filled with lilies and orchids sat to her right.

With all her inhuman strength, she peeled it from the wall. A metallic groan filled the room as the gargantuan refrigerator sailed through the air.

Hermes's failed attempt to catch it bore him to the ground with a sloppy crash peppered with a chorus of breaking glass and singing shelves.

Yellow, orange, and purple petals fluttered throughout the store like confetti. Floral scents combined with baby powder made the room reek like women's deodorant.

The abrupt quiet brought serenity to chaos. The only sound: the panting of a dying man.

She must hurry. The noise would bring curious humans, and she couldn't be caught. Not with her objective so close at hand.

She eased to the floor, her sandals transforming glass to powder.

"That was too easy," She strutted over to stare at Hermes's ruined face. Shards embedded various pockets of flesh, including his left eye. "I expected better from a demi-god."

Hermes glared contemptuously through milky tears, trying in vain to spit blood at Strife. His thoughts dimmed.

"Yes, it's too bad," she said, "but if it is any consolation…" She extended her hands to the multicolored carnage. "This is the prettiest death I've ever seen."

Strife backed away from the growing pool of blood and cocked her head to examine the damage. Hermes's bones and inner organs were crushed, she knew. But as much as she wanted Hermes to experience an excruciatingly slow and miserable demise, she couldn't permit it.

Both his parents were original denizens of Eden, angels who claimed godhood on Earth.

Grievous as his injuries were, the possibility Hermes could survive had occurred to her.

She stepped down on his Adam's apple, putting her full weight on it. Sickening popping and crunching music filled her ears as more bodily fluids gushed from Hermes's mouth.

A pleasurable sigh eased through Strife's lips when her foot came to rest on the back of Hermes's throat. The light faded from his eyes, his spirit dissipated.

Tension drained from Strife's body. She could not remember the last time she'd been so satisfied. And hungry. Murder gave her an appetite.

She straightened her clothes and checked for stains. Strife wiped talc from her face and clothes, combed it from her hair with her hands. Good thing she'd worn a paisley print blouse. The pink and red swirls would hide her sins, as would the black capris. She found a cloth to wipe blood spatter from her legs and shoes.

She'd only been here minutes, but Strife hastened. Time to get out.

She exited the store as calmly as she could manage and returned to Kyoto, sniffing her collar for tell-tale hints. Fortunately, she smelled like a fresh shower of hygiene products.

When Strife approached the table, Ranjan and Adrian were engrossed in conversation.

"I mean, I know it's just a car, but I worked so hard to get it. I loved that Bentley," Adrian said. "I am going to kick that guy's ass so hard he'll beg for jail time just to get away from me."

"I get that," Ranjan said. "Just don't do anything that might jeopardize your… Hi, Sarah." He sidled over to make room for her. "Sit here."

"Thanks." She pushed aside the menu and took a generous gulp of green tea. Its soothing heat and fresh flavor flooded her dry throat.

The server with the dark blue kimono approached.

"Did you want to look at the specials?" Ranjan asked. "Or do you know what you want?"

"I'll have the tuna sashimi." She salivated, fantasizing about the silken sensation of raw fish grazing her teeth.

This would be the nearest thing to tasting Hermes blood she would get, and she intended to partake with pleasure. She brought her teacup to her lips to hide her relish.

CHAPTER THIRTY-THREE

Poetry moaned. The echo it caused disturbed her, but she didn't open her eyes. Her head hurt too much. She wasn't up to stabbing rays of sunshine in her brain.

As consciousness returned, so did her instincts. Something was wrong.

Instead of the clammy heat of her apartment, a bone-chilling dankness embraced her. No noise of traffic, no dull roar of furnaces below.

She licked cracked lips and tasted mud. Not good. Every shift of her body resounded in her ears. Water dripped, she couldn't tell where. It seemed to be all around.

Poetry dreaded the discovery that would no doubt greet her once she risked a peek at her surroundings. But she had to know…

Panic engulfed her. She couldn't see.

Despite protesting muscles she rushed to her feet. Her screams reverberated back the sound of new horrors.

Bats.

They slapped her face and caught in her hair, squealing their united indignation and digging what must be hundreds of tiny claws into her scalp. Poetry danced to dislodge them and ran blindly in the dark.

The decision nearly popped her arms from their sockets. A cry of anguish and agony ripped from her throat and ricocheted into space. She dropped to her knees, barking as they connected with solid rock and jagged pebbles.

Poetry's head swam. Her empty stomach lurched. Tendons ached and now her legs were shredded and sore. And she was still blind.

Her heavy hands reached to rub her throbbing shoulders. Why did her arms feel like they weighed a ton?

The answer came with the rasp of metal on metal. No way. It can't be. She explored her limbs and discovered the truth.

Poetry smelled standard, every-day iron. Her touch found solid cuffs encircling her wrists. Shackles. The links were huge, almost the size of her thumb.

She groped to their source and found a stone wall. Gouges and crags scratched her palms.

Her misery complete, Poetry collapsed to the ground and wailed until she couldn't stand despair ringing in her ears.

Memories patched together. She'd been sleeping. The shadow in her room, someone she knew. Everything happened so fast, she couldn't be sure what she remembered.

The only thing she understood was that she crouched on a dirt floor covered in, she took a whiff, bat shit, and she couldn't see or move. She'd been kidnapped and locked away in a cave.

Damp air, seeping moisture, flying rodents, and utter darkness…It must be a cave.

Poetry didn't know if Edmonton had anything like that, and her worry grew. Where the hell was she? Did anyone even know she'd gone missing?

Loneliness eroded her strength. Tears welled hot in her eyes and spilled down her cheeks. No one would find her. Not her parents, not her co-workers. Her boss would probably think she just no-showed and quit. She couldn't count on Jenny to get her head out from her ass long enough to think about someone else. And Adrian had written her off as a sexual conquest.

For reasons Poetry couldn't explain, the last thought hurt the worst. If there ever existed a time when she needed a smart, compassionate warrior-type hero, it would be now.

She dismissed the guy who'd seduced and left her. In his place, Poetry wished for the brave man who'd fearlessly confronted Kevin, then searched her apartment with a broomstick. She envisioned the slender Norwegian, dressed not in the garb of a Viking, but in the blue robes of a Kendokka.

But he'd never come for her. He didn't want her anymore.

Grief tightened her chest. "Adrian." Poetry listened to the echo of her desperate whisper, and surrendered to her sorrow.

# # #

Adrian dragged himself inside and disengaged his home security system. What a gong show of a day. Ranjan had dropped him off, something about showing that Sarah girl the University of Alberta campus.

Poor guy had it bad. Adrian had resisted the urge to tell Ran he should wipe the drool from his chin and stop making eyes like a love-sick moron. It was too funny. Worse than Gary.

They'd invited him to tag along, but between lack of sleep, the trashing of his Bentley, and several hits of sake Adrian wanted shut-eye more than ever.

Light poured in through the balcony windows. Afternoon sun toasted the apartment, making him feel even lazier.

He kicked off his shoes, peeled off his socks, flopped down on the sofa, and checked the time. Two o'clock. Adrian groaned. Kendo practice didn't start until nine, but he didn't have the strength to kira-kaeshi or do any other drills, never mind kiai.

Charging across the dojo, striking motodachi opponents while yelling at the top of his lungs sounded like more work than he could handle tonight. Besides, his shinai needed maintenance.

Not a bad idea, he thought, rolling to stand again. Adrian liked oiling and waxing the bamboo sword. It recharged him and brought on a sense of pride for his sport.

He grabbed it from his bedroom closet, the safest place for the weapon, and tripped over something round and metallic.

He bent and retrieved the forgotten torque Poetry made for him. Now he winced as he remembered chucking it when he awoke this morning. She'd obviously worked really hard on it, judging from the intricate braid. How long did it take to weave metal wire into a rope? He eyed the stones, rubbing the suddenly tingling burns on his collar bone.

Guess he'd had a reaction to these rocks. But he wouldn't tell Poetry. He brought it to the coffee table and sighed. If she ever spoke to him again.

After firing off an apologetic e-mail to his sensei, Adrian assembled his tools. He gathered paper towel, a pocket knife, sandpaper, light mineral oil, and a white candle. He prepared a cup of green tea before settling to the task.

Adrian unwound the himo. The string loosened and he pulled two loops free. He removed the leather nakayuki, sakugawa, and tsuka, leaving only four staves.

He separated the set, careful not to lose the top plug or the crucial metal square that connected them from the other end.

Pausing for a sip of hot grassy brew, he checked for chips on the blades.

After filing and sanding each stave, the rest of the job went quickly. He doused the paper towel with oil, coating each piece of bamboo until they glistened. Adrian ran the candle down all edges, ensuring smooth motion between staves.

Adrian realigned all four blades, the notches on the bottom fitting with the thumbprint sized tin plate. The tsuka sleeve slid on, then the plug at the point. Nakayuki and sakugawa came next, along with the himo.

He checked his kitchen clock. Two forty-five. It wasn't out of the ordinary for Adrian to get lost in the ritual, but it took him longer than usual to scrape the dents out. Normally he'd do this in twenty minutes.

With his loops and winding done, Adrian inspected his work. The staves clicked to his satisfaction and the himo twanged like a ukulele string. Perfect.

Sipping his tea, Adrian pondered what to do next. He probably could make practice, now that he'd had a chance to relax. He leaned back on the couch, letting the leftover strain fall away. Maybe he could make practice after all. After a nap. Adrian shut his heavy eyelids.

# # #

'Message from Opticon' blared from the kitchen, harshing Kevin's rainbow haze and amping him up. Poetry's ringtone. He didn't miss it. He fucking hated that song. He couldn't wait to bash it into oblivion.

He'd caught a lift from Ares and his Batmobile, so Kevin could make her pay again.

She deserved it. That'll teach her for getting him arrested. Bitch had cost him a lot in the last week. Gonna get even this time.

He stomped across the room to the shitty table and chairs where he found the buzzing phone. He slammed it to the floor and crushed it with his heel.

"Shut the fuck up!" What was the bitch gonna do without her precious Koodo? Now she had no cell, no computer, no nothing. If he had his way, she'd get another eviction too. Kevin wouldn't be happy until she'd lost everything. Then maybe he'd take her back.

Two sounds interrupted his thoughts. First, the slow stroll of big-assed boots coming from the bathroom. The second clicking Kevin knew better, having been on the business end of a gun a few times.

Kevin glanced up to see some skinny, wrinkled fuck pointing it at him.

"And who might you be?" The old man asked, drawling out the first word.

"I don't gotta tell you, Gramps." The dope made Kevin brave. "Who the fuck are you?"

"None of your goddamn business." Geezer wasn't backing down.

Good. I could use a half decent scrap. Even if he had a revolver, Kevin could take him. He coughed up a chortle. This was gonna be fun.

Kevin feinted left, then right. Gramps couldn't keep up, his aim waggled back and forth.

He gripped the stranger by the throat and smashed his forehead into the guy's nose. Kevin lived for that crack and gush of blood. He even tasted some of it.

Both the old man and the revolver tumbled to the linoleum and Kevin's fists delivered haymakers on their own.

But Geezer wasn't done. His face was a snot smoothie, but damned if he didn't fight back. He had a lot of balls behind them bony knuckles.

Too bad Kevin couldn't feel it. He'd never been higher in his life. His numb face had a steel jaw that absorbed every hit. Like a fucking god.

Kevin let his hands slide around Grandpa's throat; time to snuff the bastard.

The man stopped hitting him as Kevin tightened his grip. Leathery, nicotine-stained fingers scratched uselessly, desperate but weakening.

This must be how Ares feels, to just take a man's life and soul. Fucking awesome. The old guy pawed around the ground with one hand.

Forget it dude, nothin's going to save you. I am all powerful.

Cartilage crunched in Kevin's palms, and he knew if he could see Grandpa's eyes through the bruising they'd be fading out. Saliva flecked Kevin's face. Grandpa gagged.

Not long now.

Kevin wasn't aware of the subtle scratch of metal against floor. Or the final clack. He didn't hear the gun go off.

CHAPTER THIRTY-FOUR

Strife bit her lip in irritation. Not another drawn out, exhaustive tour of the 'sights of Edmonton'. As if a university campus could be of any use to her. She had enough issues with Ares without continuing to gallivant around the city, but Ranjan insisted on showing her where he'd studied.

She would endure it for the simple reason that Ares never attacked in public. When it came to one-on-one situations he preferred guerilla tactics. Degradations and cruelties remained private.

Thoughts of her master's bathroom visit sent a chill throughout her body, raising goosebumps on a sweltering day. Better to stay with Ranjan and amongst other mortals. If she stayed within view of humans, Ares couldn't find a quiet place to bend her over.

"We're on Groat Road." Ranjan pointed across her nose with one hand, while steering a slight curve with the other. He smelled of curry and sandalwood.

"Down that way is Hawryluk Park. That's where they hold Heritage Days every year."

"Very interesting." She tried to inject fascination into her inflections. "Maybe I can go sometime."

"Sure. It'll be here the first week of August. I'll take you there. Of course my favorite is the Indian pavilion," he said with a sideways grin. "But every year I try to eat something I've never heard of. Last time, I had this runny purple jelly from Persia." He shook his head as he rounded a traffic circle. "I think they made it from plums. I'd like to find that again, but I couldn't pronounce it the first time."

Ranjan thumbed back to a monstrous yellow building on the left. "That's the Butterdome."

“Wow. It really does look like a giant pat of butter.” It must be the ugliest architecture this side of the world. Energy’s essence, I miss Europe.

“And we’re here,” he said, throwing the vehicle in park.

“Where?”

“I want to show you the law building where I got my degree.”

In front of her sat a three-story brown slab. Its monotonous stubbiness reflected all the excitement law school promised.

“I can’t wait to see it,” she said through a tight smile. But boredom would be easier to endure than anything Ares had planned. Strife braced herself for a long afternoon of relentless drudgery.

# # #

Grogginess clouded Adrian’s head. It took a few minutes for him to realize racket from the TV woke him. He didn’t recall switching it on.

He wiped grit from his eyes and sat up. His shinai still sat across his lap. He must have completely crashed.

Long day and not much sleep.

He heard a Global News announcement. How long had he been out?

“Police are not saying how the man died, but are treating the death as suspicious,” the female newscaster reported as the scene panned to the background. “Witnesses say a woman with long dark hair was seen leaving the establishment before the body was discovered…”

The rest of the report faded from Adrian’s hearing. He recognized the building in the shot. He’d been there only a few hours previous, buying Poetry’s good graces.

The vibrant designs on the store front perked up an otherwise grim environment crowded with police ribbons and curious onlookers.

He couldn't help but notice the woman with her back to the camera. Her waist-long golden hair and frothy tunic singled her out from a group wearing shorts and t-shirts. She resembled a genie or maybe a faerie.

As if alerted by his scrutiny, she peered over her shoulder. Her beauty stole Adrian's breath.

Eyes like the sea gushed grief without marring her pristine porcelain skin. Tears fell from her face like pearls while she kneaded her bare arms.

Adrian shuddered at the rage he saw there. She studied the camera with accusation and defiance. Adrian could almost swear she glared right at him.

Something in the room with him caught his eye. The silver circlet glowed. What the…? Adrian had a ridiculous thought, that maybe the woman on the screen had something to do with the way Poetry's piece shone like a disco ball.

He glanced back to the television, gulping hard. She was looking at him.

She dropped her arms to her side and strode toward him, never breaking eye contact. She loomed larger in the screen. Adrian clutched his shinai, sinking into the cushions of his couch in a vain attempt to kamae.

He couldn't think straight. Nothing made sense. Sweat pooled on his top lip and air became scarce. He tasted the salt of his panic, heard it as harsh swallows.

The woman grasped the edges of the television and her fingers took form, curling over the black plastic like flesh spiders. In a single stride she crawled into the living room.

Adrian quaked until his weapon blurred in his periphery. She appeared to be human, but couldn't be. Unless…

"No, mortal," she said, her soft feminine words floated through the condominium like a song on the breeze. "You are not dreaming." She advanced until Adrian toppled off the sofa trying to avoid her.

Her honeyed scent engulfed him. It was the essence of a woman's desire, the playful musk of pleasure, a sugared kiss.

Adrian released his sword to shield his stirring groin. Visions of Poetry's face, flushing in the throes of passion, surfaced in his mind until the woman leaned over him. With a dismissive gesture, she stilled his racing thoughts.

"I understand why you would think I am a figment of your imagination. You New Worlders sleep excessively." She shut her eyes and arched her brows, as though trying to gather her thoughts before she unleashed fury. "It mystifies me how you managed to build this modern empire of false joy. You are all forever sleeping as though Morpheus himself stole your will. He must be truly powerful here."

Adrian pulled himself off the hardwood floor to take a second glance at his visitor.

She waited with hands on hips, moisture still dripping from her phosphorous stare. Rain pattered at his windows.

"Wh-who are you?"

"My name is Aphrodite." Her brows furrowed and lightning flashed. "You know not who I am?" Thunder boomed. Adrian's stomach rolled. She'd read his thoughts. "I am the goddess of love. Do you New Worlders know nothing?"

"S-sorry," Adrian said, shivering. The room seemed suddenly colder. "I'm not into mythology."

"Mythology." Aphrodite spat the word. "Do I look like a myth to you?"

"No, ma'am." She resembled a long forgotten wet dream, smelled like a night of lovemaking.

The storm rivaled the news report. "...it is believed that all seven of the suspects in custody will plead temporary insanity..."

Adrian's vocal chords barely functioned. "What do you want?"

Outside the weather intensified. A deluge raged. Aphrodite seemed to radiate pain until Adrian experienced the barrage of her agony. Tiny balls of ice pelted him. He glanced outside his patio doors. It was hailing.

"She killed him," Aphrodite said, her voice barely audible above the gale. "I know it was her. Who else would use talcum powder in battle?"

"Who?" Adrian asked. "Who killed who?"

"Strife. She murdered my son."

Adrian thought about the flower shop swathed in police tape and the guy with the curly surfer hair...like hers.

"You mean Herrold?"

"That was his Earth name. His name was Hermes."

"Earth name?" Adrian's jaw dropped. What the hell was going on here? "What are you people?"

"It would take too long to clarify. And why should I? You are mere pawns."

"What?" Something was wrong with his brain. This was just too weird.

"I knew Ares would cheat. He never fights fair." Aphrodite put her hands to her face as fresh tears washed down her sallow cheeks. "But I never thought he would allow his minion to kill our child." The wind howled in empathy.

Adrian plunked down on the arm of the couch, dumbfounded. Maybe he'd eaten some bad sushi. That was it. Combine that with sake, exhaustion, and a stressful day, and bang on; instant hallucination.

But what about the evidence on his clothes? He rubbed his collar and pulled away chunks of precipitation like frozen white peas. Adrian took another peek at his balcony. The doors were closed. If this came from his sickened state, maybe he should give up law and retire to Ponoka. But of course that was just ridiculous. There had to be a logical explanation, but he couldn't wrap his head around it.

"Wait," he said as something she'd mentioned came back to him. "Pawns for what?"

The downpour reduced to a shower. Aphrodite collected herself, wiping wet trails from her jaw and straightening her clothing.

"If you must know, it was a contest between Ares and myself." Sea shells appeared in the palm of her hand and she placed them decoratively in her hair. "My task was to make you fall in love. Ares only had to prevent it."

Adrian reached for the torque as his stomach lurched. He had to squint at its brilliance. Its energy throbbed in his hand. Magick. That explains a lot.

Now he understood why Poetry went to the Rosemount; why her ex came to the restaurant, to her apartment. He'd been duped to watch out for her, to care for her and her damn cat. The whole thing had been orchestrated for the amusement of a couple of squabbling deities.

"Not everything," Aphrodite said, but Adrian ignored her.

"It was just a game…" He shifted the neckpiece this way and that, examining the tight weave Poetry had painstakingly created with her own hands. "We were under a spell."

He wanted to vomit. They'd been used as chess pieces. "None of it was real."

“I would not say that. I did not send her to meet you. Nor was Kevin dispatched to torment her.” She stroked his hair.

“You defended her of your own accord. You escorted her home and sought her enemy.” Aphrodite caressed his chin and brought his gaze to hers. “It was all you. I merely suggested you bring her to dinner.”

Adrian didn’t believe her.

“She brought you a picnic out of gratitude that you earned.” Her demeanor grew urgent. “Please. Will you not wear her gift?”

“Why?” Adrian couldn’t keep the sneer out of his voice. “So you can put me under your control?”

“No, human. That is not how it works.” She offered her open hand. “You care for Poetry without magicks, yes?”

Did he? Or was it a lie?

He thought of her deep brown eyes, her olive skin ripe with that metallic fragrance unique to her body chemistry. Not only had he grown used to it, he’d started to like it.

He remembered yesterday on the rooftop, how she’d made him forget the prison of his responsibilities. He tasted hummus every time he thought of it. His heart lifted.

“I thought as much,” Aphrodite said. “Don the jewels and bring your sword.”

“Why? What are we doing?”

Aphrodite’s face clouded. “If Strife is bold enough to kill Hermes, there is no telling what she is capable of.” Thunder growled.

“Poetry is in grave danger.”

CHAPTER THIRTY-FIVE

Regurgitated sake sloshed the back of Adrian's throat; his knees jellied. The smell of blood and feces greeted him. If he had to open his eyes, he might lose his sushi.

"Oh my Energy, what a mess," Aphrodite said, and Adrian couldn't help himself. So much for not peeking.

"Holy…" Déjà vu. They were at Poetry's new place, but it had been trashed just like the previous one. Adrian identified Kevin's condiment scrawl on the peeling walls, complete with the same derogatory notes written in ketchup. He seemed to like four-letter words beginning with 'F' and 'C'. Light from the open refrigerator door revealed broken dishes and ransacked drawers spilled all over the floor.

But what he didn't expect to find was Kevin's brain-splashed corpse next to Frank Fleisher's battered one. He recognized the musician's leather jacket and his client's cowboy boots.

Well, that's convenient.

Adrian pushed the insensitive opinion out of his head. Both men were public menaces, but they were still remotely human.

He inched forward, trying to avoid a pool of congealed fluids. Kevin's skull lay gaping like a hatched egg. No hope for him, but Adrian should examine Fleisher, just in case.

"Don't bother," Aphrodite said. "They are both quite dead." She shoved past him to lift Frank's arm and flopped the stiffening appendage at him. "See?"

"Don't touch him." He placed two fingers on Frank's neck. Nothing.

Decomposing flesh in photographs was one thing, seeing it in person required therapy afterwards. Frank's cold epidermis could only mean death. "Don't tamper with the evidence. We have to call the police."

His cell phone chirped. Adrian yanked it out of his pocket and stared at the call display. Denny's Restaurant? Who the…?

Poetry worked at Denny's. He answered with hope in his pounding chest.

"Hello?"

"Adrian, it's Jenny." The anxious babble on the line didn't sound like Jenny. Not even the slightest hint of a giggle. "Gary gave me your number."

"What's up?"

"Is Poetry with you? Have you seen her?" Hope turned to dread.

"No, I haven't." He gripped his shinai and began a search of her miniscule apartment, scanning the bathroom as he spoke. Splintered glass crunched beneath his feet. Purple dots spelling the word 'slut' painted the wall. This was getting a little too familiar for his liking, only this time a statuesque blonde trailed behind him instead of a pint-sized Mediterranean. "I'm at her place right now and…" Should he apprise Jenny of the situation? No. That would freak her out.

"She didn't show up for work. She never does that, Adrian. She never misses a shift without calling."

Adrian's already sensitive bowels squirmed. "I'll look into it." He skirted past the gore to the bedroom. "It'll be alright." He almost added I promise, but he didn't buy it himself. He hung up before he could say anything incriminating.

He stared at the empty bed, the rumpled covers. Adrian placed his hand on them. No body heat. She'd been here, he smelled her body odor. How long since she'd left?

"She is not here." Aphrodite arrived beside him.

"No shit."

“I mean she is nowhere,” Aphrodite said. “This place is complete void of her presence. I cannot sense her at all.”

Adrian’s pulse throbbed in his neck, heat rose to his cheeks. “I’m calling 911.” He punched the nine but Aphrodite stayed his hand.

“We do not have time.”

“What do you mean we don’t have time?”

“Poetry needs our help now. The sooner we find her, the better.”

“What do you think I’m trying to do?” Adrian asked. “We have to call the police.”

“What will you tell them? Will they believe you are not responsible for this?” Aphrodite gestured to the broken corpses behind them. “Two men lay dead and your lover is missing.”

She was right. They’d question him. Bring him down to the station and interrogate him for hours. Long, exhaustive, pointless hours. Even if Adrian told the truth, it would make the situation worse. He couldn’t win.

“Besides, we have no need of them. You have me.” She pointed to his neck. “And that.”

She snapped her fingers and the torque warmed his throat.

“Think of Poetry.” Her whisper coaxed Adrian to dream.

The metal vibrated. He knew if he could see it, the neckpiece would be glowing like it did at his condo.

Magick again. This had better work.

Adrian fixed Poetry’s face in his mind. Her drowsy brown eyes and blue bangs drifted through his thoughts. When she smiled, her white teeth stood in contrast with her flawless tan skin. The rhinestone on her cheek winked.

“It works,” Aphrodite said, and Adrian glanced to his left. The goddess had orange reflections in her pupils, matching the stones he wore. “Think harder,” she said.

He closed his eyes and imagined the tattoos down her shoulders and arms; foliage, hibiscus, and satyrs shone in pink, yellow, brown, and green. He could almost feel her skin beneath his fingertips, like silk scented with musk and sex.

The air chilled, oxygen vacuumed from the room with a concussive THUNK.

Adrian cried out as his ears popped. His eyelids snapped opened to a creamy blur. He covered his face with his hands, trying to get a bearing.

“Aphrodite.” The hissing voice penetrated Adrian’s ears, despite the ringing. “I sensed you tampering with my spells. This will not be permitted any longer.”

Adrian risked a glance and gaped.

A lanky woman with long snowy hair and icy eyes stood before him wearing furs that sparsely covered her breasts and legs. She held a massive broadsword. She was massive. He craned his neck to gawk at her snarling face.

He shivered from the bitter cold she emitted. And from fear. She looked every bit the Valkyrie. He peered at Aphrodite. She’d gone pale.

“Freya,” she said. What could make a goddess quake like that? Judging by the terror this woman caused, he guessed her to be another deity of some kind, but more powerful.

“I swear I did not know the stones were yours.” Aphrodite, cowering, took a step back.

“Who else would they belong to?” Freya raised her sword arm, pointing the tip of her weapon at Aphrodite’s face. “You came to me for amber.” She jerked the end in front of Adrian’s neck. His heart stuttered. “That is amber. My amber.”

"You refused me. It is true I sent Hephaestus to speak with you, but I have not heard from him. How was I to know he succeeded where I failed?"

Freya stared Aphrodite down. Clouds of vapor passed from their mouths in the frigid chill. Long moments crawled. Adrian wondered if there was a safe way to squeeze past the dresser and out the door while the women had forgotten his existence.

"I did nothing more than charm the metal she used for the jewelry," Aphrodite said. "I sought to inspire."

Adrian's shallow breathing cut through the silence, but not the tension. He'd give almost anything for something to break the stalemate.

"Meow?"

Amir?

Adrian released a frozen breath and gratefully braced for a cat bite on his ankles.

The black fuzz ball appeared from behind the bed but, instead of streaking to attack Adrian's socks, Amir paused to observe the ivory-haired giantess.

"Meeeeew!" Amir raised his tiny paws. He wanted this polar nightmare to pick him up? Crazy cat.

"Hello, little one." The transformation from frosty titan to melting angel happened so fast Adrian thought another woman must have taken Freya's place when he blinked. Even Aphrodite seemed to calm, her shoulders easing down as her rival's anger dissipated.

Freya sheathed her sword and knelt to retrieve the kitten with an open palm. Amir climbed on and settled in.

"Amir? That is your name? What a perfect name for a handsome prince." Freya straightened, bringing a handful of cat to her serene face. Amir purred and pawed at her nose.

Adrian leaned into Aphrodite's ear. "She can talk to cats?"

Aphrodite stared sideways daggers at him. "Yes, she communes with cats. Your lack of knowledge astounds me."

He shirked the rebuke, but until today Adrian didn't believe gods and goddesses existed. Why would he bother studying fantasy?

Across from him, the white deity teased the black cat under his chin. Amir addressed her with a series of meows and grrrlling sounds.

"What does he say?" Adrian asked.

"The poor boy is frightened. He has been hiding in that corner for over an hour." She tossed her head to the cupboard behind her. "Freya will not let anyone hurt you, sweet prince."

"Enough," Aphrodite said, just when Adrian thought he'd need a shot of insulin. "I like you better when you are not so soft." Her scoff of disgust amazed Adrian. Aphrodite had overcome her fear of Freya apparently. "Ask the feline if he knows the whereabouts of his human."

Freya stroked Amir's head. "Where is your mistress, little one?"

Amir let out a plaintive meow. Freya responded by cuddling him to her breast and petting him while making soothing clucking noises.

"Poor little prince."

"What did he say?" Adrian asked.

"She is lost," Freya said. "Someone stole his mommy." Mommy. Amir must be worried sick.

Adrian gave his head a shake. Amir the cat. Worried sick. This day went from bad to screwed-the-hell-up and it was only getting worse.

"Who?" Aphrodite asked. Adrian felt as hopeful and wound up as she sounded. "Did he witness the kidnapping?"

"Meow."

“He sounds sincere.”

“He is,” Freya said. “Amir recognized the villain who took her.”

“Well?” Adrian tried not to be so impatient, but while these immortals chatted Poetry could be dying. “Who is it?”

“Meowrr-rowr!”

“The forge-god.” Freya’s tone went cold. Her slate grey eyes became slivers of ice. “Smells like sweat, metal, and smoke.”

Aphrodite sucked in her breath, placing a delicate hand over her mouth. “That son of a demon hoarde.”

“What?” Adrian threw his hands in the air. “Who the hell is the forge-god?”

Both women favored him with a glare. “Hephaestus,” they said in unison.

“New Worlders…” Freya said with a disgruntled snort.

“Hephaestus is her mentor and landlord.” Aphrodite spread her hands over her head. “He owns this building.”

“I thought that was some guy named Hugh.”

“Same man,” Aphrodite said. “You expected him to use his true identity?”

Adrian shrugged. He had to admit, he would change his name too if he had to run around with a mouthful of a moniker like ‘Hephaestus’. How do you even spell that?

Aphrodite buried her face in her hands. “This is a disaster.”

“Why?” Adrian asked. “If we know who has her, then we can figure out where he took her and-“

“It is not that simple. I cannot feel him or her. They could be anywhere.”

“I have a suspicion,” Freya said. She examined a bracelet on her wrist, twisting her hand back and forth, making the gems twinkle like unspoiled snow. “Hephaestus gave me this.”

Aphrodite’s lip curled over long, glistening teeth, marring her beauty even as her eyes flashed from green to yellow. “So he gave you a bauble.” Distain dripped from her lips. “Everyone is aware of how you obtain your trinkets. What do I care?”

“You will.” A grin crept up her smug face. “But not because I slept with your husband.” She returned Amir to the floor and caressed her sparkling diamonds as Aphrodite glared.

“When Hephaestus presented me with this prize, he told me of the Cadomin mines in the north where he obtained these as lumps of coal.” Aphrodite extended her hand to touch it but Freya pulled away, wagging a finger in Aphrodite’s glowering face. “I should think that if he were to abduct someone, where better to hide them than in abandoned caves?”

The room quieted as Aphrodite appeared to consider this information. Her brows knit and color returned to her cheeks.

“He once preferred to make his home in the belly of the world,” she said.

Adrian licked salt from his lips. They wasted precious minutes, yet he couldn’t move.

“Why are you helping me?” Aphrodite asked. “You do not like me. This is none of your concern.”

Freya placed a hand on her hip and cocked her head. “I am not doing this for you. The young prince needs his human.”

She pointed at Amir, who gazed up at her with feline adoration, blinking sleepily.

“And for the Norwegian.” She leered at Adrian, and he got butterflies in his gut.

“Do you love your smithy?” she asked.

Adrian couldn’t speak. His words swelled in his throat until he couldn’t express them without anguish. He nodded instead.

Freya tilted his face up to meet hers. “Enough to fight for her?”

“You will not face an addict this time, Adrian Olsen,” Aphrodite said. “You challenge a god.”

Both deities stared, awaiting his decision with hushed patience. Adrian had never felt so alone as he did now. Once he’d been content to live like that, a permanent bachelor. Now the idea of existing without Poetry tightened his chest. The thought of her languishing in a bleak prison of rock twanged every fiber of his being.

What choice did he have?

“I’ll do what I have to.” He still had his shinai and the conviction to use it. Time to put his Kendo skills to work. “I’m going to bring her home.”

CHAPTER THIRTY-SIX

Both goddesses appeared pleased with Adrian.

"Spoken like a faithful lover," Aphrodite said.

"And a true warrior." Freya nodded her satisfaction. "But you will not get very far with that pathetic stick."

She tapped the shinai with her sword. The bamboo flared blue, like a light saber, and began to burn. Adrian caught the hitch in his throat, anticipating disaster but instead of the insubstantial weight of ashes, the weapon grew heavier. A white glow enveloped the dinginess, heating the small bedroom and warping the linoleum. It dispersed as quickly as it had come.

A clock ticked in the kitchen, counting heartbeats. For long moments Adrian saw only green spots in his vision. No one spoke as he hefted not bamboo, but steel.

Giddiness in his gut threatened to unleash stunned laughter. Instead, he ran his tongue inside his stale-tasting mouth before he spoke. "It's beautiful."

Freya crinkled her sharp nose. "What manner of sword is that?"

"It is a skinny thing," Aphrodite said, sharing Freya's obvious concern. "How will you fight with it?"

"It's a Japanese katana," Adrian said. "The shinai is used to represent it, and kendokka are trained to wield it." He took two strides to his right and tested the blade. "It's a weapon of grace and precision."

Adrian went into kamae--feet parallel, right before left, and balanced forward on the balls of his feet. He placed his hands on the hilt in the proper grip, right hand above left, and centered himself.

He gauged the cracked ceiling. Three meters; just enough space to swing. Adrian began with shomen-suburi, slicing straight down to his would-be opponent's cranium. He stepped back, taking the sword to near horizontal above his head.

A few more strikes. "Ichi, ni, san, shi…"

"You count in Japanese?" Freya asked.

"It's a Japanese sport," Adrian said, returning to kamae position. Time to try sayu-men.

He struck an imaginary motodatchi once again, aiming instead for a man's temples at a forty-five degree angle.

"Ichi, ni, san-"

"Are you going to do this all day?" Aphrodite asked, hands on hips. "Or are you ready to rescue the woman you love?"

Adrian twitched in embarrassment. "I guess I'd better get started."

He hesitated. He had no sheath for his new katana, and no bogu.

No problem. He wanted to travel light anyway, all he needed was…

"Shit. I don't have a car."

Before despair could settle in Adrian's heart, Aphrodite snapped her fingers. A brief sunburst stung his eyes. He pried them open again to see a pair of gold sandals in her hand.

Adrian yelped when they sprang to life, straining at the laces Aphrodite held like leashes. A flutter echoed; the smell of disturbed dust made him want to sneeze. The sound came from the shoes, and on closer inspection he noticed metallic wings on the heels.

"Interesting," Freya said. "Where did you get them?"

Aphrodite's tormented glare, filled with grief and hatred, compelled the larger woman to withdraw a step. Something passed between them for long seconds as the deities spoke with their eyes. The wind resumed its mournful keening, rain continued to pound at the window.

Freya ducked her head. “I am truly sorry.”

Aphrodite ignored her adversary’s token sympathy and set her sights on Adrian. Once again she became the heartbroken mother who’d emerged from the television and into his life.

“These belonged to Hermes.” Her sorrow formed a lump in Adrian’s chest. “When he was our young messenger, before he peddled flowers, he wore these to bring our word to mortals and to steal prized artifacts.”

She stroked each sole in turn and the anxious flapping ceased. The magick pair drooped, nearly passing for ordinary footwear.

“They remember Hephaestus and will help you find him. They are faster than a car, but not as quick as a jet.”

Aphrodite dropped the shoes, and they strolled to him of their own accord.

“Hey!” Adrian almost tripped as the sandals wrestled themselves onto his feet and strapped in.

A shining hat appeared in Aphrodite’s other hand. It also bore feathered accents. Adrian recognized it from a florist’s logo.

“Mercury’s helmet,” he said.

“That was his Roman name, yes.” Aphrodite placed the ornamental headgear firmly on Adrian’s skull. It felt snug and confining, but he was grateful to have it. Better than nothing.

“I have said the sandals are not as quick as a jet. That does not mean you will not need protection. This will shield you from the elements.”

Freya eyed him with humor and approval. “Not the ideal uniform,” she said. “But it will do. It is courage that counts.”

Adrian tried to picture himself; rumpled shirt, skewed tie, and a hodge-podge of enchanted gear. Perfect costume for a Bruce Campbell movie. Lucky him.

“I feel like a goof.” He took a deep stabilizing breath. “Doesn’t matter.” He set his shoulders and corrected his posture. “Now. Where do we go from here? What happens next?”

Aphrodite looked uncomfortable. Thunder rolled from a distance but the rain slowed to a patter. Freya’s face grew somber, as though she knew something unpleasant.

“I cannot go with you,” Aphrodite said, her gaze dropping to the floor.

“What?” Adrian asked, his resolve fading. “Why not?”

“I understand now that Strife killed Hermes, but not Poetry. Knowing the apple monger and Ares this means they have a more sinister agenda, one that does not involve our game.”

“Like what?”

“Ares is the god of war, Strife sows discord wherever she treads. She poisons the minds of the masses and incites violent civil upheavals.”

Adrian’s gut twisted for the umpteenth time that day. Pieces of the puzzle crammed into place in his brain. The riots, the explosions…As hard as it was for him to believe, Aphrodite’s theories made sense of the chaos in the last two weeks.

“I won. You love Poetry.” Aphrodite didn’t look victorious. “But it means nothing if Ares conquers this world. He will not stop at North America. He will crush your democracies and divide the races. Disband the United Nations and strike indiscriminately at the rest of the planet. He will become too mighty to stop and Earth will suffer in war.”

Weariness etched lines in Aphrodite’s face, leeching away her loveliness. Behind her, Freya also paled.

“I have been a fool.” The love goddess shook her golden curls. “And my son paid with his life.” When she looked upon Adrian, her green eyes shone liquid angst. “It is my fault, and I must make amends.”

Adrian accepted her refusal, but choked on his dread. “Freya?”

The Norse titan sighed. “I like you, New Worlder, but I will not join you.” She blessed him with a smile that would melt ice. “This is your hero’s quest. You will succeed, or die trying.” She shrugged, unconcerned. “If you and your lover die, it is of no consequence.”

Freya tilted her hand like a scale. “However, a victory for Ares would mean a dangerous shift of power for all of our kind and the mortals who feed our strength.” Her lips curled in an imitation of camaraderie. “Aphrodite will need my help.”

Judging from the shocked ‘o’ of Aphrodite’s mouth, she hadn’t foreseen the offer.

“You would help me?”

“I understand vengeance. My brethren and I have as much to lose as yours. Unless you do not wish for my assistance?” Her tone was coy. Only Amir’s contented purr disturbed the quiet. Another staring contest ensued.

“I accept.”

Adrian sucked in oxygen. He really didn’t want to know what would happen if a fight broke out between these two.

“Adrian.” Aphrodite pointed to his shoes, and they buzzed with life. He felt light on his feet, almost airborne. “It is time for you to go.”

Amir streaked forward and bit Adrian’s toe. The mischievous kitten blinked up at him.

“Ow, dammit.” Adrian rubbed his smarting foot. “Stop doing that.”

Amir mewed a song. Adrian straightened and looked askance at Frcya.

“What did he say?”

Freya chuckled. “He says he shall stop biting your tasty feet if you bring his mommy home.”

Adrian sighed. “I’ll do my best, buddy.” The promise felt hollow. He didn’t know what frightened him more, challenging a god alone or war on a global scale. Either way, his chances of survival were slim.

“Enough,” Aphrodite said. “Time to go, Adrian. May the Energy be with you.”

The bedroom window opened to the cleansing after scents of a rain. Adrian crunched into a ball as the animated sandals propelled him through the screen and into the damp dusk.

# # #

“Adrian, Adrian.” The mocking sneer floated to Poetry across the inky black. She still couldn’t see. “What could he do for you that I could not?”

Poetry snuffled and tried to pull herself together. She attempted to wipe her eyes but the weight of shackles on her wrists made the motion arduous. She struggled to her feet to greet her visitor. She recognized that voice.

“Hugh? Where are you? Why did you do this to me?”

The quiet continued for so long Poetry wondered if the taunt was a figment of her imagination. She only heard the laughing trickle of dirty smelling water and the incessant squeaking of hundreds of bats.

She heard a click and a single beam of light pierced the absolute darkness so abruptly Poetry winced at the stab of pain in her temples.

“I’ve done everything for you,” Hugh said. Why was he angry? “You horde my favors.”

Poetry waited for her vision to adjust to the unpleasant surroundings. Not much to see but the shine of rocks and beady red eyes everywhere she looked. “I thought we were friends.”

“Friends?” Hugh’s grim laughter rang hollow through the cave. “Friendship is reciprocity. What have you ever offered me?”

His footfalls grew louder. Rank body odor drifted to Poetry’s twitching nostrils despite the mucus clogging them. Hugh smelled ripe.

Once her eyes adjusted, Poetry stole a glance at her jailer. A sheen of sweat covered Hugh’s face and head like glitter, but there was no beauty in that visage. His pupils and irises darkened with resentment. The whites glowed in the flashlight’s beam.

“Human females are so entitled. Always expecting something for nothing.”

Poetry shook her head. “I don’t understand.”

“I gave you my time, my expertise. I mentored you,” Hugh said, bucking his head like an angry bull. “In your moment of need I gave you shelter.”

“But I thought…” I thought he cared about me.

She rubbed the gooseflesh on her arms, adrenaline sharpening her senses and tensing her muscles.

What was it about her that attracted crazies? Poetry hadn’t missed how Hugh referred to her as a ‘human’, and when she peered into Hugh’s face, she didn’t recognize him. Hugh was gone, leaving some bitter nut-job in his place.

“I loved you,” Hugh said. “I tried to make you want me. I resorted to magicks.”

Poetry struggled against the chains. She really didn’t like the direction of this conversation.

“But you gave the gems away to this…” Hugh’s lips tightened. “Adrian. They were meant to be worn by you, not him.”

“I’m sorry,” she said. How was she supposed to know? But she’d say almost anything to get out of this infested mushroom farm. “I thought you gave them to me to use any way I…”

“Shut up!” He closed the gap between them, shouting her down. “When will you stupid mortals learn that everything comes with a price? Did you think I gifted them to you just so you could throw them at another?”

He gripped her jaw, forcing her to stare into his deep pools of madness. His fingers pinched her flesh and bruised her gums. His breath reeked like old meat. When Hugh spoke again his sinister hissing weakened Poetry’s knees.

“There are other ways I could have you.” Now Poetry understood the real threat behind his words, his true intentions. Still clutching her chin, he set the flashlight on the ground. The gleam resembled moonlight on a lake in Poetry’s watering vision.

He cupped one her breasts, brushing a thumb over the cold-sharpened nipple. Poetry tried to wriggle free but Hugh covered her mouth with his, sliding his pasty tongue past her teeth.

She resisted the kiss, pushing both hands against his naked chest while trying to wrench her face away. If he didn’t let her go, she’d puke.

She slapped him across the cheek as hard as her chains allowed and he shoved her backward.

His brutal retaliation sent her to the ground. Her ears rang from the blow.

“Bitch.” In the shadows, Poetry saw Hugh rubbing at the red handprint she left. Building rage clouded his features.

“You will learn gratitude, little whore,” he said with a growl. “By the time I am finished with you, you’ll beg to suck my cock for a sip of water.”

Poetry said nothing as he retrieved the only illumination and stomped away. She listened to his withdrawal until she knew she was alone. Her head throbbed and her body ached, but the physical pain meant nothing in comparison to her lost hope.

CHAPTER THIRTY-SEVEN

Sarah threw back her head and laughed for the first time in what felt like years. Her face hurt from smiling. She savored the wind drifting in through the car's open windows, letting it scatter her hair.

She'd enjoyed herself immensely with Ranjan. She brushed away strands to gaze at his cuteness as he drove. He'd been sweet enough to invite her to dinner at his parent's house. What a noisy, silly, and heart-warming experience.

"They can be a real handful," he said. "Sorry about my nephews. They're both really friendly and curious. Especially little Hammad."

Sarah remembered how the chubby toddler had crawled into her lap, grinned at her with his brown saucer-eyes wide, and squeezed one of her breasts.

"They're adorable." She recalled their boisterous shouts. "Honestly. Your sister and her family are wonderful."

Ranjan's face split with love and pride, exposing flawless teeth. "Yeah, they're a loud bunch but I'm crazy about them."

"Do you have other brothers and sisters?" she asked. "Or just Nadia?" Even as the question left her lips, Sarah experienced a pang of confusion. She'd asked about Ranjan's siblings. Her face tightened and for a moment she wondered why she cared.

"My older brother, Pulak, lives in Calgary," Ranjan was saying, distracting her from her confusion. "He's an engineer and has two boys as well. Hopefully you'll get to meet him one of these days."

"I'd like that."

Sarah let her misgivings ride and stretched like a cat. It wasn't quite dusk, but the city twinkled with life. The breeze smelled of dust and petunias. The temperature had dropped to a comfortable level. It was a gorgeous summer night and she didn't want it to end.

She licked her lips, tasting curry once again.

"Your mother is a fantastic cook. I can't remember the last time I had Indian food." Sarah pictured the robust woman in the blue sari with a charming smile and thick accent, piling food on her plate and imploring her to eat. Sarah developed an instant bond with her.

"You enjoyed it?"

"Loved it. What was that dip again? With the chillies?"

"Dal Nawabi. With Naan. I swear she makes the best flatbread this side of the world. And her coconut rice…" His obnoxious smacking sounds made Sarah giggle.

"I could get used to that," she said, and let the implication hang. She glanced over to see Ranjan's mouth turn up. A comfortable silence passed. Nothing disturbed it but the hush of vehicles driving by and the drone of rubber on pavement.

"Listen, Sarah," He finally broke the silence. "Do you have anything planned for tonight?"

"I hadn't thought about it," she said, but Sarah had a nagging feeling.

I'm forgetting something.

After a short pause she dismissed the idea. If it was important, it would come to her.

"I live across from the University campus. Would you like to see the house, do some research?" He wiped a hand down his mouth. "I mean, you said you're good at chemistry, right? Maybe you'd like to look into attending?"

He'd mentioned that earlier, and she found herself warming to the subject.

“That sounds like a great plan.”

Ranjan took a ramp off the freeway marked 112 Street. “Great. We’re almost there.”

Sarah stuck her hand out the window to let summer air flow through her splayed fingers. The clanging of the LRT crossing faded as they sped away. Picture-perfect houses with immaculate yards whizzed past, and Sarah daydreamed of a future.

One that involved an education in a green city, a career, and a handsome Indian man.

# # #

“Here we are,” Ranjan said, welcoming Sarah inside with a flourish. “This is home.”

Like many of the properties on the street, this one had been updated with new siding and old-fashioned embellishments such as woodworked arches and restored windows.

“It’s beautiful,” she said, taking in the tasteful décor as she perched on the sofa. Not what she expected from a man. She’d anticipated a sloppier environment, a bachelor pad full of dirty laundry and empty beer cans. “I love what you did with it. Is the hardwood floor original?”

“Yes, Adrian helped me stain it to match the furniture.”

Adrian. His blonde friend. Why did she feel like she had to remember him? Something about him…

Ranjan pointed to the ceiling, where solid wood struts supported textured panels. “And the rafters too.”

“Oh, wow…” Sarah studied the rest of the living room. Tiffany replica lamps graced two corners. She guessed the fixtures to be oak. The brown cushions on the furniture had a luxurious silky texture. "Looks expensive."

"It is," Ranjan said. He strolled to a massive cabinet. It housed an entertainment system, complete with a sixty-inch flat screen TV and a state-of-the-art stereo system. Sarah caught a glimpse of his PS3 and a stack of video games."I really wanted to keep the character of the house, but I didn't want it to be, you know," He smirked. "girly."

Sarah laughed. "Trust me, it's very masculine."

Ranjan pressed a button and Sarah hid a grimace as Black-Eyed-Peas filled the room with their peppy synthesizers and rap lyrics. She hated this trendy happy crap. Irritation tugged at her mouth despite her efforts.

"Thanks." Ranjan headed to the kitchen. "Would you like a drink? A beer or maybe a cooler?"

Sarah followed him to get a peek at the other room. "What kind of coolers?"

"I've got raspberry and green apple."

"Green apple, please." Sarah stared at the polished surfaces, the stainless steel appliances and the glass fronted cupboards displaying neat rows of dishes. "That looks fantastic."

"Thanks." Ranjan handed her the bottle of pale golden liquid. "Adrian did the counters too. He has the same kind in his condo." That name again. Sarah knew it was significant, but why?

She took a sip of her drink, allowing the fizzy sharpness to roll over her tongue. Her lips puckered, but not because of the flavor. Her mind raced with disjointed visions.

She saw a garden of tattoos and explosions. Resentment and animosity welled from within. Familiar but somehow out of place. Where did all this come from? She was having a great time with a super nice guy. What on Earth had come over her?

Sarah fingered the condensation building on the glass vessel. Maybe she shouldn't drink after eating spicy food. She took another tiny sip to be polite, but after shaking off the second burst of anguish, she decided against more. She'd hold it just for show. She didn't want Ran to see her as wasteful or rude.

"Hey, you want to see my office? We can Google the university, get some info about registrations and options."

"Sure," Her shoulders slacked at having something else to dwell on. "Lead the way."

They went back through the living room and up a flight of stairs.

"This is the bathroom," Ranjan said, waving to his right. "To the left is my room. This is my office."

He opened the middle door to a simple work area. The waning sunlight exposed bookshelves full of law textbooks on one side while a glass desk dominated the other. Several photos adorned the walls. Sarah recognized Ranjan's sister, nephews, and parents among them.

He sat down at the tweed-covered chair and switched on the computer. He pulled up a stool for her while the monitor went from blue to a screen saver depicting a view of planet earth from space.

"Have a seat."

She waited beside him while he typed in the University of Alberta's home page. He spoke of the campus, scholarships and tuition, but Sarah found it hard to concentrate.

Ranjan's cologne mixed with the musk of a long day in the sun and his mother's cooking. Her sights wandered to his neck. If she only leaned forward she could lick away the sweat.

The monitor's gleam sparkled in his eyes and hair. Sarah tried not to smile, but the butterflies in her stomach fought her efforts.

He seemed unaware of her scrutiny as he babbled. She had no clue what he said. Didn't care. She watched his lips form the words.

He did a double take at her.

"Sarah, are you even listening?" A blushing grin wormed across his features. He'd caught her leering.

"Hmm? What were you saying again?"

"I said we should get your transcripts as soon as…" Ranjan's sentence petered out. Sarah could stare into those chocolate wells for hours. She wanted to press her lips against his.

What was he thinking right now?

Ranjan closed the gap between them and kissed her. His mouth began a gentle dance, his tongue exploring. Sarah's eyelids fluttered shut as she surrendered.

Her hands laced into his coarse hair. He ran his mouth along her throat and she arched in pleasure. Her hardened nipples brushed his chest, making her whimper.

Ranjan dug his hands into her buttocks. She spread her legs and he dragged her over his lap until his heat bulged against her sex.

He slipped her shirt over her head. She caught a whiff of perfume and the faint odor of blood. It jolted her senses, sparking aggression.

She rushed to devour him. She hungered. She wanted to sink her teeth into him, to claw his back and make him hers.

Ranjan grasped her shoulders, pulling her back and biting her bare nipple. Sarah yelped, struggling. The more she writhed, the harder he clamped down.

Sarah forced herself to calm and he rewarded her with tender suckling. He shifted to its twin, giving it the same treatment. Sarah exhaled in shaky bursts as the air chilled her sensitive tips.

“Sarah.” Ranjan’s husky whisper demanded her attention. “Spend the night with me.” He bumped against her until his erection persuaded her.

“Take me to your bed.”

Ranjan lifted her with him as he left the office. He kicked open the bedroom door, letting it bounce off the wainscoting. He arranged her like a breakable doll on plush duvets the color of sapphires and whipped off her capris.

Sarah imagined she must be lounging on a cloud as she sank into the soft covers. It was heaven to watch Ranjan shed his suit to reveal a taut brown physique and strong cock.

He retrieved a foil square from a dresser drawer. He rolled the sheath over his member, stroking it into place with a throaty growl.

In one stride he’d lunged to the bed and tore at her thong. It bit into her skin before snapping into a damp scrap of cotton. He sniffed it like an animal.

Then he eased her thighs apart and dove into her wetness.

She cried out as her nerves grew to full, tantalizing alert. She lurched, but he wrapped his arms around her legs and held tight, dipping and probing without mercy.

Ranjan took his time, bringing her to the edge of orgasm. He used his fingers, his stubble, everything. Repeatedly. His composure infuriated her. She’d brace for the rush and he would stop teasing, only to begin again when the tension subsided.

“Ran.” She couldn’t endure any more. Her swollen pussy couldn’t wait. “Don’t make me beg.”

He grinned at her, a devilish expression. “You’re not enjoying this?” He knelt down and Sarah squirmed at his warm breath.

Time to take matters into her own hands.

Sarah gathered her strength, stretched forth, and spun Ranjan on his back. She didn't have the patience to torture him in kind. She had desires to fulfill.

She straddled him without hesitation, gasping as she lowered onto his thickness.

"Mmmmm…" She rode him slowly, savoring the glide of each inch. His grunting was music.

She had to come. She was more than ready. A scream built in her throat.

Just as her wailing began, Ranjan sat up, squeezing her nether regions against his sac, grinding her clitoris into his pubic hair.

"Oh please…" Guttural shrieks echoed. Hers, she realized, but she was no longer in control of her senses. Waves of pleasure bordered on pain.

The glimmer remained in his eyes and she was hypnotized, unable to break the link between them. He guided her onto his cock again and again. Aftershocks of ecstasy coaxed more squeals from her lips as she slowed the pace.

"Is that all you got, Sarah? Or do you want more?"

She wasn't sure she could handle more. Her limbs ached, her heart raced, her entire body quivered.

He tossed her, bracing her legs over his shoulders. She moaned when another jarring ripple of bliss erupted with his penetration.

As agonizing as his restraint had been, his insistence proved her undoing. She gathered handfuls of linen, trying to maintain a physical hold on sanity. Faster and faster he dragged her hips into his cock, panting until the slap of flesh against flesh drowned out her howls. He wouldn't cease.

One more orgasm claimed her, scarier than the last with its relentlessness. Above her Ranjan snarled his release.

When the last of their shouts faded, Ranjan collapsed beside her.

"That was fun." Ranjan could barely speak.

"Yeah. We should do it again."

"Definitely." He sounded wicked and playful. "First thing tomorrow."

A moment later, Ranjan's snoring dimmed Sarah's euphoria. Amazing sex like that would have been perfect with a little pillow talk and cuddling.

No matter. Let him sleep. After all, that was exhausting. Poor guy had a right to be tired.

Sarah extended her abused muscles and went limp. She couldn't wait to wake up to this incredible man in the morning.

What should she make him for breakfast? She had no idea what he had in the fridge.

Sarah mustered the energy to get out of bed. She was thirsty anyway.

She tiptoed toward the kitchen, careful not to make a racket. Even so, she knocked her shin on an end table and stifled a curse. She massaged the new bruise and straightened.

If she could just get there without bumping into anything else…

A large hand clamped over her jaw. It stank of corpses.

Don't move, Strife.

She tried to scream, but even though she strained to escape, she understood its futility. Sudden tears sprang to her eyes.

Don't make a sound, Ares said. Or I'll kill your new lover.

CHAPTER THIRTY-EIGHT

Cruel truth flashed before her eyes in a muddy blur. Sarah, the young woman new to Edmonton, never existed. She was Strife, goddess of discord, minion to Ares. Her story was a tale of perpetual viciousness that spanned centuries. The revelation brought disbelieving horror.

I should not have placed my trust in you. Ares' telepathic fury burned. You allowed this mortal to enchant you with honeyed words and promises like a love-struck fool. You consumed the food, did you not?

She had. Ranjan invited her to dinner when she needed more information. What did that have to do with anything?

The curry. The masala and turmeric… Ares spun her around to face him, crushing her arms in a painful grip. The whites of his eyes flared in contrast to his indigo skin, his beauty as terrible as it was confusing.

Do you not see? They are a mystic race. The spices and herbs they eat give Indians the ability to see our kind. It gives them immunity against your spells. And you, stupid girl, partook and rendered yourself impotent. Do you remember now who you are?

Strife licked her lips, tasting a life that didn't belong to her. The coconut rice and succulent chicken no longer lingered. In their place, the flavor of ashes.

She peered into the eyes of her master, her tormentor. She smelled his musk of wine and blood and longed to crawl back to bed and listen to Ranjan's heartbeat.

Strife realized with a pang of loss how much she'd learned to care for him. Not just the incredible sex, but the kindness he'd demonstrated, the way he'd treated her with respect. Never before had a man cherished her as Ranjan did.

A low growl from Ares distracted her. She erased all thoughts of her lover. She was in enough trouble without further aggravating the deity.

What do you want, Master? She straightened despite his bruising handprints. What must I do?

Get dressed. He released her and waved upstairs. Your human gave me an idea. We will go across the street to the Cross Cancer Institute.

Strife obeyed without a backward glance. But what could possibly be at a disease research center that could be of use to him? How would he twist tools used for the good of mankind into machines of war?

She crept to Ranjan's room, wincing inwardly as the door groaned, but he continued to slumber. Strife plucked her rumpled clothing from the floor and dressed. Her thong lay draped over a quaint beaded lamp. Dislodging the tattered remains of her underwear might cause the glass fringe to jingle.

She left it. Let Ranjan have a souvenir of their night of passion. She smiled, but her heart knew regret. She would never have his love. She didn't dare return, even if he survived whatever plot Ares devised.

Strife took a long last look at her human lover. His perfect skin shone in the moonlight, his sweaty locks plastered his brow like seaweed. His mouth tweaked upwards in his sleep and she wondered if he dreamed of her.

So perfect for a mortal. It grieved her to leave him like this.

Strife.

Her master beckoned. She wanted to kiss Ranjan's bronze cheek before departing but the risk might wake him or enrage Ares. She swallowed her sadness and tiptoed away, leaving the door ajar. Squealing hinges might thwart her exit.

Ares waited beside the front door, still bathed in azure radiance. She understood that Ares was invisible, or should have been.

Not that it mattered. The effects of the Indian cuisine made him blaze like a blue star in her vision. Strife wished dal nawabi and biryani affected all his powers, like his ability to intimidate her into committing his foul deeds.

# # #

Adrian felt like Superman.

The shoes took some getting used to. He'd spent ten dizzying minutes somersaulting until he was able to straighten out and fly right.

Fly right. He never thought he'd be attempting that in his lifetime. Jet-packs were a science-fiction fantasy; he couldn't imagine himself even bungee jumping. But he streaked through the sky hundreds of meters up, a comet with a sword pointed in front of him like a stinger. The Human Mosquito.

Adrian developed a deep appreciation for the helmet. He wasn't cold. He smelled the dust and greenery in the air, but his eyes didn't water from the wind. He watched towns roll by like shimmering lakes. Rivers meandered beneath him as ribbons through velvet trees.

The sandals changed altitude and trajectory, causing his stomach to lurch. How long had he been airborne? Hermes's footwear had done all the work, even the navigation, permitting Adrian to enjoy the trip so much he'd lost track of time.

Definitely descending. Face first.

He hadn't seen the mountain range closing in. Now the stone guardians of the foothills loomed. He headed straight for them, deep into the shadows of a valley

Panic set in. His speed decreased, and an abandoned mine shaft lay before him, darker than the coming night.

How was he supposed to fight a god with no light? Adrian pictured himself batting at a flesh piñata. Not funny.

As if commanded, the helmet clicked and a mask dropped over his eyes. Instantly, Adrian had an infrared view of the scenery and tension eased from his shoulders.

He got some bravado back. At least until the sandals tucked him upright before depositing him on the ground. Nausea returned.

He landed on gravel; crunching footfalls and scattering stones echoed throughout the crevice. Somewhere a hawk screeched.

The shoes stopped humming. Adrian listened to the lonely breeze whistling a mindless tune between the rocks. Nothing else disturbed the tomblike grace.

Daylight died, leaving Adrian to stare at the weathered struts bracing the entrance. A set of gnarled rails lay like a rusty tongue. No place he'd ever seen had such a foreboding menace to it. It looked hungry.

A last stab of doubt dug Adrian in the gut. What the hell made him think he could use his Kendo skills against a powerful being ages old? He was just a second year kendokka, a mortal human with some skill with a katana. Well…a shinai anyway. What was he doing here?

Adrian stroked the torque around his neck. The amber warmed at his touch, reminding him of his purpose.

Poetry. He was the only one who could save her now.

With that resolve Adrian moved into kamae. He positioned the sword in a relaxed grip with the tip directed at the throat of an opponent who would soon be all too real.

"Hephaestus, I know you have Poetry." Adrian muttered vulgarities when his nervous voice ricocheted from the jagged crags. Get a grip.

"I'm here for you, Hephaestus." He waited for a signal. No response.

"What's the matter, forge-god? Are you a coward?" Adrian's confidence increased. Maybe this guy wasn't so tough after all. "Come out and fight like a man."

He heard a snarl from inside the cave, shuffling lopsided steps. What would he meet? Something from a Lord of the Rings movie? A troll or an orc? Preferably something slow and stupid and easily dcfeated.

His hopes died when a muscular giant emerged, his eyes gleaming with hostile intelligence. In his meaty fist he held an axe twice the size of Adrian's head.

"You are Adrian?" Hephaestus glared with distain. "The mortal she loves?" He snorted in disgust. "Why she would choose such a puny creature is beyond my comprehension."

Adrian held his stance, dismayed by the jitter of the weapon in his sweaty hands. He squeezed harder on the tsuka to steady it.

"It is of small circumstance," Hephaestus said. "Your time has come, human. You will die."

Hephaestus raised his axe and Adrian prepared to engage.

CHAPTER THIRTY-NINE

Clang! To Adrian's relief, he succeeded in blocking and unbalancing Hephaestus, who growled as he slipped on loose stone. Adrian advanced in kamae, gliding forward to strike at the god's back. Not a kendo move, but he'd take it. He wasn't about to make this easy for the forge-god.

Hephaestus swung upward and the sword glanced off 'kote', his wrists. Adrian stumbled but kept the katana steady. He ducked in time to avoid losing his head as the hatchet trimmed his hair.

Hephaestus sneered as he hobbled sideways. "So. You have some skill with a sword." His gleaming eyes narrowed and his grin dwindled in the infrared. "I've been creating weapons since long before your ancestors understood their purpose."

"But can you use them?" Adrian said. Maybe he could anger him, throw Hephaestus off his game. "I've already drawn first blood."

Adrian glanced at the stream of crimson dribbling to the ground. A cut like that would've taken a normal person's arm off. On Hephaestus it was a scratch.

"Stupid mortal." Hephaestus drew back the axe. "Your kind doesn't appreciate greatness." The weapon came with a rush of air, but Adrian sidestepped it without losing his stance. "You will tire, and I will destroy you."

Adrian pivoted to square off with the god and collided with Hephaestus's fist.

He soared two meters before slamming against the mountain. Stars danced in his dimming vision, despite the helmet's protection and enhanced capabilities. Adrian's ribs seemed to crush his lungs. He gagged and spat bile. The katana slipped from his fingers as he slumped to the ground.

A roar from above caught his attention, and he peered through bleary eyes to see Hephaestus lunge. Adrian scurried out of range on hands and knees.

The impact of metal meeting rock echoed through the valley and pierced Adrian's eardrums. He heaved, trying to catch his breath, but vomited instead. He wiped his sour mouth with a shaking hand.

Why didn't I just bring a gun?

Hephaestus grunted with effort. His blade stayed trapped.

I won't get another chance, Adrian thought. This is it.

Adrian wobbled to his feet and fell, landing with his cheek resting on grit. The scent of moss teased his nostrils. The atmosphere radiated green from the last rays of a sun long gone.

This would be a good place to die. I could just go to sleep and never wake up again. There wasn't a nerve on Adrian's body that didn't shout in agony.

Hephaestus snarled and swore in frustration, still wrestling with the stuck weapon. Dust and pebbles trickled from the jammed crack.

But what would the forge-god do with Poetry?

If Adrian didn't free Poetry she'd be left to fend for herself. In his minds eye he saw her, quaking in fear behind the cash register at Denny's. He couldn't resist her then and he wouldn't let her down now.

Determined, Adrian slithered on his belly. His katana waited just beyond. His fingers tapped the dirt. Closer...

Judging from the scraping and grinding noises, Hephaestus had nearly freed his weapon.

Cold metal graced his fingertips and Adrian inched forward until he could carefully slide the sword alongside his body to grab the leather bound hilt.

He labored to his knees. C'mon feet, don't fail me now.

The dumb cliché worked. The sandals twitched in response, and Adrian found himself vertical. The shoes hummed in expectation. Adrian shook off the dizzy spots in his sights.

Even as Hephaestus tore his axe from the crevice, Adrian smiled. This could work. Hephaestus was clumsy and pissed off, giving Adrian the advantage.

"You don't look good, human," Hephaestus said.

"Neither…do…you," Breathing became difficult for Adrian. The god's face twinkled with greasy sweat. He stank of mold and metal. "And your fighting skills suck."

Hephaestus bellowed and charged. Adrian stayed in kamae, but Hermes' sandals whisked Adrian from harm. The blade breezed past his face and nicked his sword.

Adrian stretched tall and brought his weapon straight up and back, aiming for 'do'. Hephaestus had exposed his right flank.

The blow connected with a sickening thud, churning Adrian's stomach. Blood gushed from his side, but the massive man hardly slowed. Scarlet spray peppered Adrian's shirt as the god backhanded him. The golden footwear dragged him to the precarious edge, but he didn't worry. He trusted the shoes. He wouldn't fall.

Hephaestus glared at him in bewilderment before dropping his gaze to Adrian's feet. Understanding dawned.

"I remember those wretched things. Hermes' magicks cannot save you from me." The snarl transformed into a wicked display of teeth. "Unless you wish to fly away like a coward?"

Adrian's training took over. He wouldn't let Hephaestus bait him. A kendokka must remain calm in the face of an opponent. He relaxed, tension drained from his limbs.

‘Men’ strike.

“You,” His katana plowed into the god’s skull, “talk too much.”

The clatter of Hephaestus’ dropped axe reverberated through the chill evening. Time stopped. Adrian sighed in relief. It was finally over. The blue steel was embedded to Hephaestus’s eyebrows.

Through the helmet’s enhanced mask he looked to his enemy…

The eyes twitched.

Adrian gasped, trying to dislodge the katana from brain and bone. Hephaestus slapped his hands on either edge of the blade. The cliff’s end beckoned. Pebbles tumbled and fell, never to be heard again.

Impossible.

Hephaestus yanked, and the blood-drenched weapon began to slide. His strength drove Adrian into space. His gut lurched as he plummeted, taking the god with him into the evergreen abyss.

The sting of pine-scented branches slapped Adrian. The shoes recoiled, and Adrian hovered upside down still holding the katana, Hephaestus’s fingers gripping the steel. Hermes’s sandals stuttered and lost altitude, unable to support the weight of both him and the gargantuan immortal.

Sweat and weakness loosened Adrian’s grasp. He glanced at his rival; Hephaestus’s eyes clouded with disbelief.

“I’m sorry,” Adrian already regretted killing him, but this had to end. He let go.

Hephaestus howled for an extended moment, before an earth-cracking bang ended his rage. Hopefully forever.

Adrian wiped his face with his tie. No one took a slice to the head and lived, not even in the movies. Adrenaline leaked away and sore muscles throbbed in time with Adrian’s slamming pulse.

The enchanted sandals deposited him back to the cave entrance where Adrian took stock of his situation and options. The mountain dared him to enter.

He had no weapon. What if there were minions? Or a guardian? Adrian wouldn't dismiss anything out of fairy tales to come at him.

Wait. Where was the axe? He navigated his way with infrared vision until he found the greenish heavy metal stage prop lying where Hephaestus dropped it, and hefted it with his remaining energy. Pleased with its light weight, he brandished it experimentally.

Nice. Lucky for him, the ancient smithy knew his stuff. If he didn't know better, he could swear it was made of lightweight foam rubber. One problem solved.

But his contused heart grew weary. He peered inside the never-ending vastness of the tunnel. Not even the helmet's night vision aided him; it offered only residual heat of the waning day.

"Poetry." He felt the stirrings of despair. How would he find her?

New light materialized from…beneath him? No. He looked down. The ground hadn't lit up, but he still saw the flare. Where did it come from? He stroked his neck, even as warmth bathed his skin.

The amber. Of course. The gems were ensorcelled. Aphrodite said thoughts of Poetry would lead him to her.

"Yes." Adrian hissed his excitement. For the first time since arriving at Poetry's apartment Adrian believed he could win.

"Come on, fancy feet," he said with a laugh. "Follow the pretty rocks."

#   #   #

"Why can't you just do this yourself?" Strife kept her volume low, but the corridor's emptiness amplified her words. She shivered despite her stolen lab coat, and wished more than once that she were safe and warm in Ranjan's arms. "No one can see you but me."

She'd discovered that fact when, upon entering the hospital, a nurse attempted to send her away. She strolled right past Ares and addressed Strife directly.

"Visiting hours are over," the nurse had said. "You'll have to come b…" Her words were cut off as her master backtracked and casually snapped her neck. The same fate befell both desk clerks and a doctor. Not one human spotted him under his invisibility.

Why did Ares drag her into this? Why couldn't he leave her in peace?

Because, dear Strife, your performance at the flower merchant's compromised the mission. Not only is Aphrodite alert to your presence, but she will suspect the larger plan. She knows me well.

Ares' lip curled in distaste. And stop speaking like a simpleton. Your speech is lazy and distasteful. You spend too much time among the humans.

Strife wanted to run screaming from her fate. She recognized her foolishness in killing Aphrodite's favorite son. When the goddess discovered her, Strife would plead for a merciful death that wouldn't… would not…come.

You should thank me, Ares said. I shall protect you when she finds us.

Strife almost laughed and sucked in sterile, chemically tainted air that irritated her nose instead. Ares defending her. And Hades would leave the realm of death for women and song. She sneezed and cast Ares a doubtful glare as she wiped her nose.

You cannot challenge her alone.

True. But Strife found it more likely that he only needed her to perform the final tasks while Ares battled the woman he once loved… had he ever been capable of that emotion. She no longer believed it to be possible.

Strife never conceived she would experience it herself. The soothing atmosphere of the Cross Cancer Institute's walls, with its handmade art and sunny paint, mocked her. The guilt for her spinelessness paled in comparison to the bitter flavor of loss.

Ranjan offered her a dream. And she would reward him with death and destruction. She hoped they did not cross another human before they arrived at the cyclotron. She could not bear to watch another soul expire. Not anymore.

Ares' derisive snort startled her. The New World has made you soft, Strife. For centuries you were a nightmare on the battlefield. Now you behave like a mortal. Ares clucked his tongue. Why would you wish to be one of them?

Why indeed? But in a few short days she experienced more than she had in several hundred years. She had explored a vibrant city, tasted but a few of its delights, and viewed Earth from worldly eyes. She had been seduced by a man who wanted her love.

For the first time since leaving Eden she had truly lived. Maybe humankind, with their brief duration on Earth, realized something her kind did not: the pure joy of existing. The thought that she would never learn that lesson grieved her.

"Are we there yet?" Although Ares could hear her thoughts, she loathed sharing them. Speaking aloud gave her the illusion that perhaps the sound of her morose voice could hide them. False optimism, but a small comfort.

Almost. Ares grinned. Never a good sign. Mayhem went hand-in-hand with Ares' good humor. The door to the lab is here. He gestured to the left.

The jiggle of a doorknob interrupted the drone of Strife's footfalls. A dark-skinned man wearing a white jacket matching hers poked his head out from the doorway Ares had pointed out. His pocket tagged him as Dr. Mehra. She thought she had been quiet enough to avoid arousing awareness.

"Hello?" In that instant he reminded Strife of how Ranjan might mature twenty years from now, with a slight paunch and double chin. Bifocals perched on a generous nose. She smiled.

"No one else is supposed to be in this area," he said, sliding his glasses up. "Are you lost?"

"Yes. I, uh…" Strife lost his attention.

He stared at Ares with his mouth agape.

"My God." His hoarse whisper filled the vacant hall. Incredulity and wonder transformed his face from tired doctor to fascinated child. The scent of turmeric and curry wafted from his skin.

Ares eyed him with malice. "Guess again."

CHAPTER FORTY

"Poetry."

She raised her aching head at the call of her name. She must be hearing things, that sounded like Adrian.

Demonic eyes peered through the pitch. She gauged the approaching monster at three meters tall. Or maybe it flew. She heard no footsteps.

Maybe Hugh decided not to keep her after all. Maybe he'd sent some hell-spawned minion to finish her off. The idea almost made her laugh. Now she'd started thinking crazy.

She no longer cared. Her bloodied hands were cramped from tapping rocks into unyielding links for hours.

Death would be preferable to rotting in a dank cave, wasting away from hunger and thirst. Or worse, submitting to Hugh's warped idea of worship. Whatever that was. She'd rather go out kicking and screaming than find out.

She lobbed a stone at the creature, and hit a random stalactite. She heard it crumble several meters away.

"Poetry?"

She mustered the fortitude to stand. This thing wasn't going to take her quietly. Her chains rasped along the ground, stirring up dust. She sneezed, spitting mucus and dirt.

"Poetry, say something. Is that you?"

The orbs brightened, burning her light-deprived eyes.

Must be the mother of all flying vermin. Even through her dizziness, she watched the lights hover and land. Subtle flapping preceded the steps she'd expected earlier.

Poetry swallowed painfully. She presented her shaking fists, weaving like a drunken boxer. She had no fear. She just wanted to get this over with.

"Poetry, it's me. Adrian."

It advanced, and the surrounding radiance became tolerable as her sight adjusted.

Her brow twitched. Since when do mythological beasts wear ties? With gold sandals, helmet and a mask? Wielding a battleaxe.

Worst. Super-villain costume. Ever.

A cough interrupted her thoughts and the faceplate rose to expose human features.

"Adrian?" She didn't recognize the pathetic croak from her mouth, but she'd know that intense gaze anywhere. Her eyes stung with unshed tears. "Is it really you?"

His grin empowered her to lift her arms. Adrian tossed the weapon aside and leapt into her clutches, squeezing her until she couldn't breathe.

He's here. He's right here holding me. He came for me.

"You found me." Every word gnawed at her throat. "How did you ever find me?"

Adrian held her at arms length and cupped her chin. His eyes sparkled with happiness and relief. She fought the urge to pinch herself, despite the damp softness of his shirt beneath her palms. Could this be real?

"Divine intervention," he said, and folded her into his embrace once more. "Lucky me."

In the intimate silence Poetry bathed in Adrian's love, and she understood it was love. She went weak with the tenderness of his kiss, the warmth of his affection. She buried her nose in his fresh musk.

All the terror of her ordeal faded. Even her shackles felt feather light. But not for long.

"Adrian?" She pulled away and intertwined her fingers with his. "Can you get me out of here?"

He glanced to her wrists as if noticing her chains for the first time. "Oh. Yeah." Adrian let go and retrieved the blade. "The best way to break bindings from a forge-god is with a forge-god's weapon."

She gave him plenty of room, shielding her face from sparks as Adrian cleaved into steel.

"Watch the hands," she said. "I kind of need those."

She shrugged her ears into her collarbone, flinching with every ringing blow until he freed both arms.

Adrian gestured with the remains of the tool. "We can probably remove those cuffs when we get home." He inspected the ruined metal chunks clinging to the handle. They resembled shards of broken glass. He cast them aside.

Poetry had so many questions. "What do you mean 'forge-god'? Where is Hugh?" She took in Adrian's blood drenched get-up, with gold on his head and feet. "What the hell are you wearing?"

"Where do I begin?" He left her field of vision, but she heard stones banging together as he rummaged. "Today has been interesting. Your ex trashed my Bentley. I bought you a bouquet of roses, but someone killed Hermes." His shuffling ceased with the yip of a zipper. "I met a goddess who says you and I are part of some game she has going with another god and-Hey, look what I found."

Adrian returned, up to his elbows in a duffle.

"Is that water?" Poetry asked. She slid her sandpaper tongue over the dry cracks and flakes on her lips. To think, sustenance sat only meters away all this time. Hugh was a bastard.

Adrian opened the bottle and she snatched it from his fingers. Cool rivers bathed her cheeks. She gulped greedily, drenching her parched gullet. Clarity returned with hydration.

Kevin wrecked Adrian's car. Jerk. Poetry felt terrible, as if she brought it upon Adrian herself. And who was Hermes?

"I don't understand," she said, wiping away spills with the remnants of her dress. "You've been talking to gods? About us?" Had she heard correctly? Or was her mind playing tricks on her?

He handed her a Granny Smith apple, and she rolled her eyes in pleasure with the first bite. Normally she didn't care for its sharpness, but right now it tasted like the crisp outdoors she'd thought she'd never see again.

"Aphrodite, yeah. And Freya. Amir told us Hephaestus took you, and Aphrodite said…"

"Amir told you Hugh is a god named Hephaestus?"

"Actually, he told Freya. She speaks cat."

"Really…" A deity Dr. Dolittle. Why not?

"Weird, huh?"

"Let me guess," Poetry chewed slowly, trying to process Adrian's bizarre tale. "It's going to get weirder, isn't it?"

Trepidation spread across Adrian's face. "Ares has been causing the riots and bombings. Aphrodite and Freya are going to confront him."

He wasn't joking. Had Adrian lost his sanity while she'd been gone? Maybe this was just an elaborate hallucination her overwrought brain dreamed up, complete with sensory details and legends from ancient Greece and Scandinavia.

"I had no idea how to find you. But I did, thanks to this necklace." He lifted it with a thumb and the glimmer played along cave walls. "I only had to think of you." Adrian leaned forward and planted a gentle kiss that stung her abused mouth.

That didn't feel like her imagination.

Adrian made a shoulder check before taking her hand. "You ready to leave?"

Poetry took her first uncertain steps from her prison. Pebbles, cold and pointy, poked the soles of her bare feet. Small price to pay for liberty. She was weak but determined to walk.

"Let me." Adrian placed her arm over his back, trying to carry her.

"No," she said, taking his hand. "I need to leave on my own." Then she could believe this rescue for herself. Only then would this be reality.

After about fifteen minutes of hesitant inching, a worrisome thought occurred to her. "Where is Hugh? I mean, Hephaestus? Did you…" She didn't want to ask, but the blood on Adrian's shirt begged the question. "Did you kill him?"

Poetry sensed weary tension in Adrian's taut muscles.

"God, I hope so."

No sooner had the words left his lips, than they heard an unearthly roar. Startled bats swooped and dove over their heads.

Poetry peered through the gloom to see the starry sky.

And the hulking shadow that barred their exit.

"Shit." Adrian's grip grew clammy. "Asshole won't stay dead."

The beast she'd once called friend stomped toward them, his unbalanced tread thudding throughout the cavern. He panted like a vicious dog.

"What do I do?" Poetry stole a glance at Adrian. He'd gone white and shook as though he would come apart. Sweat spotted his nose and chin.

"I already killed him once." His resignation and hopelessness frightened her more than Hephaestus' approach.

She smelled fresh mountain air, so close. They'd almost made it. But weaponless and exhausted, they were easy pickings.

Poetry resented it. To just die like sitting ducks after everything she'd endured, after Adrian's victory in the name of love. It wasn't fair.

The god's gore-encrusted face materialized like a butchered jack o' lantern.

Gathering her courage, Poetry pried her fingers from Adrian's. She wanted payback before checking out. She surged ahead to deliver a final act of defiance.

A satisfying thud filled her ears as her foot connected with Hephaestus' testicles. It halted him in mid-charge, and he hit the ground with a moan. Apparently immortals had vulnerabilities too.

"Ohh…" Adrian's hands shielded his groin. She gawped in amazement. She didn't think that would work.

"That's for kidnapping me, you prick."

Hephaestus curled into a fetal position. Poetry prepared to boot his unprotected back, but Adrian dragged her toward freedom. "He's down. We gotta go. Now."

He hoisted her legs around his hips. She buried her head in his back and held tight.

With a flurry of wing beats they swam to meet the clouds.

CHAPTER FORTY-ONE

"Was that necessary?" Strife choked down tears and regurgitated turmeric, thinking of the poor man who had the misfortune of having his head roasted at Ares' touch. She could still smell the acrid odor of charred flesh and hair.

He could see me.

As if that alone justified his actions. But that was Ares; eye contact with the almighty war-god meant death.

Are you just going to stand there sniveling? He admired a contraption of metal, bolts, and wires enclosed in a plexiglass room. Or must I do everything myself?

Strife would prefer the latter, but it was a rhetorical question. Disobedience was not an option.

"What is your bidding, Master?"

Flip the switch. He pointed to the control panel on the wall. It housed a large red handle, presumably for powering the isotope processing apparatus.

Ares sounded so casual. Never mind that thousands of humans would die by those words. Strife remembered when his impudent remarks would cause her to squirm with glee. She once loved mayhem. Now it tortured her heart.

Strife shuffled to the other side of the sterile room and yanked the lever down. The lights flickered. No going back now. This was her lot in life. Her existence.

The mechanical cylinder, the cyclotron, spun into action. The hum rapidly built to a crescendo. It exuded tremendous energy for such a small engine. No wonder they kept it enclosed.

“I fail to understand how this will accomplish your objective,” she said, sauntering her way to the computer in a very sloth-like manner. “Despite its power, it is rather puny.”

Ares smiled, a sight that made her nerves tingle with fear.

Have you heard the term ‘dirty bomb’ Strife? This is merely another instrument of jihad.

“But why here? Extremists do not war against Canada. It is the Americans they hate.”

It is time they united with their allies in war. This city is ripe with ethnicity. As we speak, tourists from all over the world are visiting Earth’s largest retail establishment, complete with amusement park and waterslides. Ares winked. Strife’s insides rolled with awful realization. This may as well have been her idea.

Thank you for the inspiration, even though your water-tampering potions are wearing off. Tonight we attack on a larger scale. This act of aggression will eclipse 9/11. Watch and learn.

He raised his arms and lightning crackled from his hands. The jagged strings of fire seeped into the plexiglass, leaving melted pock marks as they engulfed the machine inside.

Strife did not think it possible, but the cylinder rolled even faster and whined at a higher pitch that pained her ears. The noise and vibration rattled her teeth. Metal went from silver to black to sunset orange. The heat warmed her skin like an impending sunburn.

Strife, monitor the current velocity. Ares dropped his stance and peered warily around the room. We have guests.

She experienced it as well, the influx of new power.

It was the tell-tale sign, an inside hurricane, stealing the breath from her lungs. Papers flew in all directions; staplers, pens, and various office supplies clattered and tumbled to the floor.

Aphrodite materialized across from Ares. Her magnificence bathed the lab in the color of sunrise.

She was not alone. An abnormally tall woman joined her. She radiated moonlight, creating an eerie silver contrast. She wore winter rabbit pelts to match her braids and carried a heavy-looking sword.

Strife had never met a Norse deity before, but she had no doubts about her identity. That intense, passionate potency could only belong to the lust and fertility goddess, Freya.

How did that bitch recruit such a valuable ally?

"I have been expecting you, my love." Ares oily grin mocked Aphrodite.

Her expression held equal condescension. "Your crude theatrics are difficult to ignore."

"You are too late. There is nothing you and your comrade can do to stop me."

Strife tore her gaze from the trio to the bellowing cylinder. It revolved faster than her eyes could follow. Neon purple arcs ebbed and flowed over its surface like animated lace. Ozone saturated her nostrils.

"Perhaps not," Freya said. "But we will prevent you from gaining superiority from this disaster."

Aphrodite's sorrowful eyes glimmered like faceted jewels in the kaleidoscopic light show. "And I will avenge the death of our son."

Strife noted the distinction. Ares had never been much of a father, and Aphrodite acknowledged him only for spite.

Her anger and hatred rippled like a sonic boom. Strife prayed to the Energy that Ares would destroy his nemesis before Aphrodite turned wrath in her direction.

"He was a boy-loving milksop," Ares' mouth curled in distain. "reared to inadequacy by a slut."

Aphrodite's screech rivaled the racket of the engine as she launched a brilliant bolt of pure rage at Ares. Anticipating it, he blocked with a shield of crimson electricity.

Freya bellowed a war-cry and pointed her weapon at Ares. A blue beam mingled with Aphrodite's to create a twisted sapphire and gold chain of the women's essence.

Strife squinted and covered her ears. The atmosphere grew unbearably bright and hot. Thunder roared. The Dell already displayed dangerous levels of radiation.

Three deities fought for control before her in a blaze of prime colors, beautiful and terrifying.

Alarms whined as the sprinkler system rained rust and dirty water upon them. She snatched her hands from the sparking computer.

She barely endured the sights and sounds, but at last Strife understood her role in the chaos. Nothing could prevent the annihilation. Ares did not need her to insure its success.

As she watched, Ares' shield wavered. If she remained idle, he might be defeated.

Leaving her to Aphrodite's relentless vengeance.

Although a lesser god and Ares' underling, Strife was not without resources. Rarely had she used her meager stores of power. She survived on her talents and cunning alone.

But with her master in danger she needed to tap into those strengths. She spared another glance at Aphrodite, with her flawless face contorted with insanity. She would rather serve a monster like Ares than deal with her.

Now was the time. All but forgotten in the heat of battle, no one noticed as she outstretched her hand, willing a strand of ozone through the plexiglass. She concentrated, and let the bolt fly.

Missed.

Freya dropped to the floor, unconscious. Not Strife's intended target, but it had the desired effect. Aphrodite faltered. Her brilliant light wobbled and waned, but the deity's will strengthened. Her determination was palpable.

Strife sat struck with indecision. Her first strike lacked accuracy. What if her next attempt made the situation worse? Her fingernails dug crescents into her palms.

"Sarah?"

Strife whirled at the sound of her Earth name. Ranjan slumped in the doorway.

"Ranjan…" Strife recognized sorrow in her own voice. She could not bear the terror etched on his sweet face. "What are you doing here?"

"I woke up, and you were gone." His disheveled hair plastered his head. Sweat and water weighted his shirt and hugged it to his body.

The crackle and buzz of battle seemed to fade like television static. Ares and his harpy could go to Tartarus for all she cared.

"I knew you were special, Sarah," Ranjan said. His expression of astonishment morphed to one of affection. "Like a typhoon at sunrise. And now I understand why. You truly are a goddess." He smiled, and Strife saw herself in his mind's eye the day they met. He viewed her not as a woman to bed, or a monster, but a delicate flower. She fought hard not to cry.

"You left me alone in my bed, but I could still feel you. You left a perfumed trail."

Her fragrance spell. Damn it. But if her magicks had no effect on him…

"How did you find me?

“I followed my heart.” He ventured toward her in the sizzling downpour. “This isn’t you, Sarah. The woman I know wouldn’t jeopardize lives. This,” he waved at the havoc behind her as though it were a distasteful scene in a movie, “is beneath you. You are an independent woman, a chemist. Not a servant of evil.”

“This is what I am,” Strife said. Tears evaporated from her face. “Sarah does not exist.”

“She does,” Ranjan said. “She is a part of your personality. I’ve fallen hard and I want to love all of you.”

Strife bit down nausea and laughter, but not because of Ranjan’s desperation. She could not believe that, in all her hundreds of years, she had finally found the perfect man; one so generous with his heart. He understood her flaws and still wanted her.

And it was too late. She would never find happiness. The Energy had a disturbing sense of humor. It must delight in her comeuppance.

The machine’s insistent thump rose to a crescendo. She risked a glance through the humid fog. Ares appeared to gain momentum. Aphrodite used both hands to hold off his scarlet assault. Sparks bounced and died from her palms.

The cyclotron glowed volcanic.

“Ranjan, you must go.” Strife scurried to grasp his shoulders. She tried to nudge him into the hall. “Get in your car and drive as far and as fast as you can.”

He shook Strife off and folded her into his arms. His grip crushed her, his thoughts were frantic. “Not without you. I don’t know what you’ve done, but I don’t want you to die.”

She wrenched herself free and smacked her forehead in frustration. “Do not be a fool.” She gestured at the power struggle and roaring mechanics. “You see what is happening here? You will be killed.”

“I know what you are,” Ranjan said, tugging her hand. “But I still want to be with you.” He pleaded with his irresistible brown eyes. “I’m a lawyer. I can find a way out of this for you. All you have to do is run away with me.”

Stupid human. These were forces he could never comprehend. If he did not leave, he would be vaporized with everyone else unless…

Strife stared into that exotic gaze. She longed for the life ‘Sarah’ had set in motion. No more spells or drugs; she could fill her days with school or career, spend her nights with a real family. One of her own.

It would require all of her godly resources to spirit them away, but it did not matter. She would forsake them for mortality. She would rather live as a human than reclaim her past.

Strife stood on her toes to kiss him. His mouth still tasted of her lust.

“Close your eyes and hold tight,” she said, squeezing his fingers. “We are leaving.”

CHAPTER FORTY-TWO

A spine-jangling screech ruined Strife's focus. She spun in time to see Aphrodite's limp body slam into the far wall and slide to the floor. Blood and skin painted the drywall.

Her chest and face were charred meat scraps, her hands black talons. Strife gaped in astonishment as Aphrodite convulsed and moaned. Ranjan retched.

Throughout her entire existence on Earth Strife hated Aphrodite. The love-goddess' death throes should have pleased her immensely, but compassion struck Strife like a hammer to the chest.

The man that Aphrodite had loved did this. He left her broken, hideous, and straining to breath.

Destroyed.

I am no better. I killed her child in his name. I am just as guilty. A new sentiment pervaded Strife's heart. This must be shame.

She wanted to go to Aphrodite, comfort her. But someone else's sense of urgency prevented her.

"Uh…Sarah?"

Strife peered through grief at Ranjan, whose trembling hand motioned to Ares.

All thoughts of mourning evaporated as she beheld that terrifying visage.

Ares seethed through clenched teeth, his ruby eyes beamed like a demon's. The ammonia scent of urine, hers or Ranjan's, she could not be certain, drifted past her nose.

“There will be no escape, Strife,” Ares said. She barely heard him over the pandemonium, but she understood the malice in those words. “You belong to me.”

He raised a handful of raw current, a compressed ball of hate, pink as watered blood. It writhed like neon snakes in a mating frenzy, hissing and spitting in the sprinklers. At once Strife knew his thoughts.

No! Not him. Strife beseeched with her eyes, forgetting to correct her speech and conceal her thoughts, but Ares took no notice. He directed his anger at Ranjan. I’ll do anything. Please, Master, don’t kill him.

Catching movement from the corner of her eye, Strife peered through heat waves and steam. Aphrodite? No. Freya had regained consciousness. If Ares knew, he demonstrated no concern.

What should she do? Think.

Freya hobbled to her feet, zeroing in on Ares’ flank with her sword raised. Strife’s own energy swelled within. Did she have a moment to steal Ranjan?

Ares drew back to throw the sphere of death. Strife lacked options.

She could not bear the outcome. Her lover would be incinerated. She would be Ares’ unwilling minion once more, doomed to enact atrocities and suffer his deviant sexual whims. She would be left to fantasize and lament for the love that slipped through her fingers for the rest of her endless immortality.

She couldn’t allow that.

Her master launched the globe, and Strife stepped into its path.

Her nerves blistered. Her screams ceased as her larynx burned. Strife’s eardrums and eyeballs burst. The odor of cooked flesh assaulted her nostrils, briefly, as the last of her faculties withered. Yet it still hurt to hit the floor.

Ranjan's life force pulsed several meters away. She prayed to the Energy that he'd flown clear.

She felt a sting of shock from Ares. What happened? Without tactile sensations Strife relied on telepathy, but the emotions were vague and brief. He'd been…she couldn't tell. Stabbed? His presence dissolved before she learned the answer.

Did Freya best him? She strained for a sign. Did she manage to catch Ares by surprise and kill him?

I am afraid not, Strife. Freya's voice came to her mind. Strife no longer heard the cacophony of alarms or the droning thud of the overheated cyclotron. Nothing but Freya's words broke the profound silence. He is a coward. Only the Energy knows where he went.

Strife gnashed her shattered teeth. Typical of him to leave her to die in agony while he skulks away to live another day. But she didn't have the luxury of wallowing in bitterness.

Where is Ranjan? Strife asked.

He is shaken, bones broken but he lives.

Had she any lips, Strife would have smiled. Ranjan, injured but whole. She wished to mend him, but had no power to spare.

You must take him with you. He is an innocent.

Freya didn't reply, but Strife felt her conflicting emotions. She weighed Strife's final request with her instincts for secrecy. Strife began to despair that the goddess would deny her. Ranjan had seen too much.

Take the human, Freya. Aphrodite said.

You live? Strife shared Freya's amazement. She also believed the deity to be more or less deceased, her soul not more than a blink in Strife's conscience.

Help me stand. She pictured Freya peeling Aphrodite's seeping carcass from the wall. Not a pleasant visual.

Bring me to the cyclotron, then remove the mortal.

Strife heard her Earth name in Ranjan's panicked thoughts. He'd discovered her. She longed to hear him call to her, to see his noble brown face. Perhaps it was just as well. She didn't need to witness his torment as he gazed upon her ruin, or hear his sobs of disbelief.

But just once more she longed to feel his tender caress, one more sniff of his cologne, one last kiss to take her to an unknown fate the Energy reserved for fallen angels. Perhaps her creator would have mercy.

She did not fear her next incarnation. Strife would never know a crueler Hell than she experienced now. To truly understand everything she would leave behind, with nothing but regret and memories.

Was the Earth quaking? So hard to discern in this empty nothingness. The device must be ready to detonate.

Ranjan. She could think of nothing else but him. Freya, you must save Ranjan.

I will prevent the discharge, Aphrodite said to her thoughts. Do as she asks and withdraw with her man.

If Ranjan's startled bafflement were any indication, Freya wasted no time. Strife hesitated to be hopeful that Freya decided to respect her wishes.

Ares will be brought to justice, I promise. Strife found comfort in Freya's oath. Your sacrifices will not be in vain.

Their departure brought emptiness. Strife would never know Ranjan's love again. Disturbing as it was, she accepted it. She'd guaranteed his survival.

She wanted to help thwart Ares, but Strife was spent. She must trust that Aphrodite would avenge her losses.

Aphrodite. Could her nemesis hear her? Would she heed her words? May the Energy forgive me for everything I have done. I deserve my fate. It is an honor to die beside you.

Strife took a shallow, tortuous breath and surrendered to her grave.

# # #

Aphrodite wobbled blindly toward the intense heat. Stopping Ares' war machine would be the last thing she would ever do, but she must persevere long enough to complete the task.

Every exposed nerve throbbed miserably, causing her pain the likes she had never endured before. Only single-minded purpose kept her from collapse.

Tears and fluids dripped from her aching eye sockets, stinging her damaged tissues. The man-made rain offered relief to her burns. She considered herself fortunate; at least she would have revenge. Strife had no such pleasure.

Aphrodite heard her pleas for absolution before she expired, something Aphrodite had not expected. Or wanted. It was of little consequence now. The Energy knew what kind of restitution Strife must make, whatever became of dead gods.

Aphrodite would find out soon enough, but not before she terminated this abomination.

Agony gave way to numb indifference. She had become deaf to the warning system, but still felt the thrum of the cyclotron. She found it mostly by instinct. Courage was all she had left.

She fumbled for it, using the last of her might to rip it from the melted fasteners. It keened, a high-pitched wail like a swarm of angry bees.

Aphrodite dropped to her knees, cradling it, shielding Ares' mutated child from the world as it thrashed against her battered torso.

She prepared to absorb the weapon. Her final thoughts were of Hermes, gone forever. As Ares' instrument of chaos burst, Aphrodite remembered the love of her son, how all her hopes and dreams came to fruition because of him.

Aphrodite endured the dissolution of her body with bravery and pride. She had defeated Ares, once and for all. She saw herself as gold sparks in the night sky over the Institute as her essence faded into the ether.

CHAPTER FORTY-THREE

Adrian unlocked the door to his condo and Poetry let her nerves unwind. A healthy stretch caused several joints to crackle in her arms and shoulders. Every bone in her body ached from endless hours in the damp cave, not to mention the white-knuckled flight home. The shackles still chafed, but at least she wasn't burdened with chains anymore. Though no longer dehydrated, her stomach roared protest.

Adrian stroked her hair before dialing his voicemail. Subtle beeps chimed in the empty hall.

"Inbox is full," he said. "Most of the messages are from Gary and Jenny. I'd better call them. They're worried about you."

"Really? That doesn't sound like Jenny." Well, she could be protective… sometimes.

Adrian smirked, but didn't look up. He pried the helmet from his sweaty head and trudged inside. Poetry smiled at the way his damp hair stood up in tufts.

"Jenny's the one who told me you were missing. She called me in a panic because you hadn't shown up for work. I hate to tell you this, but I found two dead bodies when I got to your place."

"Dead bodies?" She groped for a seat before her knees gave way. "Who are they? Why didn't you tell me?"

The journey home had been quiet. Even the streets of Edmonton were serene: no fires, screams, or explosions. Things must have settled down. Poetry hadn't had the energy to talk, and she'd used her adrenaline to hold on for dear life. She'd assumed Adrian needed to focus on controlling the shoes; she didn't dare disturb him.

But now she wanted answers.

Adrian placed the headgear on the coffee table before crumpling next to her. "Shoes off," he said, and frowned when they remained on his feet. "Shoes, we're done now. Off."

Normally Poetry would question the wisdom of commanding footwear. But having flown with them, the lack of response seemed odd to her too.

Adrian groaned, leaning forward to untie them. Poetry winced in sympathy at the painful grunts he emitted while removing the now inanimate sandals. They seemed ordinary, dangling from his fists like plain leather soles and straps.

But depleted magicks were not her concern.

"We'll call Gary and Jenny," she said, "after you tell me what happened."

"That's just it. I don't know what happened." He shut his eyes and rubbed his temples. Poetry felt bad for him, he must be wiped out. "I fell asleep, and when I woke, Aphrodite popped through my TV and beamed me to your suite like in an episode of Star Trek."

He peered straight into her eyes and Poetry didn't see any hints of untruths. "When we got there, Kevin and my client were dead."

She should have experienced some sort of sadness for her ex, but couldn't muster any.

Good, she thought. He deserved it. Now she could stop checking over her shoulder and everything would go back to…Wait a minute…

"You mean Frank Fleisher? What was he doing there?"

Adrian shrugged. "Who knows? He was a racist and he didn't like… anybody." His expression turned severe. "I think you dodged a bullet. Literally." A shiver rolled over Poetry's skin.

The phone chirped. "Jenny again. I'd better get this, now that I can actually give her some good news."

"You do that." Poetry extracted herself from the sofa. Her arms had little strength left, but she'd muster some if it meant getting food in her belly and not dealing with Jenny. "I'm starving. Got breakfast fixings?"

"Lots. Bacon would be great, if you don't mind." Adrian pushed a button and placed the phone to his ear. "Hi, Jen."

Poetry glanced back to see Adrian yank the phone to a safe distance as Jenny's squirrel-like scolding rattled through the receiver.

"Good morning to you too, Jenny."

Poetry buried her head in the refrigerator before he volunteered her to take the call.

More angry chittering from the other line.

"I found her. She's alright."

Poetry strained to listen over the banging of pots and pans as she raided the cupboard.

"It's a long story. We're both going to need some time to rest and process everything…." A long pause. "No, Poetry's fine." A short interlude. "No, that isn't necess… Jenny? You're breaking up…"

Poetry heard the disconnect and Adrian's weary muttering about yappy people.

He joined her in the kitchen and headed for the coffee maker.

"That was quick. You handled that like a pro."

"You think that got rid of her?"

"Absolutely. If there's anything Jenny hates, it's being cut off mid-rant." Poetry mustered a grin. "Enjoy the silent treatment."

The Melita burbled and the savory scent of cured pork drifted. Poetry switched the burner to low and added pepper and seasoned salt to a bowl of beaten eggs.

Adrian massaged her back and arms before digging around for plates. It felt good, the whole domestic scene. They worked quietly and efficiently, like it was a routine they'd enjoyed countless times. There was only one thing missing.

"Where is Amir?"

"Freya promised to take care of him," Adrian said. "Now that I think of it…" He left the dishes on the counter and grasped the torque he still wore.

With closed eyes and a muttered request Adrian resembled a praying monk.

What was he doing?

Within a minute, Poetry heard a hiss and oxygen rushed from her lungs. Her hair danced like grass in a gale force. The strange phenomenon ended with a pop and the smell of broken halogen light bulbs filled the air. Adrian hurried to the living room. Curious, Poetry followed.

And let her mouth drop as she craned her neck. A gorgeous woman dressed in animal skins waited.

"I am pleased to see you survived, human," she said. Strange way to say hello. "And you brought your lover home alive as well." She spared Poetry a nod.

Her snowy hair shone like moonlight. Her lightning eyes pierced the murk of the coming dawn.

Poetry shut her mouth and swallowed her disbelief. Freya, I presume?

In one arm she held a weary-looking Ranjan. In her other hand, a fluffy black cat.

Poetry forgot her awe. "Amir!"

At the sound of his name, the kitten leapt from his perch and raced to Poetry's feet. She scooped him up for cuddles.

"Amir, baby, I missed you so much." His rumbling purr and plush fur tickled her chin. She didn't realize until now just how much she loved him. How much she loved Amir and Adrian.

"Ranjan?" Adrian's concern grabbed her attention. "Freya, what's he doing with you?"

Poetry glanced up to observe the tenderness in which the ivory deity settled Adrian's friend to the couch.

"His presence at the battle was unexpected. I fear he has witnessed events no mortal should." She parted the hair from Ranjan's forehead. The gentle gesture seemed uncharacteristic for the severity of her face.

"Back up a bit," Adrian parked on the lacquered table across from Ranjan, and looked him over. "What battle? What happened to Ran?"

"Aphrodite confronted Ares and died in the struggle." Freya observed Ranjan, affection and amazement evident in her gaze. "Strife made the same sacrifice for this man."

Ranjan peered up from his lap, but his expression remained empty. "Sarah's dead."

Poetry quit petting Amir. "Oh my God, I'm so sorry."

Adrian ran his hand down his jaw. "Jesus, Ran." He gripped Ranjan's shoulder and squeezed. "Me too."

"I brought him to Asgard," Freya said. "We healed his burns and bones, but only time will soothe his heart."

A hush fell. The sounds and smells of sizzling bacon and fresh percolating coffee seemed inappropriate for the somber mood.

Freya waved her hand over Ranjan's head. He collapsed like a toppled tree and began snoring.

"He needs rest. It has been a long night." Freya said, all softness denied. "You must continue in secrecy. Never speak of your association with our kind or the things you have seen."

Adrian twisted to face Freya. “That’s going to be tough. There are two dead bodies at Poetry’s place. Not to mention her disappearance. How do we explain that?”

Good point.

“There will be no evidence. Hephaestus’ forge is charred rubble.” Freya snapped her fingers, and a blue flame danced on her palm. “Arson. Frank Fleisher is the perpetrator.

She peered sideways at Poetry. “He did not appreciate his lawyer consorting with you. You are not Caucasian.”

Poetry’s face warmed with anger. She’d felt guilty for his death. Not so much now.

Freya closed her hand to douse the fire. “Kevin Ferris had the unfortunate luck to be there, vandalizing. No one shall mourn him.”

“Convenient,” Adrian said. “But it’s not that simple. We could still be suspects. We have no alibi.”

He’s such a lawyer. But in this case, Poetry was grateful.

“You spent the entire evening at a bar called McNasty’s,” Freya said. An unlikely grin warped her pale lips. “A red-haired biker who calls himself ‘Thor’ is willing to testify to your bickering and groping each other for hours. He remembers you well. Your constant racket disturbed his game of pool. He wished you would find accommodations.”

“Whatever.” Poetry rolled her eyes. “It’s a cliché but it works.”

“Fine,” Adrian said, throwing his hands up with a sigh and a sidelong glance. “I’ve heard dumber excuses. I’d better get Ran a blanket.”

When he left, Freya turned to Poetry and grasped hold of her cuffs. The manacles dissolved into dust. The raw skin beneath the goddess’s fingers healed.

Freya released her and Poetry placed Amir on a cushion to inspect her clean wrists. No scarring. “Thanks!”

The titan tilted her head. "You must tend to your stove, lest your meal burn."

"Oh, right. But wait…Hugh." Poetry had almost forgotten him. But before she could voice her fears, the goddess held up her hand.

"I will take good care of him." Something in the way Freya licked her lips, the way she stroked her breasts suggested she'd make Hephaestus forget all about them. "He won't bother you anymore."

Poetry nodded her gratitude and hurried to the oven. She grumbled under her breath as she flipped the rigid contents in the pan with a spatula.

Hope everyone likes their bacon crispy. Poetry snagged the mixing bowl on her way back, but the goddess had departed without a sound.

Adrian brushed past her with a duvet. He covered Ranjan before entering the kitchen. Poetry accompanied him.

"Interesting people you know."

"Look who's talking." He had a right to be bitter. He'd nearly been killed saving her, but his voice held humor, not spite.

I can't believe he came for me. Warm and fuzzy didn't begin to describe her giddiness. But it was contaminated by anxiety. They weren't in the clear yet.

"So what do we tell our friends?" she asked.

"Exactly what Freya told us to; we argued all night and came here to have incredible, mind-blowing sex."

Poetry laughed. "Works for me." Her mood shifted again when Ranjan's wheezing reminded her of his despair. "But what about him?"

Adrian stopped pouring. "Ran buzzed in after last call, babbling about breaking up with Sarah." He placed the carafe on the warmer. "When he gets up we'll fill him in, and help him as best we can. But don't say anything to Jen and Gary. They wouldn't understand."

Poetry dropped the well-done bacon on a paper towel and tipped the scrambled mixture into the leftover grease. “I’ve probably lost my job.” Oddly enough, the thought didn’t bother her. “And you lost your biggest client.”

“I don’t know about you, but I don’t really care.”

“What do you mean, you don’t care?”

He dug around the fridge. “It was a long ride home, and I’ve been thinking.” Adrian sidled closer to Poetry’s side and wrapped his free arm around her.

“This last case did it for me. Defending creeps like Frank Fleisher isn’t really what I signed up for.” Poetry stared into the sapphire windows to his soul and saw resignation. He planted a delicious, lingering kiss on her lips, and pressed his forehead to hers. “I don’t want to do it anymore.”

Poetry wanted to jump for joy. This was great news. But…

“What will you do instead?”

Adrian released her and scrounged through various containers on a wooden shelf next to her.

“I have a lot of money saved and invested-ah, here it is.” He retrieved a ceramic sugar bowl. “You know what I’ve always wanted to do?

“What?”

“Flip houses and sell them.”

Poetry slid her fingers along the stone countertop. “If this is any indication of your talents,” Adrian could succeed at this kind of thing. She knew it. “Then I think it’s a fantastic idea.” She gave him an encouraging kiss.

You know,” he said, curling a lock of her hair around his finger. “I could use the help of a real artist.”

"Who?" Poetry stepped back. "Me?" His mouth widened in a grin. He was serious.

"Just think about it." He tasted her tongue lovingly and strolled away to set the table. Poetry stirred eggs and thoughts.

Her future just changed for the better. This sunrise announced a new beginning with a great guy. Not a psycho.

Lucky her.

EPILOGUE I

Freya absorbed the opulence of Olympus as she marched, it distracted from her cramping stomach. She would never admit fear, even though she would not be the only one to succumb to it.

She gazed upon the marble pillars and gold statues with distain. The excessive ornamentation spoke of decadence. Freya snorted indelicately. Small wonder these Mediterraneans were so weak; they spent too much of their energies on luxuries. She preferred the bitter haunts of Asgard. It kept her kin humble and strong.

A deep, fragrant breath stabilized her before entering the hall. Ares' howls raged from within.

Once inside, Freya ignored the throng of celestial beings to observe the hideousness contained within. It lifted her heart to witness Ares tethered like a common mutt, a crimson ribbon tight around his neck.

Despite her confidence in the magick fetter, she drew her sword.

"Its name is Gleipnir," Freya said, indicating his restraint. "A gift from my people to yours in recognition of a mutual enemy."

She admired the handiwork of the impossible thread from a safe distance. "It is fashioned of commodities that cannot exist. Mountain roots and bird spittle, a cat's footfall and the breath of a fish to name but a few. You cannot escape our sorcery."

Ares ceased thrashing and glared at her; a smile crawled over his perspiring face. His unwashed odor and grim visage defied the pleasant surroundings.

"Ah, but that is not true, is it?" Ares said. He had lost none of his bravado. "Is this not the same way you bound the Fenris wolf?"

Freya maintained a façade of indifference even as her blood chilled and last evening's mead soured in her mouth.

He knew of their legends. And a god of Ares' power could break the magick. Freya sent a rare prayer to the Energy for time enough before Ares escaped.

"I am stronger than some overgrown beast," His voice clamored to a shout. "When I am free, I shall take my revenge on all of you."

"You will not be given the chance." The booming voice could belong to none other than Zeus. Every assembled entity shifted as one to view his manifestation from the clouds.

"Your crimes are many," he said. "Your judgment is at hand."

"What crimes?" Ares directed his sneers at the assembly. "I am the god of war. I have done nothing untoward." He drew himself tall. "I destroyed my challenger, therefore I won. I should be rewarded, not disciplined."

Freya's lip curled. She expected this kind of arrogance from Ares, but his callousness astounded her.

"Sacrilege!" Zeus' temper manifested as lightening crackled in his eyes. "You sought to extinguish thousands of human lives to create a war not of their making. You murdered mortals." His voice softened with sadness. The wind silenced. No one stirred. "You killed Strife. You brought about the deaths of Hermes and Aphrodite, your wife and son."

Ares appeared unmoved. He slouched with crossed arms. Freya sensed his apathy, and she was not alone. Though no soul spoke, the air thickened with their combined wrath.

"You cannot continue," Zeus said. "Your existence endangers us all."

"You intend to eradicate me?" Ares laughed until he struggled to stand. The crowd muttered amongst themselves. Others circled the demented titan.

"That amuses me." Ares wiped a tear of mirth from his filthy cheek. "There is a dictum on Earth that applies here." He set his hands on his hips and puffed out his chest. "You and what army?"

Zeus frowned and thunder bellowed. "You challenge me for the last time." He raised two fingers. "Summon the others."

At his signal, Freya conveyed Zeus' will to her kin.

The great room filled with newcomers; many Freya identified only by regional clothing or reputation.

Asian gods appeared in silken embroidered finery, their kimonos swishing with each movement. Razor sharp fans flicked and fluttered.

Bejeweled Indian deities proudly displayed their luminescent blue skin, an accepted mark of their station. Many boasted additional appendages or eyes.

The Egyptians emerged in gold and lapis, their animal faces resolute.

Her brothers arrived at her side; Thor with his hammer and scarlet braids, one-eyed Odin, one-handed Tyr, and even the infamous Loki.

The intense concentration of power raised the hair on Freya's arms. Her confidence returned.

One by one they merged around Ares. His eyes darted with an expression Freya had never seen him wear; concern.

Zeus elevated his fist. Pale lightning raced over his forearm and through his clenched fingers.

"On my command," he said.

The sound of broadswords, spears, bows, axes and hammers coming to bear clattered throughout the cramped space.

Freya raised her weapon, savoring the vibration of narrowly contained strength. For the first time in history, Mount Olympus would erupt. Justice would taste sweet.

Zeus dropped his arm.

"Fire."

EPILOGUE II

This must be Tartarus, Aphrodite thought. Hades for disposable gods.

It was the horror she always imagined it would be. No light, no sound, no salvation. The endless night stretched beyond fathoming.

She screamed in terror and despair, only to realize she had no voice. She clenched her fists in impotent rage to discover she had no fingers, no body at all.

And no pain. This should have soothed her. Her last moments were excruciating. She had embraced death willingly. But the thought of floating forever without sensations unnerved Aphrodite to the edge of madness. She would drift as an everlasting bubble. No one would ever see her. No one would hear her cries. No one would know she existed in this cocoon of misery.

How did it come to this?

Millennia ago she was a new soul, a servant to the Energy. Her discontent festered. She coveted the worship of the human race and the gift of childbirth.

Aphrodite abandoned Eden to live as a god.

And died like a mortal.

What would become of her son? Would the world ever learn of her desire to save them? Would they remember her?

Aphrodite.

Her plunge into dementia had begun. She grieved for her future, wishing the voice were not a figment of her already failing mind.

Aphrodite.

Her own psyche taunted her. She longed to cover non-existent ears. Leave me alone.

Aphrodite. Listen to me.

Dread.

Please, no. What new torture is this?

A speck of light twinkled in the distance. Aphrodite prepared for punishment. Her child was lost and she endured cremation at the hands of a man she once adored. She could withstand whatever came.

The mists swelled in size and brightness, but Aphrodite felt no malice, only a benevolence she recognized. The Energy.

Had she any tears, Aphrodite would have wept in elation.

My Lord, is it truly You?

Long are the years since you graced my presence, Aphrodite.

When she departed Eden, she never believed she would see the Energy again. She did not care then. But she welcomed It now.

She had no knees to fall to, no form to prostrate. It mattered not. The Energy's calming demeanor enveloped her. Darkness fled from shimmering love incarnate.

Aphrodite shed her anger and remorse. Here in the embrace of the Energy she found peace.

Could she be forgiven after centuries away? After meddling in human lives for power?

You are not like Ares and Strife, the Energy said. You did not seek to hurt mankind. You gave your existence for them without concern for your own fate.

A tingling sensation washed over Aphrodite, the feeling so odd she laughed.

Laughter. She heard her own euphoria. Her hands took shape before her. She turned them over in disbelief, pressed them to her wet cheeks.

A quiver from behind caught her attention. She spun to greet the sound, abruptly realizing the source. An experimental touch revealed soft feathers and strong sinew. The Energy had gifted her with long-lost wings. For the first time in centuries, Aphrodite took flight. She soared through the emptiness, screaming her ecstasy.

The Energy blessed her. Her Lord had returned her ability to fly. Eternity would be bearable after all.

Aphrodite.

She halted, hovering, prepared to comply. For this boon she would do whatever the Energy requested. Anything to earn the favor of her creator.

You belong in Eden.

Clouds parted to reveal skies the color of ripe peaches. Burbling waterfalls covered in lush greenery framed vast gardens of sweet scented orchids and tulips.

One angel strolled amongst the lake of blooms, a single pink rose held between long graceful fingers. His blonde curls haloed his bent head.

Hermes raised his perfect face, his mouth forming the word that shattered her.

Mom.

Aphrodite placed a hand over her lips, but a sob rasped, exposing her heartache.

If she could just touch him…

Go, Aphrodite. Your son awaits. Welcome home.

Acknowledgements

I would first like to thank the Edmonton Kendo and Naginata Club, as well as the Edmonton Japanese Community Association. Special mention to Sensei Dustin Bjorkquist, Tully Pinkerton, Steve Hladky and Keiko Marumo. Thank you for making me feel welcome from Day One, and for your mentorship. These great memories will last me a lifetime. I learned so much from *everyone*.

Thank you to my beta readers, Rebecca Bartlett-Reid, Karen Maquire, and Cathy Rogers.

Thanks to the blogging community for all your support.

Thank you to my publisher Heather Savage, my editor Sara Peterson-Johnson, and my cover designer Terra Weston-Koster. Your stellar work is much appreciated.

And thank you to my readers! I love you all!

And last, but sometimes the most important, thanks to my Dan, who assures me I'm brilliant no matter how bad the Idiot Mode feels.

CPSIA information can be obtained at www.ICGtesting.com
Printed in the USA
BVOW07s0516300913

332410BV00001B/3/P

9 780989 202763